THE HAPPY MONTH

A DOM REILLY MYSTERY

MARSHALL THORNTON

KB
KENMORE BOOKS

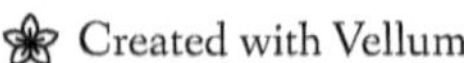 Created with Vellum

ACKNOWLEDGMENTS

A big thank you to: Joan Martinelli, Nathan Bay, Tina Greene Bevington, Randy and Valerie Trumbull, Danielle Wolff, and Ben Thompson.

The bar was called The Blue Fox and sat on the less glamorous end of the Sunset Strip. He'd been there before with an ex-Marine who'd seen combat in the Pacific. That worked out for a while, but then the ex-Marine decided to return home to Ohio.

He'd decided to go to The Blue Fox because it was less frightening than the places downtown near Pershing Square. Those places scared him, and not just because they were more likely to be raided. The people you met there—well, a lot of them were best avoided.

When it happened, he was dancing with an attractive man named Ivan. The club was a big storefront, having originally been a stationery store. The windows in front had been blacked out, the bar built on one side, with the dance floor taking up most of the space, and a collection of eight or nine tables pushed into the back. In the corners there were two large fans with streamers cooling off the dancers.

There weren't any nooks or crannies; it wasn't even that dark. Everyone could see everyone else. There were men dancing with men, women with women. The jukebox played a lot of Doris Day. Many of the men wore short sleeve shirts. He was more formal in a suit and tie. He couldn't help it. He'd been brought up that way.

After introducing himself, Ivan asked, "And you are?"

"Patrick."

"What do you do, Patrick?"

"What do you mean?"

Ivan smirked, "I mean for a living."

"Oh. I'm a lawyer."

"That's wonderful. You look like a lawyer. I love the Perry Mason books. I've read most of them. Who could read them all? I adored the most recent, *The Case of the Vagabond Virgin.* Just delicious."

"I don't practice that kind of law. Entertainment mainly. Very dull. Duller than you'd think. I suppose I'm a disappointment."

"Not at all," Ivan said, pulling him closer. "Not at all."

A few moments later, the lights flashed off, then back on. Everyone stopped dancing and quickly shuffled about. Ivan was gone and a short girl with nearly blonde hair slipped into his arms. She wore a green dress, tight in the bodice with a full skirt. It matched her eyes.

"My name is Vera. This is our third date. We met on the Santa Monica Pier. We've never been here before. Quickly, tell me about you."

"What's happening?"

"Don't worry about that, tell me who you are."

"Patrick. Patrick Gill. I work at a law firm downtown."

"Your family doesn't know about me. My last name is Korenko. My parents are Czech. Your family doesn't approve of immigrants."

The lights came on bright. Sheriff's officers streamed into the bar.

"Oh my God, I'll be disbarred," Patrick said.

"Hold my hand, stay close to me, you'll do fine."

When he looked over at the officers, he noticed they seemed surprised, uncomfortable. They'd expected to walk in on a scene of depravity, naked bodies writhing around in the dark. Instead, they found a room full of men and women who appeared to have been out on dates, now clinging to each other. They were perplexed by that.

Patrick relaxed, thinking, just be what they think you are. Something he had a great deal of experience with. Vera nestled herself more tightly under his arm. It was as though she knew what he'd just thought. Or maybe it was her mind he'd just read.

In a few minutes, they were being interviewed by an officer who was young enough to still have pimples. He asked for their names, and then, "Do you know what kind of place this is?"

Vera said, "We've never been before. A friend of mine said she and her boyfriend come here."

"You didn't notice anything strange?"

"Honestly, I didn't notice anything but Patrick." Then she looked up at him, and smiling said, "Isn't he swell?"

After declining to answer, the officer asked a few more questions. Patrick barely said anything, Vera was doing such a good job doing the talking. Finally, the officer walked over and spoke to his superior for a moment, then came back and told them they could go.

Outside, the air was cooler than in the bar but still hot and heavy. They rushed across the street. Shaken, Patrick asked, "Do you mind if I take my jacket off?"

"You can do whatever you want. Why would I care?"

Patrick took off his jacket, his white shirt underneath

was drenched in sweat. Vera said, "You should take that off, too. You'll catch cold."

"I really shouldn't."

"You're wearing an undershirt. I can see it. Why are you wearing an undershirt on a day like today?"

"I suppose I'm a bit straitlaced."

Patrick took the shirt off. He didn't know how hot it had gotten that day. He hadn't wanted to know.

Then Ivan and a girl came out of the bar. Ivan saw them and they crossed the street.

"That is such a good idea," he said, before removing his own shirt.

The girl with him started to giggle. To Vera she asked, "Are you making them strip tease?"

"This is Gigi," Vera said to Patrick. "She's my real date. Oh, take that undershirt off. It's sopping. You poor thing."

Taking the T-shirt off, he peeked at Ivan who raised his eyebrows.

Ivan said, "My car is just down here."

They followed him half a block to an almost new, cream-colored Cadillac Series 62 convertible. He'd left the top down.

"Let's go to my house," he said, opening the driver's door.

"Where is it?" Vera asked.

"Not far. Holmby Hills."

"Fancy," Gigi said.

"It's nice enough. Barbara Stanwyck lives a few blocks away. Hop in."

The girls climbed into the back, Ivan and Patrick in the front. The boys stuck to the leather seats but were still so much cooler. As they pulled away from the curb, Gigi asked, "Do you think we could drop in on Miss Stanwyck for a night cap?"

"Absolutely," Ivan said, tongue in cheek. "I know she'd like to meet a girl like you."

That made them laugh. As they drove off, the warm night air caressed them, and the sound of their laughter overflowed and spilled onto the street.

CHAPTER ONE

July 22, 1996
Monday

Happiness is an untrustworthy emotion. There is always the fear that you'll go to sleep one night only to wake up and find happiness has packed its bags and fled. Leaving you bereft, hollowed out, desperately alone. But while happiness shines on you, life is glorious, the days more beautiful, strangers kinder, laughter easy to come by. It's almost enough to make you forget the fear. Almost.

The Freedom Agenda was just a few blocks from Long Beach's struggling downtown area. It sat in a short row of stores, between an art supply store and a record shop. I always wondered how those businesses survived. I'd never seen anyone walk into them. It was a short drive from the house my lover, my partner, Ronnie and I owned on 2nd Street.

I was early. Not an uncommon occurrence since I'd stopped bartending at The Hawk, one of the gay bars over on Broadway in a section called the stroll. My boss, Lydia Gonsalez, Esquire, was giving me more hours to make up for the change, but it wasn't necessary. I was comfortable. My boyfriend made a decent living and I'd just inherited a chunk of money which we used to buy a co-op. The third piece of real estate Ronnie and I owned together. If he kept up this pace, in a few years I wouldn't have to do much more than pick up rent checks. I didn't hate that idea.

As I said, I got to work early that day. The door was unlocked, which meant Lydia was already there. I paused in the lobby after I shut the door. I did that a lot. I'd shot a man in just that spot a few months before. There's always guilt when you kill someone, no matter how right that choice. I was happy enough to only think about it for a moment.

When I walked past Lydia's office, she said, "Dom, can you come in, we've a lot to talk about."

"One sec, let me grab my project list."

"I bought you a coffee."

"Thanks," I said, as I rushed to the large open space in the back where I kept my 'desk'. I wasn't wearing a coat; it was summer and already close to eighty. I kept my keys and wallet in my Dockers. A few moments later, I was sitting across from Lydia with my project list. I took a sip of the latte she'd bought me.

Lydia was about ten years younger than I am, putting her around thirty-seven, thirty-eight. Her hair was coal black and had a tendency to fall over one of her eyes. She had a sexiness that she fought to hide. A battle she rarely won.

"We're deposing Anne Michaels on Wednesday afternoon at two o'clock. I just got the call from her attorney."

"Awfully early for calls."

"Yes, I think he was hoping to get the answering

machine. He'd leave an innocuous message, then I'd call back and he wouldn't be available. He'd try again during lunch. Then he'd be unavailable when I called back..."

"Phone tag."

"Exactly."

"But you answered the phone, so you won."

"I did win," she said with a small, satisfied smile.

Anne Michaels, née Whittemore, had been a witness in the trial of Larry Wilkes for murdering his boyfriend, Pete Michaels, in 1976. Anne perjured herself by claiming to be Pete's fiancé. She'd done so at Larry's suggestion. She'd later married the victim's brother—a story just like a movie Ronnie and I had recently watched on video, *While You Were Sleeping*. Only this was more like, *While You Were Dead*.

Anyway, she'd recently agreed to recant her testimony.

"I do have some bad news," Lydia said. "Well, not-good news. I've been doing research and the admission of artwork as evidence is challenging. It's very likely it won't be admissible."

She'd agreed to take the case based on artwork by a deceased witness which impeached his testimony. He'd done page after page of drawings, almost like one of those new graphic novel things, that showed him procuring the gun and then giving it to someone not Larry Wilkes.

"What does that mean?"

"I think we need to get a new trial without it. If I try to use it to get the new trial and a judge rejects it, then I'd have trouble trying to get it in if we got a new trial another way."

"Okay, what's the issue?" Not being a lawyer, it wasn't obviously apparent to me.

"Artwork may or may not be true. Without the artist there to testify, there's no certainty. It's possible I might be able to get it in at trial since it does support reasonable doubt. But as you know, the standard is different for a habeas corpus petition."

"Absolute certainty."

"Basically."

The artist, Andy Showalter, had killed himself several years after the trial. He'd testified that he'd bought a gun in Compton at Larry's request. The gun used to kill Pete Michaels. There were holes in Showalter's story, but the defense hadn't pointed them out.

Raymond Harris was the public defender. To date, he'd provided only a very thin file on the case. A file that should have included discovery from the AD's office but didn't. He was prominent on my project list.

"When will we have Raymond Harris in for a chat?" I asked.

"He's scheduled for Friday morning. He promises he'll bring the rest of Larry's files at that time. He's just got to find them."

Her tone was bitter. It was hard for her to respect lawyers who lost files.

"What do I need to do to prepare?"

"I'll be reading through the entire trial from beginning to end. The main focus of the meeting will be asking about the questions Harris didn't ask. There will be things you'll need to follow up on. We have a half an hour conference call with Larry on Friday afternoon."

"New cases?"

"Not until we file the habeas corpus petition. The court has sixty days to rule. We'll have several weeks to focus on other cases once we file."

"Got it."

Thinking we were finished, I stood up.

"One more thing," she said.

"Okay."

"Edwin wants to have lunch with us today."

Edwin Karpinski was an attorney affiliated with The Freedom Agenda enough to have an office with us, but not so affiliated as to actually use it. He had other offices downtown, which we sometimes borrowed. He wasn't someone I really liked.

"Us? Do I really need to be there?"

"Actually, I'm the one who doesn't need to be there. He asked that I arrange a lunch with you. I had to insist I was invited too."

"Do you know what he wants?"

"He wouldn't say over the phone. But he's driving down and we're having lunch at La Bohème at one o'clock. He wants a favor from you, obviously. I'd say it was a big one given the price of La Bohème and the fact that he hates driving down here."

"If he wants me to investigate something, I'm not sure I'm interested."

Beyond The Freedom Agenda, the kind of law Edwin practiced was mostly civil litigation, and that was mostly corporations suing some part of the government. One group of awful people suing another group of awful people; really not my thing.

"That's why I want to come along. I want to make sure you're comfortable saying no."

"I'm a big boy, Lydia."

"Even big boys need a lawyer now and then."

The rest of the morning was quiet. I spent most of it reading over Anne Michael's testimony and my notes on the things she'd said to me. I also began laying out questions I thought she should be asked. Lydia would be doing that too.

I did mine mainly to make sure she didn't miss anything. She rarely did.

Karen, Lydia's assistant, came in and the phone began ringing. Since I killed Stu Whatley, Karen had been wary, distant even. I imagine she would have told the police the truth if it weren't for her respect for Lydia. The only thing she'd ever said to me about any of it was, once at the coffeemaker, "It's never a good thing when White people start lying."

Honestly, I couldn't disagree with her.

Lydia and I left around quarter of one. She drove. On the way we talked about our partners. She was married to a man named Dwayne who was in development at one of the studios. Apparently, a film he'd worked on was premiering soon and they were going to walk the red carpet.

"I don't want to spend a lot. I'm probably going to go to a consignment shop I heard of where the stars sell off their gowns. I mean, I don't expect anyone to take our picture, but I still need to look nice."

"This is one of those moments I'm glad I'm not a woman."

"You wouldn't say that if you lived with Dwayne. He's buying a tuxedo. He's sure he'll need to wear one more often. Of course, I know better. He'll wear it twice then want a new one."

We found a place to park and then walked a block and a half to La Bohème. The building was about eight stories, yellow brick, with a few neo-classical flourishes. The restaurant was on the first floor, next to a jewelry store. The floors above seemed to be offices. We walked up two marble steps into the restaurant.

La Bohème served excellent nuevo Italian food, featuring a well-designed dining room with cloth-covered tables and lovely flatware. Each table had a tiny vase with inexpensive flowers purchased that morning.

On the far side of the room, in front of the window on the Pine Avenue side, sat two men. One of them was Edwin Karpinski. He was in his mid-thirties but looked quite boyish with blond hair, blue eyes and a well-trained body. His suit was gray, his shirt a gentle sky blue, and his tie bold with navy and purple stripes.

Across from him sat his older brother, who was clearly in his mid-forties, had started losing his wheat-colored hair, and spent less time in a gym. Despite the differences, it was easy to see the family resemblance.

Edwin stood up and made the introductions. "This is my brother John."

"Jan," his brother corrected, pronouncing it in the Polish way. Karpinski, of course they were Polish. At least on their father's side.

Nobody offered to shake hands, so we sat down. Before we could say much of anything, the waiter was there asking if we'd like cocktails. Jan ordered a Tanqueray martini with extra olives, I asked for an Arnold Palmer, while Lydia and Edwin stuck with water.

Edwin looked at me and began, "I suppose you're wondering why I asked you—"

"Oh, for Christ's sake, can't you wait until my drink gets here?" Jan said, leading us into an uncomfortable silence.

Lydia broke it by talking about the Wilkes case. As soon as she mentioned that Larry was gay and was accused of killing his lover, Jan interrupted.

"Why would you take a case like that?"

"Because I think the man is innocent."

"He may not have killed anyone, but he's certainly not innocent."

"I have the feeling if I restricted myself to clients you approved of I wouldn't be very busy at all," Lydia said. A very polite way to call him a bigot.

The drinks arrived. The waiter set Jan's down first, and he drank almost half of it in one gulp. Lydia said to the waiter, "You know, I've changed my mind. I'll have a glass of wine, red, Pinot if you have it."

The waiter left and Edwin tried again. "Well, the reason I've asked you—"

"What exactly are your qualifications?" Jan asked me.

Before I could say anything, Edwin said, "John, I asked you to be open to this process."

"I am open. Why would I ask a question like that if I wasn't open?"

"You know, I can make this easier," I said. "The answer is no."

"What do you mean the answer is no?" Jan said. "We haven't offered you a job yet."

"I have a job. I don't want another one."

"Well, now that that's settled," Lydia said, looking down at her menu. "The calamari is excellent."

"Nothing's settled. I asked your man a question and he didn't answer it. What are his qualifications?"

"His work for us at The Freedom Agenda has been exemplary," Edwin said. "I recommend him, Lydia recommends him. That should be enough for you."

"You know I'd rather go with Harmon and Coyne."

"Because you're friendly with Buddy Coyne who has the biggest mouth on the Westside."

"He wouldn't say a word, he's very discreet."

"John, you know that's not true."

"None of this matters. I've already said no," I pointed out.

"You don't get to say no to us," Jan said. "We say no. You don't."

"Actually, he does get to say no," Lydia pointed out.

At that point, Edwin and Jan slipped into Polish. I have a little Polish. My grandparents spoke it at home and forced both my parents to. I can follow simple conversations. Mostly, I know when I'm being cursed at. I let them go on for a minute or two, then said, "Głupi dupek," which means something like stupid asshole. I didn't know how to make it plural.

The stared at me.

"Reilly is an Irish name. Why do you know Polish?" Jan asked.

"I grew up in a Polish neighborhood in Detroit."

I prayed that Detroit had a Polish neighborhood and that neither of them knew anything about it. Like for instance what it was called.

The waiter returned with Lydia's wine and my iced tea, and told us the specials, one of which filet mignon. It sounded like the most expensive thing on the menu, so I decided I'd get that. We didn't order just then. He left us to decide.

"The specials sound very good," Lydia said.

"Go ahead, tell him," Jan said.

"Finally," Edwin said under his breath. He calmed himself then began, "We have an uncle named Patrick Gill. Our mother's brother. He's just turned eighty. He lives in a nursing home in Beverly Hills. He's been diagnosed with dementia. When he was young, he was engaged to a woman named Vera Korenko. The engagement was broken off and he never married."

"Our mother finds this all very romantic," Jan inserted.

"Now he's saying that he killed Vera. Which is upsetting our mother."

"Was this woman murdered?"

"Yes. She was found in an arroyo near Pasadena."

"When was this?"

"1949."

"No one's ever been charged?"

"No."

"So, he could have killed her."

"Our mother doesn't think so," Edwin said. "She thinks he walks on water. He's much older than she is."

"How would finding out who killed this woman help your situation?" I asked. "Why don't you just tell your mother he didn't do it and forget about it?"

The brothers glanced at each other, then Jan said, "Our mother requires some kind of proof. Our father was a lawyer, we're lawyers, a lot has rubbed off on her."

"In other words, she doesn't trust you as far as she can throw you," I said. That earned me a couple of frowns. "Look, it's a case that's nearly fifty years old. It wasn't solved then, it's even less likely to get solved now. I can take your money, but I can't promise you'll get anything for it."

"Speaking of money," Lydia said. "He gets twenty-five an hour."

"Come on, Lydia," Edwin said. "I know you pay him less than that."

"You're not a not-for-profit, though."

I was tempted to say no again. I didn't need the money. Except, I was thinking I kind of did. I liked to keep a stash of cash, around ten thousand, a gun, and alternate identification in case I needed to leave suddenly. Ronnie had found my last stash and put it into the bank. Now that I didn't get tips, it was going to be a lot harder to squirrel money away.

"I'd need to be paid in cash," I said.

"Hiding it from Uncle Sam?" Jan guessed. For a moment, he seemed to like me better.

"Something like that."

The waiter came back asking if we'd like to order. Jan tried to send him away, but Lydia said, "I do, but I have to get back to the office. I have to work this afternoon."

After that we ordered. Lydia asked for the Caesar salad with shrimp, Edwin the cod, Jan chose lobster ravioli and I stuck with the filet—I mean, why not? When the waiter left, I said, "I'm going to need to speak to your mother and your uncle."

"Of course," Jan said. "But you'll have to promise not to upset Mother."

"You know I can't promise that."

Jan looked like he had indigestion, and the food hadn't arrived yet.

CHAPTER TWO

July 22, 1996
Evening

El Matador was a Spanish-style courtyard building built in the twenties. The stucco was a fading terra cotta with reddish brown trim and woodwork. There was a fountain, which no longer worked but still had wonderful handmade tilework. The stairs, both up to the back of the building and up to our unit, had red tiles as tread and those same handmade tiles between.

Our co-op was on the west side of the building, in the front on the second floor. It was one of four larger two-bedroom units, with a dining room, a large living room, a kitchen with a tiny breakfast nook and three Juliet balconies.

We'd closed early in June. It was an all-cash offer, sixty thousand dollars, so it was an easy closing. Ronnie immediately began rehabbing the apartment and volunteered to be on the homeowner's board. He fully intended to turn the place condo within a year, which would double or triple the value. Not that we would sell it, but we could easily get a second that would provide down payment money for another... Even thinking about it is a little exhausting.

Ronnie was sure we'd be in by Thanksgiving. I thought spring '97 more likely. We'd already had the floors sanded, stained and varnished. Given the age of the building, we were told that was the last time it could be done. In twenty or twenty-five years the wood itself would need to be replaced. To Ronnie, who was more than twenty years younger than I am, that seemed an eon. Something we'd never have to worry about. To me, it was just around the corner, just the way my life of twenty years ago felt. Reachable. Touchable. Yesterday. Tomorrow.

Painters were next; the kitchen and bathroom were both being retiled. As was the tiny breakfast nook. Ronnie had decided that walls in there should be tiled too. Halfway up in light blue with painted Mexican tiles on the edge. We were using lots of Mexican tiles which sort of matched the tilework on the fountain and steps in the courtyard. At least, in spirit. Ronnie had even figured out a way to put in a stackable washer and dryer on the landing right outside the kitchen door. Technically a 'common' space, but he'd already worked his magic with the board.

I'd left work at four-thirty for a meeting with a painter. I didn't really need to be there. Ronnie was making the decisions—though I suppose it was nice of him to pretend I had a say. I would have begged off except there wasn't that much going on at The Freedom Agenda. We were ready for the deposition on Wednesday. Karen had run Vera Korenko's name through Lexis/Nexis and not found anything too old, and the avalanche of mail we got from prisoners wanting to be freed had slowed almost to a stop after Lydia (or rather I) had shot one of our clients.

Still, I was late. When I walked in I stopped to look at the floors, which I hadn't seen. They looked amazing. It was the first thing we'd done which hinted at what the place would be like someday. I was getting excited about living there, just Ronnie and me.

Ronnie Chen, a swirling mix of Chinese, Vietnamese, Irish, Native American and a few more ethnicities, was small, in his late twenties, and, to me at least, gorgeous. I found him in the kitchen with the painter.

"My tile guy says we should tile first," he said to the painter. He was roughly around my age, growing in the middle and dressed in overalls that advertised his trade.

"Yeah, they always do," he said. "They just want to make a mess and leave it for me to clean up."

"I see," Ronnie said skeptically.

"Since you're on a tight deadline, you should let schedules decide. Whoever's available first goes first."

When I stepped into the small kitchen, the first thing I noticed was a Kelly-green sink sitting on the counter. I didn't remember talking about that.

Ronnie said, "This is my partner, Dom Reilly."

"Hey," he said to me. "Bob Flannigan. You guys flipping this place?"

I almost said 'not that kind of partner,' but we were also that kind of partner. Ronnie breezed through it saying, "Oh no, we'll be living here. That's why everything matters so much. It's going to be our home."

Flannigan just said, "Oh. Okay." He had to have encountered this before. It was Long Beach after all.

"Let me show you the color I've chosen for the kitchen," Ronnie said, picking up a handful of swatches.

"It's this one," he said, pointing to a very pinky beige.

"Isn't that a bit subtle for you?" I asked. He hadn't

shown me this. Nor had he talked to me about the green sink.

"This is the tile," he said, picking up a tile off the counter. It was a mix of cobalt blue, Kelly green and the pinky beige. It was pretty, but...

"Wow. Isn't that going to be a lot?"

"If we had more counter space, yes. But we only have ten feet of countertop with a sink in the middle. It's exactly the kind of kitchen where you can make this kind of statement."

I didn't know what that statement was going to be, but he was right, the kitchen was small. All the cupboards and counter were on the one side. The other side had space for a range and the refrigerator. There was a door to the dining room, another to the breakfast nook and a third out to the landing. A small kitchen with that many doors did take some cleverness, so maybe he was right.

"What about the other rooms?" Flannigan asked.

"Well, we just need you to paint the bedrooms, the dining room and hallway, and the bathroom. We're going to do the living room ourselves."

"We are?"

"It'll be easy. Trust me."

I had no idea what he meant. If it was that easy, why weren't we painting the whole apartment ourselves? Ronnie led the painter out of the kitchen, through the dining room to the bedrooms and the bathroom. I wandered back to the living room. It did not look easy to paint. For one thing, it had ceilings that needed to be painted, cathedral ceilings. I told myself it didn't matter. Would I climb to the top of a ladder for Ronnie? Yes, of course. Would I make him explain why I had to do that? Also, yes.

Standing in there, I wondered if we'd be taking the

furniture from 2nd Street or if we'd be buying new? And then, Ronnie and Flannigan were back. Before the painter could leave, I said, "Make sure the ceilings are on the quote. All of them."

"Got it," he said, and slipped out the door.

I turned to Ronnie and asked, "What do you mean it's going to be easy?"

"We're going to rag-roll it. The walls are perfect for it."

The walls were textured plaster made to look like it had just been applied.

He continued, "We'll get pigment from Home Depot and mix it with white paint. Then we dilute it with water and roll it on to the wall with rags. I'm thinking a pale buttery yellow, a lemon-y yellow, and a honey color."

"You're making me hungry," I said, honestly.

"Perfect. It's dinner time. Where do you want to go?"

"Let's just stop at the Park Pantry."

Ten minutes later, we were in a booth at the Park Pantry, which was an upscale diner on the corner of Junipero and Broadway. We were seated in a teal-colored booth on the Junipero side. I asked for an Arnold Palmer while Ronnie got a glass of the house white. Before the wait-ress could slip away, Ronnie said, "We can order. I know what we want. I'll have the salmon, baked potato, and a salad with ranch. Dom will have the chicken Caesar, chopped and tossed. You can bring it all at once. Thanks!"

After the waitress wandered off, I told Ronnie all about the 'favor' I'd been asked to do for Edwin and his brother. Skipping the part about my getting an extra cash payment.

"So, you're not getting paid extra?" he asked right off the bat.

Avoiding a direct lie, I said, "Things are pretty slow right now." Which was true. I did have time to do it.

"This guy, their uncle, had a fiancé in the forties and then never married afterward," he said skeptically. "Ping. Ping. Ping. My gaydar is going off."

"I think they would have mentioned if they thought he was gay," I said, though even as I said it, I realized they probably wouldn't. Jan was definitely a homophobe. Often, homophobes had an incredible ability to not see the obvious.

"But it has crossed *your* mind, hasn't it?"

"He says he killed his fiancé. That doesn't seem very gay to me."

"Maybe she was going to expose him. Wouldn't he have lost his law license for being gay? Gay sex has only been legal in California since the seventies."

"How do you know that?"

"It's in one of the brochures at The Center."

"Oh. Well, I'm going to have to find out about this guy one way or the other."

"Should we bet?"

"No," I said. "You always win."

"You're no fun."

The waitress brought our drinks.

"When exactly do you think we're going to paint the co-op?"

"Saturday morning. I'm not scheduling clients all day. We have that commitment ceremony in the afternoon."

"That's not enough time to paint."

"Well, I don't expect to finish. What are you going to wear?"

"Something old."

"I mean to the commitment ceremony."

"Something like this. It's not black tie, is it?"

"God, no. We need to buy Hawaiian shirts."

"Is that on the invitation?"

"No, but that's what everyone's doing. Robert and Doug met in Hawaii. Don't you think that will be cute if we all show up that way?"

I knew Robert and Doug from working at The Hawk. Actually, I knew most everyone in town from working at The Hawk. They were more Ronnie's friends though. He'd helped them buy a three-bedroom Spanish house in California Heights and they all volunteered at The Center. I was pretty sure they were the ones trying to get Ronnie onto the board of directors.

After dinner, I drove Ronnie the three blocks back to the co-op and dropped him off in front of his car. He kissed me and said, "See you at home."

I got there and found a parking spot before he did. Walking up the front steps, I grabbed the mail and went inside. In the living room, Junior Clybourne was watching *Jeopardy!* as he did most every night. He loved the show and spent most of the half an hour shouting out the wrong answers.

I shuffled through the mail as I walked across the room.

"Hello, darling," Junior said. "The questions are so easy tonight."

"Mmmm-hmmm," I said.

Our electric bill, an invitation to a charity event for Ronnie, a credit card statement for our roommate John, something official looking for Junior, and a card for me. I spread it all out on the breakfast bar in the kitchen.

The card had an Illinois postmark and no return address. I got them from time to time, though it was unexpected since we weren't close to any holidays. I opened it. The front of the card was a bodybuilder in a tiny speedo. Inside, it said 'I know what you want for Christmas.' Beneath that, handwritten, it said, 'Going on a cruise. Will be at the Westin for one night. Can you meet at the lobby bar around four on Sunday afternoon?' Per our agreement, it wasn't signed.

When I heard the front door open and Ronnie come in, I threw the card into the trash. I didn't want him to see it. Usually, when the cards came he'd tease me and sometimes ask to see them. If he saw this one, he'd want to go with me to the Westin. And that couldn't happen.

Ronnie usually had clients most of Sunday. I could probably go and he'd have no idea. But that wasn't the question. The question was, did it feel safe?

CHAPTER THREE

July 23, 1996
Tuesday morning

Every morning now, I have coffee and read the *Los Angeles Times*. I could read the *Press-Telegram*, but it's a little too conservative for me. That Tuesday morning, the Olympics in Atlanta took up a lot of space. I didn't bother reading it, I wasn't interested. They'd found some big chunks of the plane that had gone down off Long Island. People were still saying someone had taken it down with a missile from the shore. There was a little article about the problems they were having establishing a new area code for the valley. Which reminded me, I needed to take my cellular phone with me. I had a habit of forgetting it.

Instead of going to the office, I drove past it to the Long Beach Public Library. I parked in the parking structure and walked out to the bunker-style building, which was nearly buried in the ground. It looked as though someone had said,

"Hey, let's build a library that will survive nuclear war." I was sure it would.

The reference area was downstairs, even deeper into the bunker, and to the right. I looked for the thick *Los Angeles Times* index that would tell me the dates of any articles that mentioned Vera Korenko but couldn't find them. Stopping at the reference desk, I asked about that and was told that the index had been computerized. That didn't make me happy. I was much better at turning real pages than digital ones.

The nice young woman pointed me toward a computer. I put in Vera Korenko's name and got one result. I took me a moment to realize what had happened. I'd accidentally put her name into the card catalogue and gotten a book titled *Canyon Girl* from nineteen eighty-one. I wrote down the call number and walked around until I found it.

I sat down at a table and looked it over. The cover was lurid. The jacket black-and-white with red bars over the intimate parts of a reclining woman. The author was a man named Wallace Philburn. I flipped the book over and read the blurb on the back:

> "Not since the Black Dahlia has there been a crime so shocking in its depravity. On a clear, crisp morning in the fall of 1949, Vera Korenko's brutally beaten body was found in Pasadena's Arroyo Seco. For more than two decades, the Los Angeles Police Department has been flummoxed. Clue after clue has failed to lead to Vera's killer. Now, after years of exhaustive research, *Canyon Girl* presents the likely killer of poor Vera Korenko."

My first question was, *Are canyons and arroyos the same*

thing? It bugged me so much I went and grabbed a dictionary. No, they are not the same thing. A canyon is a small valley with steep, hilly sides. An arroyo is a generally dry riverbed, basically one of the 'now-you-see-em, now-you-don't' rivers that surround Los Angeles. Of course, Canyon Girl was a better title than Arroyo Girl, since ninety percent of the country—me included—didn't even know what an arroyo was.

Getting back to the book, I read the author's biography which was on the back below the blurb:

"Wallace Philburn, a noted Harvard graduate, has spent decades in Hollywood. He has worked under distinguished producers Roger Corman and William Castle, writing films for each: *Rock-N-Roll Werewolf* and *Curse of the Space Alien*. All the while, building a career as a noted journalist contributing to monthlies like *Confidential*, *The Q.T.* and *The Lowdown*. He is also the author of the well-reviewed novel, *Penny's Plight*. He lives in Hollywood, California with his wife, actress Sophia Hadley."

Okay, that was a lot of hot air. I mean, I didn't know much about the industry but none of this rang any bells. If you were good at writing movies, then why work at cheesy sounding magazines? And why write a true crime book that I was dubious of even before reading the first page.

I flipped to the back of the book to see if there was an index. There was. I scanned through it looking for Patrick Gill's name. I didn't find it. Next, I looked for the word engagement. It wasn't there. Something here was fictional. But was it Patrick Gill's engagement or was it *Canyon Girl?* For that matter, was it both?

Opening the book, I noticed that the pages in the middle were glossy. That meant there were photos. I skipped to those. The first was a black-and-white photo from the mid-twenties. A woman in a black dress with a scarf on her head held a fat, surprised looking infant. That suggested to me that Wallace had spoken to Vera's family. The next photo was Vera's high school graduation in 1942, also black-and-white. She wore a soft-looking sweater with three buttons at the neck, a gold cross and a big smile. Curls framed her face, she wore dark lipstick—most likely red— and had a mischievous glint in her eye. There was another photo, taken around the same time with Vera seated on the wrought iron railing of a couple of concrete steps. The entrance to some building? A different sweater, fluffier, tighter, but the same big smile and curls framing her face. Could that also have come from a family member? Or did Wallace have other sources?

On the next two pages were four crime scene photos that all showed a naked woman from different angles, lying on the ground as though thrown. Black bars, like the red ones on the cover, had been added to each photograph to hide her breasts and genitalia. It appeared she was lying under a tree, some kind of evergreen. There was trash around her body. Photos like this never looked real. It was a person reduced to a thing. That alone made it disturbing and unreal.

Turning the page, I found photographs of a Detective Andrew Schmidt taken around the time of the case. He looked to be in his mid-forties. He'd be over ninety now. It seemed unlikely he was alive. Also on that page was a photo of a teenage boy named Carmichael Crampton on a bicycle. He'd found the body. Then there was a couple named Harper and Georgia Dawson who were described as friends. The photo, one of the few in color, was taken some time in the fifties. Clearly after Vera's death. Last was a nice color shot of Vera Korenko's grave at Forest Lawn. 1924-1949. She was only twenty-five when she died.

I didn't have time to look at the book any further. I went upstairs to the checkout counter and gave the librarian my card. I had two weeks to read the book and return it without a fine. In the parking garage, I found my Jeep Wrangler on the second floor where I'd left it. I tossed the book into the backseat.

Before I got in, I reached under the seat and touched my gun. It wasn't the Beretta 92S I used to own, the one I'd killed Stu Whatley with. The police had taken that one from Lydia. Of course, it wasn't legally registered, so they'd asked her a lot of questions about where she'd gotten it. She'd steadfastly claimed attorney client privilege making them think she'd gotten it from a client. Given the some-what political nature of the situation, they decided not to prosecute the nice lady lawyer who'd killed a rapist in self-defense for having an illegal gun. None of that got me my gun back.

I went up to South Central and bought myself another gun on the street. This one was a Colt Detective Special, which had a certain irony to it. It was older model, used 38 caliber bullets which was a lot of bang for the buck. It cost me five hundred dollars, which was my last paycheck at The Hawk and some other money I'd put into a hidey-hole or two. It's never a bad idea to hide some cash no matter how your life is going.

So, yeah, I liked to know it was still there. After I checked, I climbed in and took the 710 all the way up to the 5. The thing that was nice about living in Long Beach was that you had pretty easy access to the Eastside and surrounding suburbs: Burbank, Glendale, Pasadena. And also, the Westside: Santa Monica, Venice and the beach cities. Silverlake and Hollywood weren't too bad. West Hollywood, Beverly Hills and the like were pretty awkward. They were far away from any freeways, which is probably why people lived there.

When I called Sheila Karpinski, she'd given me an address in Burbank. 1830 Riverside Drive. I'd assumed it was a house. One with pillars and a couple of floors. I didn't know Burbank well. Actually, not at all. What I hadn't expected was a stable.

It looked like a long red barn and had a sign over the front double door that said SHEILA K'S STABLE. Below the name it offered horse boarding and riding lessons. There were a few parking spaces in front, so I pulled in and parked. By the time I climbed out of my Jeep, a woman in her later-sixties came out of the stable. She wore stiff jeans rolled up at the bottom and a loose-fitting blue gingham shirt. Her hair was cut in a severe page boy, and her skin was dark and wrinkled, as you'd expect on someone who'd spent a great deal of time outside.

"I assume you're Dominick Reilly?" she said.

"I am. Sheila?"

"You betcha. You weren't expecting a stable, were you?"

"No, I wasn't."

"Sorry, it's one of my favorite jokes. People expect a house or an apartment. 'Course it wasn't like this when I bought the place thirty years ago. Thirty years ago, this was the middle of nowhere if you can imagine that."

"Is there someplace we can chat for a few minutes?" I asked.

"Why don't I show you around?"

I wasn't what you'd call keen on that. The place was

dusty and it smelled. I'd rather sit in the car, but I followed her into the stable. Inside it was dark, much cooler than it was outside where it had to be ninety degrees. When I left Long Beach, it was in the mid-seventies. Thirty miles made a big difference.

"I don't know what it is, but I've always loved horses. I didn't grow up around them, never sat one until I was well into my thirties, but I'd always dreamed of them. I wanted my oldest, Lorraine, to ride. I actually thought I'd get her into dressage. But she wasn't interested. She didn't even want to ride the horse we bought her. Copperhead she was called. Good name for her actually. If you crossed her, she bit like a snake. My husband complained about the cost, especially when Lorraine lost interest. I was coming out, though, every day to exercise Copperhead. Beautiful horse. Seventeen hands. Then in 1966 I heard this place was for sale. I mentioned it to my husband, didn't really say much but he knew me. Boy, that man knew me. Bought the place for me. Said he did it to save money. And you know what, he was right? At different times I've had up to five of my own horses. I don't pay any fees. Everyone else does. Their fees pay for mine."

"Your husband is gone?"

"He is. Rest his soul."

"You don't live here, do you?"

"Oh no, I still have the house I raised my kids in over in Toluca Lake."

We came out of the stable and were standing in front of a large corral. "This is where we teach kids to ride," she said. "That over there is The Equestrian Center. The horse trails in Griffith Park are just beyond. It used to be easier to get to them, but we manage."

"Did your brother ride?"

She seemed to withdraw for a moment, and then said, "We should go and see Patrick." Before I could agree she started walking over to an old pickup truck from the sixties. A Dodge. I think it had originally been blue but was now a sun-scorched gray. The paint on the hood was peeling off.

Sheila climbed into the driver's seat while I walked around to the passenger side. I got in. The interior was nicer than the outside: clean, cigarette butts in the ashtray but nothing like the mess I used to make; the thirty-year-old blue vinyl seats were in good condition. It was a four-speed with the shift sticking up from the floor. Four on the floor as they used to say. She fired it up and threw it into first before I'd gotten my seat belt on.

There was no air conditioning, but she drove about fifteen miles above whatever the speed limit was so there was plenty of air coming in the windows. I quickly decided it would be wise not to watch the road, so I asked her to tell me about her brother. Which prompted her to tell me about herself.

"Well, Patrick is almost fifteen years older than I am. I was barely in grade school when he started college. USC. I think I was nine or ten when he got his law license. That was just before the war. He was in the Navy, doing something important. I'm not even sure he could say what, but it was stateside. D.C. And then, let's see, after the war I was a bobby-soxer, boy crazy, God I loved Frank Sinatra. I got to see him at the Hollywood Bowl, forty-seven, forty-eight, I don't remember. It was scorching hot, and I screamed so hard I gave myself laryngitis. I went to USC just like Patrick. Only for a year though, that's how long it took me to find a husband. Jacek Karpinski. Jack. He was a senior. My parents were appalled, my marrying a Polack, but he was a Catholic so what could they say. I had Janie in 1950, John in '53, Karen in '54, Becky in '56, Lorraine in '58 and Edwin in '60—the year we elected Kennedy."

At Barham we basically ran a red light. Being the middle of the day there wasn't a lot of traffic. I tightened my seat belt, and asked,

"Do you remember Vera Korenko?"

"I only met her once. Patrick brought her to the house to meet my parents. It must have been 1948, maybe. Thanksgiving or Christmas. I'm not sure. I was already in college, so I'd met Jack. It wasn't serious yet so I wouldn't have asked him to dinner."

"What do you remember about Vera?"

"Oh, she was a beauty. And they were in love. The way they looked at each other. It was like they had a secret that only they shared. They smiled and giggled through dinner."

"Do you know why the engagement wasn't announced in the newspapers?"

"Well, they were taking it slow. She was only a few years older than me. And Patrick wanted to give her time to grow up some. Which I think is awfully wise. I started having kids so young that I missed a lot. Oh, I didn't think that then, but I do now. I wish that we could be nineteen more than once. Like two or three times. No one *needs* to be sixty-five. I mean, people started telling me I was old at thirty, which means I've been old for most of my life."

"Did he buy her an engagement ring?"

"He must have. I mean, I didn't see it when they came to dinner. I remember he said it was being made. He'd designed it himself, you see. I couldn't imagine Jack doing something like that. My ring was large but nothing to write home about. Which doesn't mean Jack wasn't a wonderful husband. He was, he really was."

"So did you see a lot of your brother?"

"I'm a terrible sister. I mean, six children and then a stable to run. No, I didn't see him often. Not until the last ten years. After Jack died. I started to make more of an effort. Patrick was already starting to decline, though... I suppose I was there when he needed me."

"Can you tell me about the things he's saying that disturb you?"

"He says he killed her. He says, 'I killed Vera.' I've tried asking him to explain but he gets agitated easily."

We were in the Cahuenga Pass. We'd crossed the bridge over the 101 and were on the west side. I was gripping the door as subtly as possible.

"I found a book at the library called *Canyon Girl*. Have you heard of it?"

"I have. I've even read parts of it."

"Does it mention your brother? I couldn't find his name in the index."

"No, it doesn't. But it wouldn't. The author, terrible little man, contacted us several times. Finally, Jack threatened to sue if he mentioned any of us. I mean, the whole thing was ridiculous. I think he made the entire book up."

"What kind of law did your husband practice?"

"Jack was the kind of lawyer who was always in the background doing things for his clients, very rich, very powerful people. I could never quite put my finger on what he did for them, but he charged a fortune for it whatever it was. Now Patrick was an entertainment lawyer. Contracts and things. That I understood."

"What was it like when you found out Vera had been killed?"

"Oh, it was awful. Jack and I had already gotten married, and I was pregnant with my first having the worst morning sickness. You know, now that I'm thinking about it,

Vera wasn't at the wedding. She was supposed to come, but she'd gotten sick. Stomach flu, food poisoning. Something with vomit."

"I'm guessing the police interviewed your brother."

"My goodness, I have no idea. Would they have done that?"

"Boyfriends, fiancés, husbands. They're usually the first suspect."

"Oh, but this was so violent, so horrible what was done to her. No one who cared about her would have done those things. They couldn't."

I decided not to contradict her on that. We were passing the Hollywood Bowl.

"Last year, my girls got together and took me to Palm Springs to see Frank Sinatra at a hotel there. I mean, he's a fat old man now, but my God, he's still got it."

"What did your parents think of Vera?"

"Oh, well, they thought it was horrible that both of their children were marrying Poles. Even though we explained that she was Czech, they just never remembered that. She barely had an accent at all. I remember that. And she smelled lovely. Patrick was destroyed of course."

"By her perfume?"

"Oh my God, no. Don't be ridiculous. You asked about what it was like when Vera was killed. Patrick was like a ghost. And he was still that way at Janie's christening. I wanted to ask him to be the godfather, but I was afraid it would remind him of Vera. I mean, if she'd been alive, I'd have asked them both. I asked a friend of mine from USC and her husband. Not that they did much. I haven't seen them in years. And Janie certainly hasn't."

We turned right at Hollywood Boulevard, heading west.

She was tailgating a Buick LeSabre when she asked me, "Do you mind if I smoke?"

Given the way she drove, the thought of adding a cigarette to the mix was terrifying. I said, "Actually, I kind of have asthma."

I didn't.

"Oh, but the windows—" she said and then thought better of it. "It's fine. We're almost there."

She seemed more emotional about having to postpone a cigarette than anything she'd talked about.

CHAPTER FOUR

July 23, 1996
Late Tuesday morning

"You're too young to remember, but in the fifties there were a lot of really trashy newspapers and magazines. Far worse than what you see at the grocery store today. They'd run stories about Vera every so often. A lot in the fifties and then less and less. It was always a little frightening, worrying that they'd mention Patrick. That one of them might decide he was the one who'd killed her."

"Your brother never married?"

"Oh no, there was no one but Vera. He was too heart-broken. I tried to fix him up with one of my girlfriends once, nice girl, divorced only one kid, but he was mortified. Couldn't face the idea. It's so romantic, don't you think?"

I wasn't sure I agreed but decided to say "Yes," since disagreeing with her seemed a bad idea. I did wonder if it was possible he *had* killed Vera. If he regretted it that would explain why he never married. Ronnie's theory aside.

And then we were in the small parking lot for Our Lady of Angels Care Home. It looked like a country club. The architecture was Spanish, in the same vein as the co-op Ronnie and I just bought. Except, well, it was a whole lot nicer. Perfectly maintained. Even before I walked inside, I was thinking the place must cost a fortune.

Sheila lit an unfiltered cigarette the minute we got out of the truck. We walked over to the steps and paused while she smoked. At one point she picked a piece of tobacco off her lip like an old-fashioned movie star.

"This place looks pretty pricey," I said.

"Patrick had some investments, certainly. The boys set up a trust and we moved those over and then sold the house. Patrick can live to a hundred and ten if he wants. Of course, he won't. Which I suppose is a blessing."

Sheila stomped out her cigarette, and we walked up the steps and into the lobby. The lobby was large and had a half dozen empty sofas for patients and visitors to sit on—though it looked like no one ever sat there. We stopped at the reception desk and signed in. We walked across the lobby and into a hallway that seemed to have patient rooms on either side.

At the end of the hallway was a large dining room with tables covered in white tablecloths. It was about a quarter full of patients eating their lunches. We turned a corner and walked down another hallway with rooms on either side. Halfway down Sheila stopped and opened a door.

"Patrick, darling, it's Sheila. I've brought a friend with me."

We stepped into the room. It was quite large with a full-sized hospital bed. Something I wasn't sure I'd ever seen before. There was a small table with a couple of chairs, a dresser big enough to hold a new nineteen-inch Sony Trinitron on top. The TV was on, playing a soap opera. There was a reclining chair in which a very old man sat. He had very little hair left, and his scalp was a shocking pink with a couple of scabs in the front. His eyes were rheumy and his lips slack.

In front of him was one of those hospital-style trays on wheels. It held his lunch tray; he hadn't touched it. He seemed to be focusing all his attention on understanding the soap opera on the TV.

"Patrick, say hello to my friend Dominick Reilly."

He looked up just a bit and asked, "Who are you?" It took me a moment to realize the question was directed at his sister.

"It's me, Sheila, your sister."

"No," he said simply.

"Patrick don't be like that. You know it's me."

"No."

To me she said, "He gets like this. I'm never sure if he's forgotten me completely or if he's just being stubborn. Patrick, Mr. Reilly wants to ask you a few questions about Vera."

"Vera. I killed Vera."

"No, dear, you couldn't poss—"

I held up my hand to stop her, then said, "Patrick, can you tell me about killing Vera?"

Sheila gasped. She must have been worried he'd launch into some macabre, detailed account of killing the poor girl. It was such an obvious question I wondered why no one had asked it.

"I killed her."

"Can you tell me more than that?"

"We went to Malibu."

"It happened in Malibu?"

"Ocean. Beach. Bathing suits."

"You went to Malibu with Vera?"

"No."

I glanced at Sheila. She shrugged. I decided to change directions.

"How did you meet Vera?"

He struggled. He seemed to be digging around in his mind for an answer. Finally, he said, "Dancing."

"Do you remember when that was?"

"Hot."

"Summer. What year was it?"

That was met with silence.

"Do you remember what car you were driving?"

"Cadillac convertible. Ivan's."

"Who's Ivan?"

"Ivan."

I looked again at Sheila. She was frowning. "Ivan was a friend of his from when he was younger. He mentions him from time to time."

"Ivan was there the night you met Vera?"

"Doris Day."

Sheila shrugged. "It's always like this."

Patrick said, "'Buttons and Bows'."

"Ah. That's what you were dancing to?"

He closed his eyes and looked like he was remembering something important.

"What are you thinking about, Patrick?"

His eyes sprung open. He seemed angry I'd interrupted him. "Who are you?" he asked. This time it was directed to me.

"You can call me Dom. I'm trying to find out what happened to Vera Korenko."

"I killed her," he said, as though that was apparent.

Sheila sighed, frustrated and upset. "I'm going to step out for another cigarette. I'll be on the front steps when you're finished." She kissed Patrick on his forehead, saying, "Goodbye Patrick. I'll be back soon."

I waited until she left the room, then I said, "You haven't touched your lunch."

He gave his lunch the raspberry. It looked like meatloaf with gravy, mashed potatoes and green beans. On the side was a Jell-O cup and a tiny milk carton. His review might be deserved.

"Do you like Mexican?"

His eyes lit up.

"If I come again, I'll bring you tacos."

"Come back."

He stared at me for a long moment. For a moment I felt like he really saw me, though I wasn't sure what he saw. He licked his lips.

"I want Ivan. Where is he?"

"I'm sorry, I don't know."

That made me wonder if Ronnie's gaydar had been on point. And if he and Ivan were lovers, well, what would that have to do with Vera's death? And Patrick thinking he was the one who killed her?

Now he was looking at the television again. It was obvious he couldn't follow whichever soap opera it was. Honestly, I wasn't sure I could. I decided I'd gotten as far as I could. Which was not very far. I tried one more question. "Patrick, how did you kill Vera?"

That seemed to confuse him. Then he said, "It was my fault."

And there it was. Something a little bit different. It was his fault Vera was dead. He killed her. But did he murder her? Or did he just feel responsible for her death?

"Why was it your fault?"

"I killed Vera."

"But you didn't. You just said it was your fault. That's different."

"I did it. I killed her."

"It was your fault. But you didn't actually kill her, did you?"

More confusion.

"Who actually killed her?"

He flinched, as though I might hit him, and said, "Me. It was me."

I thought about asking more questions but, honestly, I wasn't getting anywhere. I said good-bye and left the room.

Working my way back to the lobby, I found Sheila standing near the receptionist's desk with a short, wide woman holding a clipboard. Sheila was a bit red in the face. She was saying, "I don't know what I can do about it. He barely knows who I am. I don't think I can influence his behavior." She glanced at me and said to the woman, "Mrs. Carper, this is Dominick Reilly."

"Hello," she said.

"Apparently, Patrick has been touching the nurses inappropriately. They want us to do something about it, but... he doesn't listen to me. I don't know what I'd say if he could understand what I was saying. Do you think if a man said something..."

It took me a moment to realize she meant me. "Oh." I thought about it, I didn't really want to walk all the way back there. Then I had a hunch. To Sheila I said, "Do you mind if speak with Mrs. Carper alone?"

"Please. I'll be outside." She walked away.

"So, Mrs. Carper, can you tell me, are we talking about the female nurses or the male?"

She blushed. "The male nurses. I didn't want to say that to Mrs. Karpinski. Not directly."

"No, that's fine. Are they really upset or are they just reporting what happens?"

"They have to report it. We have rules about such things."

"When does it happen? What time of day?"

"Around dinner mostly, I think. The three to eleven shift."

"I've only spoken to Patrick once. I think Mrs. Karpinski is right. I don't think anyone can say something that will get through to him. But... I'll talk to the family and see if they can't think of something to balance things out."

"I don't know what you mean by that."

"I'm not sure I know either. Let me work on it, though." I walked away and out of the building.

Outside, Sheila was just putting out another cigarette. "What did she say?"

"Not much really. If I were you, I'd try sending a nice basket every few weeks: muffins, candies, one of those fruit bouquets. Put in a card about how much your family appreciates them caring for your brother. Make sure it's delivered in the evening. That'll probably take care of it."

"Are you sure?"

"They want your brother's money. They'll smooth it over," I said, just as something else occurred to me. "You sold his house; did you get rid of all his things?"

"I haven't had the heart to go through it all. The boys had it put into storage."

"Do you think I could look through it?"

"Certainly. What would you be looking for?"

"I don't know. But if there's something to find it will probably be there."

On the drive home, I said to Sheila, "While you were out of the room, your brother said, 'It was my fault.' That makes me think that when he says he killed Vera it's more that his actions may have led to her death. But he didn't murder her."

"Yes, he's said things like that before."

"You don't think he killed that girl, do you?"

"No, of course not."

"Then what do need from me?"

"I need to know what to say to him. You saw him. I need to be able to say, you didn't kill Vera. This person killed Vera."

"You realize you could just lie? Just pick a name and say that's the killer."

"I'm not sure he doesn't know who the killer really is, though. That's why he's saying it's his fault. I think somehow he sent her to her death."

A little more than an hour later I was sitting down to lunch with a book. Well, sitting down in my Jeep with chicken tacos from Poquito Mas and *Canyon Girl* propped on the steering wheel with the engine running and the air conditioner going full blast.

The first chapter of the book covered the discovery of Vera Korenko's body and details from the autopsy. Her hyoid bone was broken, which often happens during a strangling. Her cheek bone, her jaw and two vertebrae in her neck were also fractured, a severe beating. Had she lived through that she'd have had a long, painful road to recovery.

Halfway through the tacos, I set the book aside. Taking a long gulp of Coke, I worried about whether I should continue with this. It was interesting enough, certainly. But could I give the Karpinskis what they wanted? They wanted me to find out who killed Vera Korenko. Despite all the interest in the case, no one had solved it in nearly fifty years. Let's face it, I was unlikely to find the killer.

Then again, I shouldn't quit on the first day. They wouldn't be satisfied by that. I should wait until I was sure Patrick didn't do it. Rather, when I could *prove* he didn't do it. They were probably going to have to be satisfied with that. As I took my last few bites of taco, I opened the book back up.

Toward the end of the first chapter, it talked about the fact that Vera had been raped. They knew this because they found semen inside of her. That stopped me. Would they have kept it in 1949? Would we be able to test it now? I knew that semen used to be tested to tell what blood type the rapist had, which meant it really only worked to exclude suspects. Did they do that in 1949? And did that mean they kept the semen? Where was it? And could it be tested again? Then I remembered I'd seen that they'd gotten DNA from dinosaur bones, so fifty-year-old semen had to be a snap—right?

I let the idea drift to the back of my mind and continued the book. The second chapter went back to Vera's birth and told the story of her parents arriving in 1912 from the Czech speaking part of Austria-Hungry. There was no Czechoslovakia until after World War I. Philburn noted the family said they were from Czechoslovakia after 1918. Again, this suggested Philburn having contact with Vera's family. They settled for a while in Chicago and Vera was born in 1924. I remembered something Sheila had just said to me, that Vera barely had an accent. But she was born in Chicago, she wouldn't have a Czech accent. Even if she'd grown up speaking Czech, she wouldn't have an accent. Bilingual kids rarely did.

When Vera was a girl her father drove an ice truck—which he continued to do through the Second World War, while her mother took in laundry. She didn't do well in school and was considered 'boy crazy' in high school. That's when it hit me that Vera was only a few years older than Sheila. She was twenty-five when she was killed, so she'd have been twenty-three or four when she became engaged to Patrick Gill. He was eight years older. Early thirties. Then I wondered, *Did Vera know he was gay?* Probably not. It wasn't talked about the way it was now. People wouldn't have thought it was possible. He wouldn't have been the first gay man to become involved with an unsuspecting young woman.

> "Tempted by the glitter of tinseltown, Vera came West at seventeen to take her chances with stardom."

The book was certainly cheesy. Sheila had said it wasn't exactly true, so I took this with a grain of salt. Either Vera did want to be an actress or it made a better story. It could have been that she just hated snow, but that was hardly dramatic.

Once she got to Los Angeles, she quickly got a job at a munitions factory producing ammunition for the war effort. She was clever and a good typist, so she spent most of the war as a secretary to the company's president. After the war she found work at Security First National Bank and worked in their Hollywood office.

I'd finished eating so it was time to drive home. There would be just enough of the afternoon left to go into the office and help Karen pull together everything we needed for the Anne Michaels deposition. We'd make copies of her testimony from the original trial, my notes from the interviews I'd done with her, my suggested questions along with Lydia's, and finally a statement we'd taken from Larry himself covering the important details of their relationship in 1976.

As I was driving home, I got out the cellular phone Ronnie insisted I carry—mainly, I think, because that gave him a better deal on his—and called him.

"Hey," I said when he picked up.

"Where are you?"

"On the 710. Your gaydar was right. Patrick Gill is gay."

"I won the bet. Yay! What did I win?"

"I never actually took that bet. You didn't win anything."

"Bummer. How did you find out he's gay?"

"He's been making passes at the male nurses."

"Ick. Isn't he like, eighty?"

"Careful. You're in love with an old man. Remember?"

"It's different. When you're disgusting and eighty, I'll be disgusting and sixty-four. It evens out."

I wasn't sure it would work out that way, but I figured I'd let him think what he wanted.

"Anyway, I'm wondering if you can take Thursday off?"

"How come?"

"All this guy's stuff is in a couple of storage facilities, and I could use some help looking through it all."

"A treasure hunt? That's fabulous. I'm in!"

CHAPTER FIVE

July 24, 1996
Wednesday afternoon

At one fifty, the bell over the door rang, a relic from the office's retail days, and in came Anne Michaels née Whittemore. She was a hard looking woman in her late thirties, with haunted eyes and thin brown hair. She'd had a baby about eight weeks before and wore a loose top to hide what was probably a loose belly. A baby carrier hung from one arm. In it an infant dressed in pink.

She gave me a 'you again' look and said, "Well, I'm here."

Karen got up from her desk and said, "I'll get Lydia."

"Thank you for coming," I said. "This will mean the world for Larry."

"Yeah," she said, without enthusiasm.

I tried a different tact, "What's the baby's name?"

"Pete. The ultrasound wasn't accurate, so all his clothes

are pink." She seemed to cringe as she said it, as though imagining the untold damage she was doing to her child.

Lydia came out and introduced herself. Then asked, "Is your attorney on his way?"

"Ha. At two hundred and fifty dollars an hour, no thank you. Do you know they charge in fifteen minutes chunks and nothing smaller? A five-minute phone call costs sixty-two-fifty. Oh, I guess you know that. Stupid question."

"It is expensive, I know. It is often worth it, though."

"I'm just going to tell the truth. I mean, he billed me for two hours just to tell me that's what I should do."

"Well, we want you to tell the truth so this should be pretty easy. We have a table set up in the back. Nothing fancy but we thought you might not want to drive to down-town L.A."

"No way. I can't stand L.A."

"We're going to be videotaping your deposition. I assume your lawyer told you that?"

"Yeah, he did."

"Well, come on back."

We walked back to the open area behind the offices. We'd set up a folding banquet table as the conference table. A woman named Elaine Joy from Eyes on Justice was standing next to a video camera on a tripod. She looked bored already. We'd had her before. She wanted to use more interesting camera angles, but we wouldn't let her. It was one set up per deposition, period. She could feel her Academy Award slipping through her fingers.

"Can we get you anything?" Lydia asked. "Water, coffee, soda?"

Anne shook her head. Lydia and I sat down on one side of the table. She had the file we'd prepared in front of her along with a pad of yellow legal paper. I had the same file and a pad too, for notes. Karen hurried in and sat down.

"I forwarded the phones to voicemail."

Anne had set her baby on the floor next to her chair and was making herself comfortable. She looked lonely across the table all by herself.

"Okay. Today's questions will focus on your testimony at trial," Lydia said. "After we're done, Dom may have some additional questions we'd like you to answer."

"Will I be charged with perjury? My lawyer said I wouldn't be, but I'm not sure I trust him."

"Perjury is rarely charged. We'll be making a motion to give Larry a new trial based on your deposition today, a deposition we plan to do with Larry's defense attorney and Larry's own statements. It's possible, even likely the district attorney will say that your deposition is false and that your original testimony was correct. Once they've done that, they're in a precarious position. As long as you're telling the truth today, they can't prove you lied now. And it would be unwise to prosecute you for your original statements since they're on record claiming you were truthful then. Do you understand?"

"I think so."

"Do you have any questions before we begin?"

"No, I think I'm fine."

Lydia nodded at Elaine Joy to turn on the camera. Then in a loud voice she said, "This is the deposition of Anne Michaels in the matter of Larry Wilkes v. State of California writ of habeas corpus. Present are Elaine Joy, videographer; Karen Addison, notary public; Dominick Reilly, investigator for The Freedom Agenda; and myself, Lydia Gonsalez, Esquire."

She paused and sipped the coffee she'd brought with her.

"First, I'd like to say that I advised the witness to bring an attorney and she has chosen not to. That is correct, Mrs. Michaels?"

"Yes, that's right."

"Mrs. Michaels, this is a deposition in which I will ask questions regarding your testimony in the trial of Larry Wilkes for the murder of Pete Michaels. You must answer those questions truthfully. This is a formal legal proceeding just like testifying in court. You are under the same obligation to tell the truth, the whole truth and nothing but the truth. Do you swear to tell the truth?"

"I do."

"You can ask questions at any time, and you will receive a written transcript of the deposition to which you will be allowed to make changes. Do you understand?"

"Yes."

"Let's begin. You gave testimony in Larry Wilkes trial for the murder of Pete Michaels."

"I did."

"How would you characterize that testimony?"

"It was false. I lied."

"Why did you lie?"

"Because Larry wanted me to."

"And why was that?"

"Larry and Pete were boyfriends, lovers, whatever. I've always thought it would be worse for him if the jury knew that. I think that's why he wanted me to say I was Pete's fiancé."

"Why are you coming forward now?"

"Honestly, to save my marriage. I married Pete's brother, Paul. I never told him the truth until... It's almost been a year. I went to the dentist and I was messed up afterward. From the gas. I told him the truth then. That I was never his brother's fiancée. I'm trying to make everything better. For me. For my husband. For Larry."

I scratched an X on the top of my pad so that Lydia could see it. To Anne she said, "To clarify, when you say husband you mean ex-husband. You and Paul Michaels are divorced."

"We're talking about getting back together. I guess I was being optimistic. Is there a law against that?"

"We just need to be accurate. You never know what a prosecutor might latch on to."

"Whatever."

"When did you find out Larry and Pete were in a relationship?"

"Larry told me. Sometime over the summer, I think."

"The summer of 1976?"

"Yes."

"You never saw them together?"

"No. But—"

"But?"

"I'd seen them talking to each other at school once. It just made sense."

"In your testimony you said that Pete was beating Larry up, is that true?"

"It's true that I said it, but no I don't think Pete ever beat Larry up." She was smiling. Happy that she'd answered exactly.

"In your testimony, it seems like you truly believe Larry killed Pete. Didn't you go further than Larry wanted you to go? He didn't want to be convicted, did he?"

She hesitated. After a deep breath she said, "I don't remember that. I wouldn't have said anything like that."

Lydia opened the file in front of her, flipped over a couple of pages, then said, "From your testimony, 'I guess Larry got tired of getting beat-up because that's when he killed Pete.' That sounds like you believed Larry killed Pete, doesn't it?"

"I didn't mean it."

"Why did you say it? Larry wanted you to say Pete was your fiancé, but he didn't ask you to say he killed Pete, did he?"

"No, he didn't."

"Did someone ask you to say that?"

"I was just a kid. Barely eighteen. I didn't have a lot of friends. Didn't get along with my parents. I was interviewed by the police a couple times, the DA four times, maybe five. Each time they seemed to want me to go further. Make more definitive statements. So, I did."

"Are you saying they coached you?"

"I guess you could call it that, yes."

"Did they tell you what to say?"

"Not exactly."

"What did they say?"

"They kept asking me if I thought Larry killed Pete. I knew they wanted me to think that."

Lydia glanced at me. If they coached her that might be a violation of some kind, I wasn't sure which. It was also going to be hard to prove.

I made a note on my pad, it just said "think." I wanted to ask Anne who she thought killed Pete all those years ago. I knew that Lydia deliberately avoided asking that since we didn't know the answer. It wouldn't be good if she said she thought Larry killed Pete.

Lydia continued. "You say that Larry asked you to say

you were Pete's fiancée, when was that? Did you visit him in jail?"

"No. He called me."

Lydia glanced at me again, and I knew we were in trouble but didn't immediately know why.

"How are you feeling, Anne?" she asked. "Do you feel all right?"

"I'm fine thank you."

There was a pause. I could tell Lydia was trying to decide how to move forward. I still wasn't sure what the problem was.

"When Larry asked you to say Pete was your fiancé, how did he phrase it?"

Anne seemed surprised for a moment and then said, "Oh, well, it was weird I guess. He said he was sorry about what happened to Pete, and that he didn't do it. He thought it would be okay if I told people I was engaged to him. That I didn't have to keep it a secret anymore."

"You took that to mean you should lie and say Pete was your fiancé?"

"Yes. At some point, I don't remember whether it was before he said that or after, but he said that I shouldn't curse because we were being listened to. So I knew why he couldn't just ask."

Ah, that was what had made Lydia pause. Their conversation would have gone to the police. And he knew that, so he couldn't say anything directly. If Anne said he asked her directly that would not be believable. Lydia had been worried she was about to expose a lie.

Carefully, she asked, "How did you respond when Larry said that you and Pete were engaged?"

"You know, he must have told me they were listening

before he said that. Because I didn't say much. I didn't correct him. I probably said I'd think about it."

"When did you decide to go along with the lie?"

"The police came to my house a few days later. I'd already decided I couldn't do it. I guess they heard the tape of the conversation, because they asked me directly if I was Pete's fiancée, I told the truth. I told them we weren't engaged. They didn't believe me. They called me a liar. My parents were right there, sitting next to me on the sofa. I couldn't say that Larry was gay because they'd have been upset that I was friends with him. I mean, they were already upset that I knew him. They thought he was a killer. I didn't want them to think he was a *gay* killer. I just... I had to say I was engaged to Pete. Everyone was going to be unhappy if I didn't. Even Larry."

"You've been telling a lie for twenty years," Lydia said, not exactly a question.

"Can I change something I said—or modify it, I guess?"

"Yes, of course. You're here to tell the truth."

"I think part of why I said those things at trial, making it seem like I thought Larry was the killer, I think by then I was angry. At him. And I wasn't sure he didn't kill Pete. I mean, I wasn't there so I... don't know."

"The phone call you received from Larry. Do you remember when that was?"

"A few days after the murder. Maybe three or four, I don't remember exactly. I remember he had to call a few times. My parents wouldn't accept the call."

"Just a few more questions," Lydia said. "If we get another trial for Larry, you'll be asked to testify to what you've said today. Then cross-examined. I'm going to ask a few questions a prosecutor would ask. Is that all right?"

"Yeah, sure."

"Is everything you've said today truthful?"

"Yes."

"You were lying in 1976 but you're not lying now?"

"That's correct."

"Why should we believe you?"

"Because I'm an adult now and I've had a very long time to live with the mistakes I made."

"You said you're doing this to save your marriage. That's a good reason to lie. How do we know that's not what you're doing?"

"I can't save my marriage with lies. Ask my hus—ex-husband." She was stubborn, I'll give her that. Trying to save a marriage after the divorce was final.

"If Larry asked you to lie now, would you?"

"I haven't seen Larry since he went to prison. We're not close anymore."

"All right, thank you Anne. I think we'll stop now." To the camera she said, "The deposition is over."

Then she nodded at Elaine Joy who turned off the camera. Everyone seemed to relax a little. Lydia said, "As I told you at the beginning, Dom has a few questions for you. It won't take long."

"Could I have that bottle of water now?"

"Of course."

I jumped up and grabbed a bottle from the refrigerator. Opened the bottle and set it down in front of Anne. Then I took my seat again. Lydia remained.

"Do you remember a girl named Sammy Blanchard?"

"Kind of. She was a couple years behind me in school. Isn't she the one who married a teacher?"

"Yes."

"Okay, I kind of remember her."

"Did you ever see her with Andy Showalter?"

"Oh my God. Um, it's a huge school and I'm not sure I'd remember if I did see them together. I mean, neither of them was on my radar. Or really anyone's radar. I mean, obviously Andy Showalter was... but that was only after high school. Why? Do you think she had something to do with... I mean, that doesn't make any sense."

"Do you remember anyone she might have been friends with?"

"No, not really... Well, wait. In grade school my best friend was Sharon Hawley. She had a younger sister who would be Sammy's age. She might know."

"Do you have any contact information?"

"No, it's been ages. But, we're having our twentieth high school reunion in October. I got an email about that. Well, I mean... Paul got an email about it. I can ask him to forward it to you."

"That would be great." I took a beat thinking about how I wanted to phrase this. "When I interviewed you before you said you thought your husband might have killed Pete."

"Oh God, you know, I never really believed that. I was just very angry at him."

"At this point, after twenty years, who do you think killed Pete Michaels?"

"I don't know. I'd have to say the most likely person is still Larry."

And that is why you don't ask all the questions during the deposition.

CHAPTER SIX

July 24, 1996
Late Wednesday afternoon

After Anne Michaels left, Lydia called me into her office and said, "We have to do better. I can't go into a deposition not knowing all the answers."

I was sure she was talking about when Larry asked Anne to lie. Quickly, I said, "I'm sorry about that."

"I'm not blaming you, Dom. I should have asked you about that. Ultimately, it's my responsibility."

"But I'm here to make things easier for you."

Before we broke out in an argument about which of us fucked up more, she shifted, saying, "I don't think I'm as over the shooting as I thought."

"You're safe," I said.

"That's not it. I keep thinking it through, trying to see where I went wrong. I keep seeing him with that knife at Karen's throat, knowing it was my fault."

It wasn't her fault. It was Stu Whatley's fault. But that

wasn't what she was talking about. She was talking about responsibility. She'd taken Whatley's case. He was innocent of the crime he'd been imprisoned for but had still been a violent rapist. She'd made a decision that had led to violence. I knew what that was like.

"You're helping people. That can come at a cost."

"We're helping people," she said. "The deposition still went okay. I'm pretty happy," she said, getting back to the deposition. "I think we've got what we need. We need to get the rest of the discovery provided to Raymond Harris. Hopefully, he'll have a transcript from that phone conversation. Also, notes from the interview Anne described with the police."

"What should we do to prepare for meeting him Friday?"

"I need to get him to agree to be deposed on what he knows about Larry's sexuality, and whether he said the things that Larry says he said."

"And Anne," I pointed out.

"Well, no. She didn't speak to him directly. What she said is only what Larry said. Or what she's worked out for herself. It supports his story, that's all."

The file Harris had sent over contained the letter of engagement Larry signed when he hired Harris, notes from two different visits to county jail which were cryptic and confusing, several newspaper articles about the murder, notes from an interview he'd done with Larry's parents—his father seemed to believe he killed Pete, his mother wasn't sure what to believe. And that was about it.

"You'll probably need him to walk through his notes of his visits with Larry," I said. "I haven't been able to make heads or tails of them."

"We'll need to do that eventually, but I don't know if there's anything in there that will help us get a new trial."

"If Larry said anything about his sexuality, that would help. And, when he said it. If Harris suggested he not let on that he was gay before he came up with the engagement idea—you know what, that engagement idea came from an article in *The Downey Ledger* almost immediately after the murder. A source told the newspaper that Pete had recently become engaged, but there was no mention to whom. I'm pretty sure Sammy Blanchard was the source trying to throw suspicion in another direction."

"Well, it worked," Lydia said.

"It did."

"We can't prove that, though. A journalist is not going to want to give up their source. If anything, it hurts us. Anne was vague about when she spoke to Larry. The newspaper mention of the engagement was just a couple days after the murder, right?"

"Yes, that's right."

"If their phone call happened after the newspaper article, then we have a problem we'll need to solve. How did that end up in the newspaper before Larry and Anne cooked up the idea?"

"Should we talk to the journalist? You never know, they might tell us something."

"Let's try to establish when Larry and Anne had that conversation, and we'll go from there."

Karen walked into the office and handed me a slip of paper with Wallace Philburn's name, address and phone number on it. I took a quick look and said thank you. Karen walked out of the office. Lydia didn't bother asking what that was about.

"I'm going to take off tomorrow and work on the Karpinski thing," I told her.

"Okay. Just keep track of your hours. And then add ten percent," she said, smiling meanly.

"Do you want to be kept up to speed on that?"

"Not really. I'll ask if I get curious, but I have enough bad stuff in my head."

After that, I left and went to Hot Times, the coffee shop across from Park Pantry. I ordered a large latte with whole milk, then sat down at a table on the far side of the room. There was a TV over the fireplace playing some kind of music video countdown. I opened *Canyon Girl* and turned to the third chapter, which began with a discussion of women's rights groups in the 1940s. Philburn talked about the ways in which women's entry into the workforce during the war increased their desire for more equal treatment. He mentioned several groups but eventually focused on one, Sisters of Artemis. It took about five pages, but he finally connected Vera Korenko to the group. Apparently, it was from this group that she drew most of her friendships.

My name was called and I went up to the counter to get my coffee. I tipped the barista, who'd made a pretty design in my cup, and went back to my table. Alanis Morisette was pondering irony on the TV screen. The song had prompted several discussions in my house about what was irony and what was coincidence. Honestly, I'm still fuzzy on the whole thing.

Back at my seat, I kept reading. Apparently, Philburn had tracked down and interviewed several of Vera's friends. One friend, Rochelle "Rocky" Havoc, who by the sixties was living in Long Beach, remembered Vera as being "whip smart, headstrong and sometimes reckless." Betty Brooks lived in Glendale with her husband and three kids, "Vera was the sweetest girl, a little dreamy, I think. She really believed she could make the world a better place." He spent a lot of time with Manny and Virginia Marker, who'd socialized with Vera for a time the year before she was killed. Virginia wasn't quoted in the chapter, but Manny was, "Vera was a bad influence. I put up with it for a long time and then I put my foot down. We didn't see her again after the fall of 1948. When I heard that she'd been killed, I can't say I was surprised."

I checked my pockets for a pencil to circle these names. Then I remembered it was a library book. I popped out to my Jeep and grabbed a notebook from the glove compartment. Back inside, I was about to write down the names, when I heard, "My goodness, imagine meeting you here."

I looked up and there was our roommate, Junior Clybourne. Despite the fact that it was summer in California, Junior was dressed in corduroy slacks, a black shirt and a paisley vest all topped off by an extra-long white scarf. Even though he had a brown fedora on his head, I could see from the wisps of gray hair sticking out that he needed a haircut. He looked dangerously thin—despite the surprising amount of my food he ate.

I said hello and asked how he was.

"Oh, rushed off my feet. I volunteered to help out at The Center. Horrible mistake. They've got me counseling newbies; boys who just learned they're positive. I call my little spiel 'the tour'."

He hurried off to order.

I went back to writing down the names of Vera's friends. Then I flipped back to the photo section and wrote down the name of the detective who'd worked her case, as well as the boy who'd found her body. You never know.

I'd just gone back to the book, about to start chapter

four, when Junior plunked himself down at my table, and said, "Why on earth are you reading that?"

"It's for a case I'm working on."

"I remember that poor girl. An awful thing."

"Um, she was killed in 1949. How old *are* you?"

"Never ask a lady her age. I didn't mean I remember from when it happened. I was still a child. Mostly. No, there was another murder in the late sixties. Similar. Lesbian girl. People started talking about the Canyon Girl again."

"Do you think Vera Korenko was a lesbian?"

"That's what people were saying."

"Have you ever heard of the Sisters of Artemis?"

"Of course. I'm not sure they're still around, but they were definitely around in the seventies. They used to march in the parade."

"You have quite a memory."

"Not really. The pride parade in L.A. was much different in the seventies. The last time I went, four or five years ago, my God it was three hours long. Everybody and their Aunt Sally wants to be in it now. Seriously, the last time I went I kept waiting for people to march by carrying signs that said, 'I met a gay person once.' In the seventies, the whole thing was over in half an hour. Much easier to remember who was there."

"Do you know anything about them? The book describes it as a feminist group in the forties."

"Yeah, well, when I first came out, which was nineteen —" He brushed his hand across his mouth to obscure the date. "—feminism was code for lesbian. It's not so much anymore. Unless you listen to conservative talk radio."

"You listen to conservative talk radio?"

"Of course, I do. I love a good laugh."

I have to say, the idea that Vera might be a lesbian made immediate sense to me. Patrick was gay, Vera was gay. Somehow, they met and decided to have a relationship of convenience. Telling the world they were nice normal heterosexuals planning to get married, while doing as they pleased. Of course, how that might lead to Vera's grisly death was a mystery.

While I had those thoughts, Junior had forged on. "—of course, you are keeping the house on 2nd Street, aren't you?"

Oh, he was talking about the co-op and the future. "Yes, of course, one of Ronnie's absolutes is that once you own a piece of property you never ever sell it."

"I imagine you'll be renting out your bedroom?" He didn't wait for an answer. "I hope you'll be a bit more selective than you were with me. I mean, everything worked out, but you didn't know that when you let me into your home."

"I think Ronnie's going to look for a flight attendant." Though as I said that I wondered if it was still true. He'd wanted flight attendants when we lived there because they weren't around a lot. If we're not living there, I suppose it didn't matter. We could rent to anyone.

"I wonder, would it be possible for *me* to rent your bedroom? You could rent out the one I'm in now."

Our bedroom had its own tiny bathroom. Ronnie was going to want extra for that, and Junior was already paying less than he wanted. The difference would be hundreds a month. I was not making that decision on my own.

"You'll need to ask Ronnie."

"Of course," he said, clearly disappointed. "Well, I'm off to give 'the tour.' See you at home."

I went back and reread the part about her friends. Rocky. Duh. That was definitely the kind of name a lesbian in the forties might choose. Betty said Vera dreamed of making the world a better place... for lesbians? Manny Marker said Vera was a bad influence. Well, now I knew what kind of bad influence.

I'd slipped my cellular phone into my shirt pocket rather than leave it in the Jeep. I took it out and dialed the number Karen had given me. The phone number had a 619 area code. That was most of the southern part of the state from San Diego to Nevada. Philburn's street address was in Palm Springs. I'd been trying to wait until it was time for nighttime minutes but honestly, I wasn't sure when they started. I'd have to get the bill from Ronnie so I could charge this call back to the Karpinskis.

A man picked up.

"Yes, I'm trying to reach Wallace Philburn."

"Speaking. Who is this?"

"I'm reading *Canyon Girl* right now and I wonder if I could ask you a few questions?"

"So, you're a reader?" he asked, a tiny bit of excitement in his voice. "Are you enjoying the book?"

"It's fascinating."

"Well, thank you. It's always a delight to hear from a fan. I didn't know people were still buying the book. I haven't seen it in a bookstore in forever."

"I got it from the library."

"Oh. Well, I suppose... Have you heard of this Interweb site called Amazon? Don't get the book there. They're going to destroy bookstores, which means destroying books."

"When you wrote the book, did you know the Sisters of Artemis was a lesbian organization?"

"Who are you? You didn't introduce yourself."

"Dominick Reilly."

"Let me guess, you're investigating Vera Korenko's murder?"

"I am."

"For?"

"The family of Patrick Gill."

And then he hung up on me.

CHAPTER SEVEN

July 25, 1996
Thursday morning

In the morning, Ronnie, John and I drove up to the Silver Lake area. The storage facility had turned out to be the one on Beverly Boulevard near Virgil in my old stomping ground. General Storage was housed in an Art Deco building about fifteen stories tall and made of beige stone that was ornately carved on the first floor. The entrance was just off Virgil. I parked in their lot, and we went inside.

A grumpy young man, practically a teenager, sat at the reception desk staring at us.

"Yeah?"

"We're going up to lockers 1018, 19 and 20."

"Take the elevator to the tenth floor. Shocking, I know."

He was annoying, so I said, "Have a nice day."

I'm not sure I meant it. All right, I know I didn't mean it. We walked over to the elevator and hit the button. Ronnie rolled his eyes at me.

In the elevator, John asked, "What exactly are we looking for?"

"Personal papers, diaries, photo albums, photographs, bills, taxes... Anything that might give us more information on who Patrick Gill was and who he was involved with: friends, lovers, associates. Particularly in the nineteen forties and early fifties."

"Personally, I don't have a lot of those things—mementos, I mean. I have friends and..." John said. "I do have a photo album and a box of important papers, but that's about it. I don't keep bills or taxes..."

"You're supposed to keep your tax records for seven years," Ronnie said. "In case you get audited."

"I use the EZ form. There's not a lot to audit."

I knew almost nothing about my taxes. Ronnie did them. When the elevator opened, we found ourselves in a long bland hallway. Following the numbers, we found 1018, 19 and 20. From a pocket, I took out a keychain that was labeled SHEILA K STABLES and held three keys. The locks were the kind of lock you bought for your gym bag if you weren't good at remembering numbers. Not very secure, but then simply being ten floors up was pretty secure, so it probably didn't matter.

One by one, I opened the lockups. John rolled up the doors. Once they were all open, I stood back and looked at them for a moment. Each lockup was full to the brim. I could see the ends of sofas, mattresses, dressers, some really ugly lamps, easy chairs, a dining table, a bunch of end tables, framed art, pillows, rugs, bookcases, a console television—and boxes, lots and lots of boxes. Each lockup seemed to have a path that went through to the back.

"We should each take one," I suggested. "Preferences?"

"I want the center one," Ronnie said.

"I'll take 1018," John said. It was the one to the left.

"Okay, let's get going," I said as I headed for 1020.

They'd left me the lockup with the most boxes. Which was good because what was in them was probably what I wanted. But also bad because it meant I had to lift them.

Years ago, twelve years ago, I got shot. The bullet went through my chest messing up a rib, nicking a lung, and doing a number on my right shoulder blade. That had resulted in one surgery. The doctors had such a good time with that, they wanted to do it again six months later. But by that time I was gone, and seeing a doctor was not exactly a priority.

And it's really not that bad. I have trouble getting things off the top shelf—and when you're six-foot-three people ask you to get things off the top shelf all the time. I'm a continual disappointment. I also have trouble with things like push-ups and pull-ups and lifting weights. Body-building was out of the question. And I have a problem with heavy boxes—well, heavy anything.

In lockup 1020, there were fifteen boxes lined up, five deep, three tall, right next to the door. The only way I was going to be able to open them was to move them out to the hallway. I grabbed the first one; it was just below chest height. Not too bad. But then I had to put it down. I squatted and then a pain shot through my shoulder. I got the box close to the floor and dropped it.

The box had been taped closed. I pulled out my keys and used the key to my Jeep to open the box. Inside, I found six thick, red lawbooks. I didn't bother looking at the titles, they weren't what I wanted. I pulled the next box out, the one below the first. Same thing. Law books. Different color.

I decided to leave the bottom row of boxes where they were. I opened that box. More legal books.

Then I began shifting the boxes from one stack to another, so I didn't have to move them far. I worked my way through all fifteen boxes. Nothing but legal books. It had taken a half an hour for me to look in the fifteen boxes. This was going to take a while.

I asked myself why Edwin or his brother hadn't taken the books. But then I realized they were probably outdated. Patrick was eighty. He likely stopped practicing ten, fifteen years ago. The books were out-of-date. Useless.

Why did they keep them at all, then? I couldn't imagine the Karpinskis loading up a moving van themselves. They must have hired movers and then not paid a lot of attention. I left the two boxes I'd put into the hallway out there and moved on.

Next to the boxes was an absurdly large, mahogany desk with a couple of straight-backed chairs sitting on top of the leather inlaid surface. I moved the chairs, sat down in one of them, and began opening the drawers. The drawer in the center contained things you'd expect: pencils, pens, erasers, stamps, business cards, a stapler, a staple-remover, match-books, paperclips, clamps and a cigarette lighter.

The top drawer on the left side contained stationary, both letter-sized and note-sized. The drawer directly below was full of boxed envelopes. Several sizes. And below that, manila envelopes 9x12.

On the right side, there were only two large drawers. The top drawer held an old black, rotary desk phone. The kind the telephone company used to rent. It was always the cheapest one when phones began to come in colors.

But all that was a long time ago. Patrick must have bought the phone at some point. I wondered if it still worked. The bottom drawer was filled up with cassettes. They were numbered P1, P2, P3... or at least I assumed that. They weren't in order. What I was seeing was P12, P8, P2. I suppose there were around fifteen tapes. I had no idea what they were. I'd have to look around for a tape deck somewhere.

I decided I ought to check on Ronnie and John. But as I walked out of the lockup, I took in what else was there. Beyond the desk were a couple of shovels, a stack of four tires with a toolbox sitting on top of them, rakes, gardening tools. This was starting to make some sense. These were the contents of the garage. The boxes and the desk had been in a study. There was a brown leather sofa, tufted and long. That too would have been in the study. And there were two wing-backed chairs in a brown-and-black plaid.

Stepping out, I walked the few steps over to 1019. There was no hint of Ronnie. I stepped in, noticing a large, simple sofa in a ghastly gold velvet fabric. There were more boxes against the wall, which Ronnie hadn't opened yet. That annoyed me.

"Ronnie?"

"Back here."

He was at the very back of the lockup, on the far side. He'd pushed some furniture away and was staring at two green chairs. They were trimmed in carefully carved wood —the arms, the legs, and around the back cushion. French provincial? I wasn't sure. They certainly looked like they belonged at some castle somewhere a few centuries back.

"Look at these," Ronnie said. "Aren't they fabulous?"

"If you like green." Actually, green was fine as long as it didn't look like pea soup or mint candies. These chairs were definitely pea soup.

"I'd have them reupholstered. I know a place. Do you think they'll sell them to you?"

"I have no idea. That's not why they gave me keys. What else did you find?"

"There are a lot of old albums."

"Photo albums?" I asked, getting excited.

"No, record albums. Doris Day. Frank Sinatra. Ella Fitzgerald. That kind of album. And a record player. The kind that's on legs. You slide the lid back when you're not listening to it. It's totally cool."

"My mother had one like that in the sixties."

"And I adore this sofa," he stepped past me to the simple gold sofa.

"Did you find anything that might be useful, to me?"

"Not really."

"This is the living room furniture, right?"

"On this side. That's bedroom furniture over there."

"Is that a grand piano?"

"It is."

"Don't people put photographs on top of those?"

"You want me to find the photographs?"

"I do."

"Okay. I will."

"Can you open these boxes?"

"Fine."

I'd ruined his fun. I was a terrible person. I left him and went next door to ruin whatever fun John was having. 1018 had some furniture at the front: a floral loveseat, some end tables, crazy lamps. But as you went back, boxes, and then some old typewriters and office items.

"Hey," I said. "What are you finding?"

"Dinnerware, pots and pans, utensils. But look at this..." He led me over to the typewriters, two of them: one looked like it was from the fifties, a Royal, and the other looked even older, a Remington. John moved them so we could look at what was underneath. It was basically a white table with an IBM Selectric sunk into one end and a box holding two cassette decks at the other.

"What is that?" I asked.

"I think it's some kind of word processor from the seventies. These are the tapes it uses," he said, showing me a box on the floor. "The manual is underneath."

"So, you think the tapes are like floppy disks?"

"Yeah. I think so. I mean, they can't hold much."

"I found some of those in Patrick's desk."

From where I stood, I could see that these cassettes were labeled differently: 75-106, 75-223, 75-004. Obviously, the year and then a number for the document or documents. Legal documents. I mean, that made sense, right? But what were the cassettes in Patrick's desk?

"Have you seen any bags or empty boxes?"

"Um, yeah. It's not big," he said, reaching under one of the typewriters and pulling out a yellowing Fred Segal bag.

"Thanks. Matchbooks. Business cards. Anything personal."

"Got it."

I started to walk away, and he said, "Hey, thanks for this. It's fascinating in a creepy way."

"I should be thanking you, I appreciate the help."

I walked out of 1018. On the way back to 1020, I looked into 1019 and saw that Ronnie was opening the boxes like I'd asked. "What are you finding?"

"Books."

"Law books?"

"No. Fiction."

I stood behind him and looked into the boxes. Herman

Wouk, Ira Levin, Gore Vidal, John Updike, Christopher Isherwood, Philip Roth. A who's who of American letters. The male edition. There were women who wrote in the sixties and seventies, but it didn't look like Patrick read them.

I went back into 1020. After scooping up the matchbooks and business cards and putting them into the Fred Segal bag, I looked the room over and thought this through. There had to be tax information. Bills. Patrick's library or den or home office seemed to end up in this lockup. His paperwork had to be here. The thing is, I couldn't find anything remotely like a filing cabinet. There should be nice ones, wooden ones, ones that would have matched his desk. But I didn't see anything like that.

A few minutes later, I did find another box behind the leather sofa. When I opened it up, I found five accordion files that held Patrick Giles bills from 1990-1994. Success, of a sort.

Right away, I saw that something was wrong. They were neat and organized and recent. The man I'd met the other day would not have been able to keep his records like this just two years ago. What I should have been seeing is decline. I could believe he'd be able to put together a file like this in 1990. But the files would have, should have declined with him. They should have become increasing messy and disorganized. But they weren't.

I stepped out of the lockup. Ronnie was still looking through boxes of books.

"Hey John, come here a minute."

I waited for John to come out. When he was standing with Ronnie and me, I said, "You know how when a gay guy dies, his friends go into this apartment or house before his family so they can take out all the porn and sex toys and anything else that might upset his family?"

"Been there, done that," John said.

"Do you think that's what we're looking at here? Someone's gone through Patrick's stuff and taken out anything that would tell you he's gay."

"Makes sense."

CHAPTER EIGHT

July 25, 1996
Thursday afternoon

Around lunchtime, John ran out to get us Mexican food at a place nearby. I sat on one of the boxes we'd pulled into the hallway and went through the accordion files starting in 1990. Gas, electric, telephone, long distance (MCI)—Patrick barely made any long-distance calls—American Express, bank statements (Security Pacific), service records for a 1982 Mercedes 300, maintenance on the house which was at 410 N. Faring Road—monthly landscaping bills, trash pickup, air conditioning maintenance, furnace maintenance, plumber (he came a lot) and a pool service.

There were no canceled checks. I checked the other accordion files and found nothing. I took out the bank statements and looked at them closely. They didn't give any information about who checks were written to, but I could make some guesses. For example, every week or so a check was cashed for $60. My guess was that this was a maid who came weekly.

At the beginning of each month there was a deposit of $5,000. There was also an automatic payment of $993.16 on the second Tuesday of the month. This guy was living on almost $6,000 a month, and he wasn't even spending it all. The beginning balance in January 1990 was $2,354. The closing balance was $2,987. I pulled out the January bills and was able to match the amounts for most of them. American Express was the largest bill at $1,789 for December. A number of charges from department stores, which were probably Christmas gifts, seven lunches or dinners it didn't specify. Two of them at The Ivy, which was a favorite industry haunt. Gasoline for his Mercedes. A weekly charge at Gelson's, a high-end grocery store. Nearly two hundred each time which seemed like a lot. Was he buying a lot of alcohol? There was also a charge for the florist at Forest Lawn, Hollywood Hills. That snagged me. I skipped ahead and checked the bills for the next few months. It happened every month. I skipped ahead to the latest date and it was still there. A standing order.

Ronnie came out of 1019. "Hey, look what I found." He was carrying a medium-sized bowl of matchbooks.

"Cool," I said, then went and grabbed the Fred Segal bag. "Dump them in here."

"I want everything in here, FYI. Can you offer them ten thousand for the lot?"

"Ten thousand dollars?"

"Yes. We'll use some of it to furnish the co-op and then sell the rest. We'll make enough to pay ourselves back, meaning that we'll decorate the co-op for free."

"If it's worth more than ten thousand, why would they accept that offer?"

"Convenience. It sounds like they have a lot of prob-lems. This is one problem solved."

"Do we have ten thousand?"

"Kind of." I knew him well enough to know 'kind of' meant credit cards.

"How will we *kind of* pay that off?"

"It's time to refinance the Bennett house."

The Bennett house was our first house. It was small and cute, and we rented it to a couple of lesbians and their little boy. He continued, "That mortgage is at eight point three five. I think I can get a mortgage for seven and a quarter, so it's worth it to refi. The value has gone up so we'll get good terms, and we can pay off the ten grand and a few other things."

"Okay," I said. Basically, I left the money stuff to him. "I doubt they'll take it, but I can offer."

John came back with our lunch. I had respectable carne asada tacos, a lot of chips and a Coke. Part way through, John asked, "So how big a house did this guy have? Two bedrooms? Three?"

"There are two beds," I pointed out.

"But he could have easily done something else with a third bedroom. Or even a fourth."

"I can find out," Ronnie said, and pulled his cellular phone out of his back pocket. "What's the address?"

"410 Faring in Holmby Hills."

He walked away and a moment later I heard him saying, "Hey Margie, can you run a property for me?"

She must have said yes because he gave her the address. I felt like I shouldn't just sit there listening, so I asked John how his burrito was.

"Not bad, especially for some random place."

"There's a place up here everyone goes to. La Casita Grande. It's great."

"I've heard of it."

"I didn't know you spent much time in Silver Lake."

"Oh yeah. There was this guy…"

And then Ronnie was back with us. "Eighteen hundred square feet. Two bedrooms, library, formal dining room, pool, lovely view. Not big for Holmby Hills, obviously. The house sold for over a million. And it's a tear-down."

"I guess it pays to be a lawyer," John said.

"He must have bought it a long time ago," I said. "Did you find that out?"

"No. Our system only goes back ten or twelve years. Otherwise, I'd know the last time the house changed hands and how much they paid."

"I've got some of his financial records."

"Some?"

"Yeah, there's no cancelled checks for some reason. His American Express bills are there. It seems he was paying for the florist at Forest Lawn to put flowers on a grave every month for years."

"Do you think it's Vera's grave? Do you think he's felt guilty for a long time?" Ronnie wanted to know.

"I'm pretty sure the book I found said she's buried there," I said.

"It's not still happening, is it?" John asked.

"I imagine whoever took over his finances put a stop to it."

We put our empty Styrofoam containers back into the bag they'd come in. I set it outside of 1020 with the Fred Segal bag of matchbooks. Honestly, I wasn't sure why I was taking those, other than knowing the kind of places Patrick Gill went to might tell me more about him. There were probably matches for gay bars in there. Was that where he'd met Vera? In a gay bar somewhere?

Back in the lockup, I made another inventory of what was there. The lawbooks, the weirdly deep desk, the leather sofa—if we did buy all this stuff, I'd want that sofa in the living room. But we weren't going to buy this stuff. The Karpinskis would never agree to it. Not for what we could afford.

I squeezed my way by the garage things and found a couple of dressers behind the leather sofa. I was able to pull the drawers open a bit. Each was full of clothing. Men's clothing. I pulled out a pair of slacks. From the fifties or sixties. Not something Patrick would have worn for a very long time. Not something he'd ever wear again. So, why were they here?

The whole thing was stranger and stranger. To put dressers full of clothing into storage suggested this was all done rather quickly. But then, Patrick's financial records seemed to be severely edited. As were the rooms themselves, denuded of whatever personal photos Patrick had around.

Ronnie snuck up behind me and grabbed me around the waist. "What are looking at?" he asked.

"You're supposed to be in your own lockup," I said, turning around and pulling him into my arms.

"You're going to be really happy with me," he said, giving me a quick kiss.

"Why?"

"I called the florist at Forest Lawn, told them I was Patrick Gill's son, the late Patrick Gill, said that he was sending flowers for years and I wanted to know whose grave they were put on. He didn't want to give me a name, I was like, they're both dead, what harm could it do? He still wouldn't tell me. But… he gave me like an address."

"For a grave?"

"Basically. Lot 2077, space 3. We should go after this. It's on the way home."

"The long way home."

"Do you want to make a separate trip?"

He was right. He usually was. I didn't have time to come back to L.A. until at least Monday.

"Sure, we'll go after this."

He kissed me, deep and sexy. Then he stuck his hand down my pants.

"Uh, if you wanted to do that you should have thought of it while John was getting lunch."

"You could have thought of it."

"You're the planner."

"In that case, plan to get busy on Saturday. We have to christen the co-op." He kissed me and then walked away. I had to rearrange myself and think of baseball for a couple of minutes before I could continue.

We poked around for another hour and a half without finding anything—except more things Ronnie wanted. About three, I said "Okay, let's pack up and leave. All we were taking were the matchbooks and the accordion folders, which were going to take several days to fully understand. Not to mention, I had to ask myself whether that was going to matter in the end. I'd probably discovered the most important thing: that Patrick was sending flowers to Vera's grave every month. But what did that prove? Except that he felt guilty, which I already knew.

"Can you guys put the boxes back?" I asked.

"Your shoulder hurts?" Ronnie asked.

"It'll be okay," I said, reflexively. He'd told me a million times I needed to see a doctor about it. I really didn't need to hear it again.

"Oh, I did find something. Probably nothing but..." From just inside 1019, he grabbed a big stack of greeting cards. "These were stuck in books. It's hard to say how old they are, there weren't any envelopes and it's first names only."

"Throw them in the Fred Segal bag. You never know."

Ten minutes later, everything was locked up and we carried our findings down the elevator and out to the Jeep. It's probably just as well I didn't find more, what we did have filled up the tiny space behind the back seat and the spot next to John. My Wrangler was hardly what you'd call spacious.

I suppose I could have gotten on the 101, but that was risky, rush hour would be starting soon. I took Beverly over to Western, cut up to Santa Monica, and took Cahuenga through the pass to Barham. It was the same way I'd come to see Sheila Karpinski at her Burbank stable. Before reaching Warner Brothers Studio, we turned right on to the aptly named Forest Lawn Boulevard.

We found the entrance, then immediately stopped at the information booth. A gentleman in his mid-sixties came out. Thinning hair, slight paunch, he looked straight out of central casting.

"Hi. Can you help us find Lot 2077, space 3?"

"You got a name with that?"

"Vera Korenko," I said.

"One second."

He went back into his booth and pulled out a large notebook. He opened it on a shelf which also housed a telephone and the book he was reading by Tom Clancy. He came back out and said, "Nope."

"I'm sorry?" I said, not knowing what no meant.

"Vera Korenko is in 2077. Space 1."

"Okay. Is there someone in space 3?"

He went back in, examined the page, then came out and said, "Ivan Melchor."

"And space 2?"

"Empty."

Ronnie leaned over me and asked, "Can you tell us who owns the empty plot."

"Nope. I can only give out information on the dead."

"And where are these?" I asked.

"Go down two streets, in the section called Eternal Love. East side."

"Thank you."

I drove on, his directions easy to follow. We got out of the Jeep and soon realized that, while we were in the right area the graves still weren't easy to find. We spread out and wandered around until John called out, "Over here."

It was almost ninety degrees and I'd begun to sweat. The cemetery was on a hill and rather than having markers standing up, there were plaques laid flat into the ground. The grass was well-watered and a brilliant green that went well with the bright blue sky, not to mention the few rabbit-like clouds floating by.

When I reached John, Ronnie was already there with him. They were looking down at Vera Korenko's marker. It looked just like it did in the book, except in color. There was an empty space and then the marker for Ivan Melchor, the man to whom Patrick had sent flowers for years. His marker read:

Ivan Melchor
my Hadrian

1906-1972

"Who's Hadrian?" Ronnie asked.

"Beats me," John said. "Greek God?"

I didn't know either. John wasn't right, I knew that much. But I thought he was close. Whoever Hadrian was, he was ancient. When we got back into the Jeep, I grabbed a little notebook and wrote down Ivan Melchor's dates and the name Hadrian.

When we got home, which took quite a while given that rush hour was in full force by the time we got onto the 710, I suggested we have a pizza delivered.

"Oh God," John said. "I can't have take-out twice in the same day. I'll make spaghetti. It's simple enough."

"I think there's salad fixings." Junior said. He'd run down to greet us the minute we walked in. He looked at Ronnie, assuming he'd make the salad. Knowing what was in the fridge was often Junior's contribution to meals.

John and Ronnie went into the kitchen leaving me with Junior. "What have we here?" he asked of the things we'd brought in with us.

"I told you I'm looking at the Vera Korenko murder. Well, supposedly she was engaged to this lawyer named Patrick Gill. Patrick is saying he killed her. Or at least he feels responsible for her murder. I think they were both gay and were helping each other out."

"So where did you get all this... no offense, junk."

"When they put him into a home, his family sold his house and moved his things to three lockups. We spent the day looking through his stuff."

"And this is all you found?" Peeking into the Fred Segal bag he said, "Matchbooks?"

"Somebody got there before us."

"Ominous."

"Probably not," I said. I had a pretty good idea who removed everything 'gay' related.

Junior was picking through the matchbooks. "Oh my God, a lot of these are gay bars. Look. Studio One." He was holding a purple matchbook with a silver logo. "I used to go there and dance. It was a fabulous place. The boys, oh, you would die—and then one night, I was suddenly too old. They wanted twelve pieces of identification and a promise to stand in the shadows. One of the worst nights of my life. I remember people were always complaining that they didn't let minorities or women into the disco, but the thing is, *they did*. Well, not women. But they did let Black and Asian and Hispanic boys in if they were beautiful. Which was also the criteria for White boys, by the way. It's just that no one ever formed a civil rights group for the ugly."

"Sounds like a great place," I said, facetiously.

He must have missed my tone though, because he said, "Oh, it was. It was a dream."

Then something occurred to me. "I wonder how Patrick got it? I mean, he's decades older than you are and if they wouldn't let you in."

"Money, I'm sure. Nothing makes you look younger than a hundred-dollar tip."

He was pawing through the matchbooks again. "Windup, I've heard of that, Roosterfish, Gauntlet..."

"I used to work there."

"No, this is a different one, years before that. On Highland, I think. Gaslight. Playpen. Madness, Inc. The Blue Fox —that was on Sunset somewhere. Before I was old enough to drink. Circus. You know, he can't have gone to all of these places. I mean, they're very different sorts of places."

"Maybe friends brought them to him, knowing he collected."

"That could be." Then he stopped. "Oh my."

"What."

"The Black Cat."

"Okay." Didn't ring a bell for me.

"The police raided it in the sixties, late sixties. That made people angry and they started protesting. It was a big deal. Then New York came along a few years later and stole our thunder. Now everything is Stonewall this and Stonewall that when they really should be Black Cat this and Black Cat that."

Of course, Stonewall Democratic Club—of which I'm sure there were many—had a better ring to it than Black Cat Democratic Club. Strange how things like this can come down to something as simple as a word.

Then Junior asked, "Exactly how are these helping you find Vera Korenko's killer?"

"I'm not really sure I need to find her killer. I just need to figure out why he's saying he killed her."

"It sounds easier to find her killer."

"You mentioned a lesbian who was murdered. Do you remember much about that?"

"It's been ages. I think her body was found under a bush somewhere near the Rose Bowl."

"Pasadena."

"Well, yes, of course. I don't remember much more than that. The police figured out she was lesbian and didn't do much. I think the lesbo groups put up fliers and wrote letters and things, but nothing happened."

"Except, you said people connected it to Vera Korenko?"

"Or at least they tried to. The more they said someone's killing lesbians the less interested the police became."

Ronnie stood in the doorway to the dining room and cleared his throat loudly. "Dinner is served."

Junior and I went into the dining room. The table was set and there was a salad sitting in the center. John brought in a big bowl of pasta and sauce. Ronnie followed with a bottle of red wine and a Crystal Geyser for me.

We filled our glasses, served ourselves, made the appropriate noises about how good everything looked. It really did. Finally, John said, "I have Internet Explorer. I could try to figure out who Hadrian was."

"What do you mean?" Junior asked.

"Patrick Gill had 'my Hadrian' carved on Ivan Melchor's tombstone," I said.

"Oh my God, that's the most romantic thing I've heard in ages."

"You know who Hadrian was?" Ronnie asked, skeptically.

"Children, you embarrass yourselves. Hadrian and Antinous were two of history's most famous gay lovers. Hadrian was emperor of Rome when he met Antinous, the most beautiful young man in the entire world. They fell desperately in love and Hadrian brought his lover on his military campaigns. Then, in Egypt, Antinous drowned in the Nile. Hadrian was bereft. He commissioned statues of Antinous wherever he went. His grief was as big as the world."

"Putting that on Ivan's grave means he and Patrick were lovers, doesn't it?"

"It also means Ivan was the older of the two. And very likely the top," Junior said with a smirk.

"How do you know that?" Ronnie asked, with even more skepticism.

"Because in ancient Rome, gay sex was everywhere but it was only okay if you were a top. You could fuck your slave or your neighbor's teenage son, but they couldn't fuck you."

That was just bit too close to home, given that Ronnie was much younger than I was and... Well, I decided to change the subject. "Junior's been to a lot of the bars that Patrick saved matchbooks for."

"Yes, back in the seventies. Speaking of the seventies, I remember this joke we used to tell. Why do faggots have mustaches?"

We looked at each other, none of us had mustaches. John had had a Van Dyke for a while the year before, but it had been gone for a long time.

Junior picked up on our lack of facial hair saying, "Okay, so a lot of guys had mustaches in the seventies. Come on, why do faggots have mustaches?" He paused dramatically then crowed, "To hide the stretch marks."

We didn't laugh or even chuckle. Junior frowned and said, "Somewhere along the way people lost their sense of humor."

CHAPTER NINE

July 26, 1996
Friday morning

When I arrived at The Freedom Agenda, Karen told me we'd gotten an email from Paul Michaels with the reunion information. She'd printed it out and handed it to me. I went in the back, made myself comfortable, and called the number. When I asked for the information on Sharon Hawley, I was told they couldn't give it out but that they would contact her and give her my information. It was up to her whether she called me. I gave both the number for The Freedom Agenda and my cellular number.

We were expecting Raymond Harris, Larry Wilkes' public defender, at eleven. I had some time to kill, so I went out to the front and asked Karen, "Could you check Lexis/Nexis for Ivan Melchor. He was born in 1906 and died in 1972. It's for the Karpinskis."

"When we get you a computer, I'm going to get you a login so you can do this for yourself."

"Oh God," I said. I really didn't want to get involved in things like that. I mean, a lot could go wrong, right?

Karen seemed to read my mind, saying, "Don't worry. I'm not giving you the nuclear codes. Get me a coffee and I'll probably have something by the time you get back. Two creamers, three sugars." She held out her coffee cup.

When I got back just a few minutes later, her printer was running.

"What did you find?" I asked.

"An obituary in the *L.A. Times* and a short item in the *Hollywood Reporter* about his papers being donated to the Margaret Herrick Library."

"What kind of papers?"

"Read the obituary," she said, handing it to me.

The headline read "Oscar-nominated art director dies at 66."

"Ivan Melchor, one of Hollywood's most prolific set designers, has passed away after a short illness at his Holmby Hills home, his agent reports.

"Melchor was long under contract to Monumental Pictures, an association which benefited both parties greatly. Receiving eighteen Academy Award nominations over a twenty-six-year period, Melchor is credited with the Monumental 'look' when it came to musicals, one of the most famous being *The Girl From Albany*. He's been quoted as calling his style, 'Reality-plus.' He said, 'Everything should look realistic but also be so much more than real. My designs are more about what life could be rather than what it is.'

"Showing artistic talent from a young age, Melchor was forced to leave school and worked his way up from stagehand to set dresser to set designer beginning in the days of silent pictures. Some of his most memorable films are *O'Bannion's Bluff*, *A Rose for Harriet* and all of the *Scamp* detective films.

"Though occasionally linked to Hollywood starlets, Melchor was a lifelong bachelor. In an interview just months before he died, he's quoted as saying, 'My work has been more than enough for me. Work and friends. No one needs more than that.' Services are private."

I finished reading then glanced at the brief notice about his papers. I asked, "What do you think this guy's papers would consist of?"

"Drawings, blueprints, sketch pads, business correspondence, diaries."

"Diaries," I couldn't help saying. That's what I wanted. I wanted this guy's diaries. "Where is this place?"

"The Margaret Herrick Library is in Beverly Hills. Are you going now?"

"No."

"I'll give you the street address later."

"Speaking of later. I have a list of names, people from this book. Most of them are probably dead. I don't have time to talk to them until Tuesday. I wouldn't need the list back until Tuesday morning."

She looked at me skeptically, then said, "All right. Get the list."

I went back to my makeshift desk and grabbed the piece of paper on which I'd written down the names of Vera's friends and detective who'd worked her case. I was only about a third of the way through the book, so I knew I was taking a chance. I'd peeked ahead to the next chapter and the one after—good old Wallace was going through the suspects one by one. Of course, the most likely suspect was going to be at the end of the book. Putting them in any earlier just didn't make sense.

I brought my list out to Karen. There were only eight names. She looked at me and said, "Tuesday."

"Yes."

"Okay," she said, as she set the list aside. Then she picked up a copy of *People Magazine*. Will Smith was on the cover. She saw me looking at the magazine and said, "What?"

"Nothing."

I scurried to the back. I was trying to decide if I wanted to read more of *Canyon Girl* or just make a list of all the things I had to do. Before I could decide the phone rang. Karen picked it up and then a moment later called out, "It's for you!"

I pressed the blinking plastic square on my phone, and said, "Hello, this is Dom Reilly."

"This is Sharon Hawley. You wanted to talk to me?"

"I work at The Freedom Agenda—"

"The what?"

"We attempt to free people who were unjustly convicted."

"You must not have a lot to do."

"Actually, I'm looking for your sister. I'm told she was in the same class with Sammy Blanchard."

"Someone put Sammy in prison?"

"No, we're trying to get a new trial for Larry Wilkes."

"But he's guilty. Why would you do that?"

"We have reason to believe he's innocent."

"And you want to talk to Kelly?"

"Yes. I want to know if she was friends with Sammy Blanchard or if she knew someone who was."

"What does Sammy Blanchard have to do with Larry Wilkes? They were like two grades apart."

"I'm just gathering information at this point."

Not exactly truthful but the truth might get in the way. I could almost hear her thinking on the other end. Finally, she asked, "Where are you?"

"Long Beach."

"I can bring my sister. Two o'clock?"

That was cutting it close. "Four?"

"Three."

"Okay. Three o'clock at Hot Times? Do you know it?"

"On Broadway? I've driven by it. See you then."

It was around ten-thirty. I went and stuck my head into Lydia's office. She was dressed casually in a pink blouse and navy skirt. The outfit showed off her figure, which she usually hid in more angular outfits. I wondered for a moment if the meeting had been called off.

"I should have asked this earlier," I said. "But are we set for this meeting?"

"I've read the transcript, most of it this morning. I have a list of questions." She tapped a pad next to her.

"Can I ask why we're not using Edwin's conference room?"

"Harris is a public defender. They don't have much to work with. I want to put us on the same level. Engender sympathy."

"He's a lawyer. I doubt that will work."

"Ouch. I'm a lawyer."

"Sorry. It's true though."

She couldn't help smiling. "I have something in mind—" She was interrupted by the bell over the front door ringing. "He's early. As expected."

We could hear him saying, "Raymond Harris. I'm here for the deposition."

"One moment," Karen said. Then Lydia's phone buzzed.

She picked up and said, "I'll be right out." Hanging up, she remained seated.

In the lobby, Karen said, "She'll be with you shortly."

Lydia remained in her chair. I waited for her to look at me. When she did, I mouthed the word, 'Deposition'? She smiled, a Cheshire cat.

Then, still in no hurry, she stood up. From her desk, she picked up two of four-inch three ring binders sitting there and handed them to me. For the first time, I noticed that she'd used Post-It Flags to mark the places she wanted to refer to. There were many. Very many.

She picked up the third binder and her pad, then led me out to the lobby where we found Raymond Harris. Bald with a messy fringe of hair hanging down to his collar, he was in his early sixties and looked—well, the expression 'rode hard and put away wet' came to mind. Under one arm, he held a thick manila envelope which had also seen better days.

Oddly, his suit was perfect. Simple, charcoal grey with a white shirt and a red and black 'power' tie. It had been recently dry-cleaned. I could smell the chemicals. Then I realized the suit was from the late sixties and older than my boyfriend.

"Raymond, it's a pleasure to meet you in person," Lydia said. "This is my investigator, Dom Reilly. And my office manager, Karen Addison."

"A pleasure, I'm sure," he said. He didn't shake anyone's hands. There were too many. And besides that, he'd noticed the notebooks Lydia and I were holding. His eyes narrowed.

"We're back here," Lydia said, turning to lead us to the unimproved space behind the offices. "Can we get you something to drink? Coffee? Tea? Water?"

"Water please."

Karen had followed us and went to the college dorm-style refrigerator and got him a bottle of Evian.

"No video? I thought everyone was doing video these days," he said.

"Video? Oh no, Raymond, this isn't a deposition. Just a friendly chat."

Though they seemed to make a liar out of her, she set the notebooks onto the table. I followed suit. Karen placed the Evian at the seat across from us.

"I'm sure you said it was a deposition," Harris said, clearly grumpy. Well, he had dry-cleaned his suit after all. "I distinctly remember the word."

"I'm sure—well, maybe I misspoke. I had a deposition earlier this week. I might have gotten confused. So many details."

My God, I thought. She's playing the dumb girl.

"I mean, we will be doing a deposition. After I've gone through the file you've brought. For today it's just a few questions. Shouldn't take long."

Three notebooks with dozens of flags and a pad full of questions in tiny, cramped writing said otherwise.

He sat, obviously displeased, putting the manila envelope down next to him and cracked his bottle Evian. I reached across the table and pulled the envelope over to our side.

"I was only planning to be here an hour."

"Oh goodness," Lydia said. "It definitely won't take that long. We should start, though, shouldn't we?"

He didn't respond.

"Prior to trial, was there a plea bargain offered?"

"Yes. It's in the documents I brought."

"What was it?"

"Voluntary Manslaughter."

"That's a pretty good deal."

"Yes, I told him to take it. He'd have been out of prison ten years ago. Probably more."

"Did that tell you anything?"

"That my client was an idiot?"

"That they offered him such a good deal."

"What are you getting at?"

"They wouldn't have offered him such a good deal if they had a good case."

"They had a good case. They convicted him." He set his jaw. Already this was making him angry.

"Looking at the pre-trial motions, you asked for several continuances. Can you tell me why?"

"I was giving Larry time to accept the plea deal."

"It didn't come with a time limit?"

"Of course, it did. They always say that. But if we asked before the trial started, they would have put it back on the table."

"Let's move on to testimony. Starting with Detective David Harper."

"Is this about ineffective assistance of counsel? Is that what you're trying to claim?"

"I'm sure you know that a writ of habeas corpus based solely on ineffective assistance of counsel rarely works."

"What else do you have?"

"We'll get to that," she said. By this point, I was sure he'd put the idea that she was dumb right out of his head. "Can you tell me why a detective was testifying? Wouldn't an officer have been first on scene? Why do you think they put a detective on the stand?"

"I'm sure it was meant to save time. The detective could testify to the case more fully than an officer."

"The responding officer's report is in the file you brought?"

"I believe so."

"You didn't go through the file to refresh your memory?"

"You led me to believe the deposition would be narrow in scope. I didn't feel I had to reacquaint myself with the entire file."

"You made a copy of the materials you've provided to us?"

"Yes, of course."

"Detective Harper claimed that Larry Wilkes appeared remorseful when he arrived on scene. If the responding officer's assessment disagreed with the detective that would be a reason to keep him off the stand. Do you think that was possible?"

"If I thought that I would have done something about it at the time."

"To your credit, you did object to the word remorseful twice. Did you consider calling a rebuttal witness?"

"You're assuming there was one."

"Let's move on to Andy Showalter. You questioned him on why he got a gun for Larry."

"I did."

"You didn't get a satisfactory answer and then failed to pursue it. Can you explain that?"

"I don't have the transcript. You know how much they cost. I would not have gotten one then, or now."

"Andy Showalter and Larry Wilkes were both white teenagers who would probably have been scared of going to Compton at the time. What would the advantage have been to having Andy get the gun instead of Larry getting it himself?"

"Are you kidding? It's always good for a murderer to distance himself from the murder weapon."

"You asked Andy why he did it and he said he wanted to be friends. That doesn't seem a strong motive. You made a snide remark but didn't really pursue it. Was there a reason you didn't?"

"Two decades later, I have no idea."

"Andy Showalter committed suicide a few years later. We've spoken to his mother; he had significant mental issues. During the trial he was being treated by a psychiatrist. Were you aware of that?"

"I'm a public defender. I had, and have, limited access to an investigator. I'm not sure I could have justified it in this case."

"Andy Showalter was an impeachable witness from a number of angles. You didn't pursue any of them."

That made Harris very angry. Metaphoric smoke was coming out of his ears. Lydia took a sip of water from her own Evian bottle, then said, "Larry Wilkes is gay. You were aware of that while defending him?"

"I can't recall offhand. I'd have to check the file. But I don't believe it's in there."

"Would you have written that down?"

"Possibly not."

"Possibly or probably?"

"Probably."

"Larry Wilkes and the victim were lovers. Do you recall him sharing that information with you?"

"Well, no. If I did then I'd recall that he was gay,

wouldn't I?"

"He says that you wanted him to hide that he was gay from the jury. That it would hurt his case if they knew."

"I don't recall saying that. But in nineteen seventy-six it would have been good advice. You can see that, can't you?"

"Based on your advice, Larry convinced Anne Michaels to perjure herself at trial and say that Pete Michaels was her secret fiancé."

He looked from Lydia to me and back again. He even looked at Karen. He was stalling. Trying to decide what he should say. Finally, "I never met with that girl before the trial. I had no idea what she'd say."

"And you didn't have an investigator available?"

"No, I've said that already."

"You're claiming you weren't aware Larry had convinced Anne to lie?"

"I don't recall. It's a twenty-year-old case."

"Are you saying you might have known?"

"I couldn't have known. That would be suborning perjury."

"Debatable. She wasn't your witness. Though, if you'd known you'd have had a duty to impeach her testimony."

He was silent again.

"Anne Whittemore is recanting her testimony. She remembers Larry telling her she should tell everyone she was Pete's fiancée. Larry remembers you telling him not to say he was gay in court."

"Outside of Larry's statements and possibly his friend Anne's, there's no evidence of his relationship with the victim. I would not have put that information into his file for fear that it would become discoverable to the prosecution. If I was aware of his sexuality, I would have viewed it as an even stronger motive than the love triangle the prosecution presented."

"Are you serious?" I asked, unable to help myself. "Their being in love is a stronger motive for murder?"

"In nineteen seventy-six, I think a jury would have seen it that way. I would not give that kind of advice today."

"I think we've explored that fully," Lydia said, pursing her lips in a way that told me she was not happy. I was pretty sure it was Harris she was unhappy with and not me. "Getting back to Andy Showalter, he testified that Larry asked him to get a gun at the beginning of September nineteen seventy-six, but Larry had already begun college in Santa Barbara. So he wouldn't have been in Downey. You didn't confront Showalter with this information. Was there a reason why?"

Harris explained, "Larry took a bus from Santa Barbara to Downey the day before Pete Michaels was killed. According to you, Showalter's recollection of when Larry asked him to get the gun was the beginning of September. Larry could easily have come down on the bus at any point and returned at any point. There wouldn't have been any record of that. The DA would have sliced and diced me."

"But he couldn't prove that Larry was in the area when Andy said he was, could he?"

"I didn't know that, though. For all I knew the DA could prove he was there. Certainly, Andy Showalter was saying he was."

"And then you put Larry's mother on the stand."

"She was a character witness. She was adamant that she be allowed to testify on her son's behalf."

"You didn't ask any questions about whether Larry was at home early in September."

"He could have stayed somewhere else."

"Yes, but it was your job to create doubt. You should have made the DA prove Larry was there to ask Andy to get him a gun."

"Hindsight—"

"And then you allowed his mother to testify to his relationship with Anne Michaels. She thought they made an adorable couple. She was so proud of him."

"I didn't *allow* that. The DA gets to cross examine—"

"Which is why she shouldn't have been on the stand. She did more harm than good."

"Yes. I understood that then. I understand it now. But what would you like me to have done? I couldn't tell her to lie."

"You could have kept her off the stand."

"I barely had any defense at all."

"You could have called Bernie Carrier."

"I don't know who that is."

"He was Pete Michaels' tennis coach. He'd been having a sexual relationship with the boy. One which Pete may have threatened to expose."

"How would I know anything about that? Larry never mentioned it."

"Larry didn't know. My investigator learned of it by talking with the boys on the tennis team. Did you look for other possible murderers, at all?"

"I didn't have the luxury of a full-time investigator."

"If you're saying that you couldn't properly investigate Larry's case because your office wouldn't give you an investigator, then that is clearly ineffective assistance of counsel."

"I'm afraid I'm going to have to leave. I told you I wouldn't be able to stay long."

He got up and walked out of our office.

CHAPTER TEN

July 26, 1996
Friday noon

"A re you going for ineffective assistance of council?" I asked Lydia as we were sitting there in shock that he'd actually left. Karen took it in stride though, and was already making three copies of the file he'd brought.

"No," Lydia said. "It's always a weak argument. I just wanted him to stop blaming everything on not having an investigator. He did have an investigator available; he just didn't know how to direct them."

"How much of that are you going to pull into the deposition?"

"I don't know. I'm not even sure it's worth doing a deposition."

"What do you mean?"

"Well, we have Anne saying that Larry wanted her to lie about the engagement. And Larry saying that his lawyer told him to hide his sexuality. That's all we have in our favor right now. Harris says he doesn't remember. I'm guessing there's a transcript of the phone conversation Anne and Larry had in which he mentions the engagement. That works against us. I'm not filing a writ of habeas corpus until this is stronger."

"What now?"

"Now we need to go over what he brought us. The three of us should spend the rest of the day on that."

"I have a five o'clock interview. The Karpinski thing."

"Okay, that still gives us plenty of time. We should order lunch. Does Dragon House still deliver?"

"Pick up only. I can go get it while Karen finishes the copying."

"No, she's almost done. Pizza?"

"That's fine."

Then she changed her mind. "No, you know what, the three of us should just go to Dragon House. We'll bring the file. Have a working lunch."

"Sounds good."

"My treat."

It took about half an hour to get everything together. I pulled out three more three-ring notebooks. Fortunately, we had a lot in our supply cabinet. When Karen was done, I started punching holes in the copies. Then we put two files together. Karen grabbed a bunch of tabs, while I grabbed one of the thick transcript notebooks to have with us if we needed to look at it. We took Lydia's BMW since there was room in the backseat for everything we'd decided to bring.

Dragon House was three doors down from Hot Times and right next door to Star of Siam. It was owned by a Chinese family named Long. Ronnie had explained that in Chinese Long meant dragon, so the Chinese symbols on the menu also meant Long's house. It was the family business, which was apt since the matriarch, Sue Long (whose Chinese first name was actually Shuye but—Americans...), ran the place with two sons in the kitchen and half a dozen granddaughters waiting tables.

The walls were red, adorned with gold sconces wearing little gold shades. The tables were covered in red tablecloths which themselves were covered with a circle of easily cleaned glass. The main dining room had booths on two sides and an open area for tables, double doors into the kitchen, and an ornately arched entrance into a second, roped-off dining room.

When we walked in it was crowded, but we were the only ones in the waiting area. Sue Long, small but imperious and in her mid-eighties, immediately came out from behind the cashier's desk. She knew me. I'd been in frequently with Ronnie, and sometimes with Junior and Ronnie, and a few times with Mai and Ronnie. She was famously thought to be psychic and once touched my arm and said, "There is much strife for you." She might have been reading my past, hopefully not my future, or—just as likely—the bumps and twists of my frequently broken nose.

That day, she noticed everything we were carrying and said, "Come. This way."

We followed her over to the roped-off second dining room. She pulled back the rope and sat us at the first large round table. It was set for six but could accommodate eight if necessary. She picked up three of the settings and we set down our notebooks in the now empty space. Before she left, she turned the lights on for that room, and said, "Lin will be waitress. Important work." Then she left.

Lydia asked Karen, "What did you think of him?"

"I think he's seen too many movies where stupid White men get everything they want."

Lydia looked at me. I said, "I'm not going to disagree with that. He's still a public defender, that means he's either a crappy lawyer or he's got a savior complex or both."

"We need public defenders. It's a decent thing to do. But you're right, the good ones don't stay long and the bad ones stay forever."

"You did really piss him off," Karen said.

"Was that your plan?" I asked.

"I had a feeling he might have memory problems."

Lin arrived. From a tray she took a pot of tea and three handle-less cups, setting them on the table.

Lydia said, "Could you bring us crab wontons and shrimp egg rolls? Two orders of each. And then we'll have the walnut shrimp, the crispy duck, and the scallops and peas."

She'd just ordered the most expensive things on the menu. Probably because Sue Long had given us a private room. She looked at us and asked, "We'll share. Is that okay?"

Karen and I nodded. Then Lydia added a dragon fried rice to the order, the fried rice with everything in it. Lin asked if we wanted egg flower soup or hot and sour soup. When we'd chosen, she left.

Pouring us all tea, Lydia said, "Let's find the report from the first officer on the scene."

Karen and I began flipping through the materials Harris had brought that morning. She beat me.

"Found it. Officer Jared Kelly. Arrived at 7815 Via Amorita at twelve-twenty-five. He finds Mr. and Mrs. Michaels standing outside the house. They tell him to go inside where Larry Wilkes is holding the body of Pete Michaels. Sobbing. He kept saying, "He's dead. He's dead. How can he be dead?""

"Got it," Lydia said.

I was still looking for it.

"There's nothing here about remorse. The first thing Officer Kelly did was look for the gun. He found it just by the door."

Finally, I found the report, too. As I started skimming, I asked, "What's the relationship between where the gun was found and where Pete Michaels died?"

"There's a drawing on the next page," Karen said.

I flipped the page. The drawing was of the living room. The furniture was sketched as boxes, there were X's for Larry and Pete. They were on the floor at the far end of the sofa. There was a small drawing of a gun right next to the front door.

"How far do you think they are from the gun?" I asked.

"If the living room is twenty feet, they're fifteen feet away," Lydia estimated.

"How would that happen?" I asked. "The DA is saying Larry came to the door. He would know that Pete lived with his parents and his brother. He wouldn't know where they were, so he would have knocked or rang the doorbell. Pete would have been shot very close to where his body fell."

"Are there photos?" Lydia asked.

"Copies," Karen said.

"Xerox copies?"

"Yes."

"That scum bag. We're going to need actual photographs."

"The copies are about ten pages back from the officer's report," Karen said.

Lin arrived with the appetizers. I asked for a Coke. The tea was a bit thin for me. I kept my eyes on the copy of the crime scene photo. The quality was terrible. I could make out Pete's body in a pool of blood. But then, most of the carpet was very dark. I couldn't tell if there was a trail of blood leading across the room. I flipped through the photos. There was something I didn't see.

"If he was shot at the door, there would be blood on other parts of the carpet, and they would have taken specific photos of those stains. And there aren't any."

"So he couldn't have been shot at the door and then walked over to the sofa," Lydia said, munching on a wonton.

"How close was the killer when Pete was shot?"

"The coroner and the ballistic expert both testified within a few feet."

"So, the killer is allowed into the house. They walk deeper into the living room. They may have talked for a short period and then Pete is shot. The killer then wipes the gun clean and leaves the house, dropping the gun next to the door. But their version is that Larry wiped the gun clean, dropped it by the door, and then returned to Pete's body."

"I've got the ballistics report," Karen said. "It says they found smudged fingerprints, none that could be identified. Oh, wait, they did find a fingerprint on the barrel. There was a fingerprint guy who testified, right?"

"Yes," Lydia said. "That fingerprint does not belong to Larry or Andy Showalter. They assumed it belonged to the person who sold the gun to Andy."

"It could belong to Sammy Blanchard," I said.

Karen asked. "Is that the girl in the sketches?"

"Yes," I said, then asked. "How did Harris handle that at trial?"

"Badly," Lydia said. "He could have suggested the fingerprint as proof of another killer but didn't. He just accepted the prosecution's theory about its being the seller's fingerprint."

I picked up a wonton and set it on the tiny plate Lin had brought. I spooned on some of the delicious sauce that was mainly sugar and red dye. Taking a bite, it was wonderful, as I knew it would be. Chewing, I flipped through to the witness statements. Karen and Lydia were discussing whether the size of the fingerprint could tell you whether it was a sixteen-year-old girl. Lydia had never heard of anything like that; Karen said she'd research it.

The Downey Police Department had canvased the neighborhood and taken statements from the Michaels' surrounding neighbors. There were eight reports. I was able to quickly determine that three of those neighbors had not been home. Two others were home but didn't notice anything. There were three valuable statements: two on Irwingrove Drive, 7812 and 7816, behind the Michaels house. Each heard what might have been a gunshot around a quarter to twelve. Neither called the police, uncertain of what they'd heard.

The most helpful of the three was from a Celia Wickers, who lived at 7816 Via Amorita directly across the street from the Michaels. She was in her front yard gardening. Planting sweet peas. I was pretty sure that was a flower rather than a vegetable. She was asked specifically about Larry Wilkes and shown a photo. She said he arrived in a large brown car at noon. The officer quizzed her about the time, but she stuck to her guns, saying she took a pill every day at noon. She went into her house for a few minutes and when she came out the Michaels car was in the driveway. Then, about twelve thirty the police arrived. The officer asked whether she'd heard a gunshot after the brown car arrived, but she hadn't. Then she said a little yellow car had driven up around eleven thirty with a very young girl inside. She was pretty sure the girl went into the Michaels house. She'd gotten busy with her gardening, gone behind her house to get a shovel and didn't see the girl leave. In blue pen, the officer made a note in the margin of the report. He was certain Mrs. Wickers was hard of hearing.

I came up for air, grabbing an egg roll just as the soups and my Coke arrived. We still had more than half the appetizers to eat. I took a big bite of my egg roll waited until Lin left and I'd finished chewing before I could say anything.

Lydia and Karen were back talking about the gun. It was a Smith & Wesson that had been stolen from a couple in Alhambra about two years before the murder. It had been traced to an attempted murder in Carson prior to it showing up in the Michaels murder.

"I just read the statements from the neighbors. The woman across the street saw Larry arrive around noon. The neighbors behind the Michaels heard a gunshot about twenty minutes earlier."

Lydia looked at me suspiciously. Of course, her suspicions weren't directed at me. "The woman across the street, her name was Wicker, right?"

"Wickers."

"Okay, at trial she said she heard a gunshot *after* Larry arrived."

"But she was inside," I pointed out.

"She said the door was open."

"And she said she didn't hear a gunshot in her statement."

"Did Harris challenge her?" I asked. I must have read her testimony, but I couldn't remember. I grabbed another bite of my egg roll and a sip of my Coke.

"I can't remember," Lydia said. Now I didn't feel too

bad. Karen grabbed the transcript I'd brought and began flipping through it. "I don't think so though."

I swallowed. Hard. Then, "The officer taking her statement made a note that he thought she was hard of hearing. And she was inside the house when she supposedly heard the noise. Or didn't hear the noise."

"It could have been the Michaels closing a car door," Karen suggested. "She might have misremembered."

Lydia looked at her strangely. "Karen, you know how loud a gunshot is?"

And of course, she did.

"I don't know what a gunshot sounds like from across the street if you're half deaf. And she probably didn't either."

"Point taken."

I tried the soup. It was okay, but nothing compared to the wontons. I grabbed two more of those. I was ready to dig in when Lydia said to me, "We might need to interview this woman."

"She was probably pretty old if she was going deaf." I pointed out. "I don't know if she'd still be alive."

"We're going to have to check. Karen, can you look to see if she's still in that house? If she's dead, maybe there's a son or daughter who remembers what she said at the time."

"What about the other neighbors. Did either of them testify for the defense?" I asked.

"Hold on, I'm writing this woman's name down," Karen said.

"I don't remember any other neighbors taking the stand," Lydia said.

"So we need to ask Harris why he didn't put them on the stand to refute the Wickers woman's testimony. Since they both heard the gunshot fifteen minutes earlier."

"And about that yellow car," Lydia said. "I know Harris didn't bring that up."

"No," Karen said definitively. "Neither of the neighbors who heard the gunshot earlier were put on the stand. And yes, I'll find out if they still live there."

And then the entrees arrived with bowls of white rice and more plates for us to use as we shared. As soon as Lin walked away, I said, "Can I make a suggestion?"

"Go ahead," Lydia said.

"Let's not let this wonderful food go to waste. All this talk is getting in the way. How about we read and eat? We can talk afterward."

And that's what we did.

CHAPTER ELEVEN

July 26, 1996
Friday afternoon

The food was delicious. I might have taken more than my share of the walnut shrimp. As I ate, I compared Anne Michaels' deposition to the interviews she'd given twenty years before. There were six interviews, two with the police and four with the district attorney. The interviews with the police were held at her house, and there were only the notes of the officers. I didn't bother much with the first interview, it was the second that was important. That interview took place after Larry tipped her off to say she was Pete's fiancée.

We had the notes of a Detective Jacobs. He'd typed them up. His original, handwritten notes were not included. The most important statement was "interviewee originally denied being victim's fiancée, but after questioning admitted the truth." That matched with what Anne said in the deposition. She had attempted to tell the truth but was not believed.

Then I looked through the file again to see if I could find a transcript of the jailhouse phone conversation. It wasn't there and it should have been. Even if phone conversations from jail weren't normally included in discovery, this one should have been. It was the reason detectives showed up at Anne's house. It's the reason they believed she was Pete's fiancée.

I took a bite of the duck. It was good, but not as good as the walnut shrimp. Unfortunately, that was gone. I scooped some of the scallops onto my plate and said, "The transcript for the phone call Anne described is not in the file."

"What?" Lydia said.

"I can't find it."

"That's not good."

"For us?" Karen asked.

"No. For them. If they didn't provide it, it could be a Brady violation."

"But there's nothing exculpatory in the conversation," I said.

"We don't know that for sure. We haven't seen it. All we know is what Anne said. Now it's an integral part of her recanting. We need that. I'll call Harris on Monday. What else?"

"The notes of the detective who interviewed her after the call support her version."

"Good. She tried to tell the truth but couldn't. That'll help a lot."

"Are we going to depose him?"

"Probably not. Let me read his notes and if they're strong enough we'll go with that. We don't want to risk him saying anything that won't help."

We ate for a moment, then Lydia said, "I read the Showalter boy's original statements. There are a number of inconsistencies which should have been brought out at trial. He confused Carson and Compton a couple of times. He messed up the price of the gun, going back between forty and fifty. And he originally said he went in the afternoon."

"Do you think he didn't get the gun in Compton?"

"The art he drew suggests he did. He could just be a kid who wasn't used to lying. What are you reading, Karen?"

"There are a couple of interviews with Paul Michaels. Boy is he a fool. Didn't know his wife was lying to him. Didn't know his brother was lying to him."

"Sometimes people know what they want to know and nothing else."

"Isn't that the definition of a fool?"

"More important than that," Lydia said. "Is that he's not going to be any use to us."

Karen shook her head.

Lin came over and asked if we'd like the rest boxed up to go home. Lydia said, "Yes, please." To us she added, "This way I won't have to make Dwayne dinner."

"Does he ever make you dinner?" I asked. I mean, really, she was my boss and an attorney. She shouldn't have to make dinner every night for a man whose big effort was reading a script.

"Dwayne is a disaster in the kitchen. Believe me, I cook in self-defense."

"Men are a disaster because we let them be," Karen said. "You need to tell that man he needs to learn to cook something. Anything. Spaghetti."

That was an awkward moment.

Karen said, "We have to go. You have a conference call with Larry at two thirty."

"I'm probably not going to be there," I said. "I have an interview at three. A woman named Sharon Hawley. She's bringing her sister who was in school with Sammy Blanchard."

Lin returned with our leftovers all boxed up. She put down the check, and a plate of three fortune cookies and some chalky mints. Lydia quickly gave her an American Express card.

After she was gone, Lydia said, "Take a cookie. Let's see what the future holds."

I broke mine open and read my fortune: Look over your shoulder, happiness is trying to catch you.

"Karen, you go first," Lydia said.

She had a sour look on her face. "Your ability to juggle many tasks will take you far."

"Well, that's certainly true."

"I wouldn't mind a frog I could turn into a prince."

"That's not a Chinese fairy tale," Lydia pointed out. "Dom, what does yours say?"

I told her.

"That's lovely. You deserve to be happy. Mine says, Eat chocolate to make a sweeter life."

I made it to Hot Times about a quarter to three. At the counter, I ordered a latte with whole milk. I hadn't bothered looking around when I walked in. I wasn't expecting them to be there. While I waited for my coffee, there wasn't anything else to do but look around.

The place was about half full. There were a couple of guys working on laptops. One had decorated his with lots of stickies: a rainbow flag, a pink triangle, silence=death— which made me think he was older than he looked. In the corner there was a lesbian couple talking intently.

There were tables outside. Most of them were empty, but then I noticed two women in their later thirties. Two straight women. The sisters were here already. I'd walked right by them without seeing them. My name was called and I took my coffee, made in a gigantic teacup and nicely decorated with a milk tree, outside.

"Sharon?" I asked when I approached them.

Sharon, who was the older sister, thin, tall and fidgety. Her sister, Kelly, was several years younger and much more tentative. Both were bottle blondes with sharp features that betrayed their relationship.

"Yes. You're Dom?" She sounded surprised for some reason.

"I am," I said, putting my coffee on the table, and then sitting down.

"This is my sister, Dr. Kelly Wallpole."

Kelly blushed.

I said, "Thank you for coming. Did Sharon explain what I—"

Sharon interrupted, "This is the gays neighborhood, isn't it?"

"Yeah. I mean, you don't have to take an entrance exam or anything."

"We parked over in that park—" She pointed to Bixby Park. "The signs. They'll really arrest you if you drive by the same spot three times?"

"I don't know. I've never put it to the test."

She gave me a funny look at then asked, "Are *you* gay?"

"Sharon!" Kelly exclaimed. "You're being rude."

"Why is that rude? It's just a question."

"Yes, I am. Are you?"

She laughed at the question. "Of course not. Is this why you're helping Larry Wilkes? Because you're both gay?"

To be honest, it was. At least a little bit. I'd paid a little more attention to his case than I might have otherwise. My way of leveling the playing field, just a tiny bit. I didn't tell her that though.

"We help all sorts of people at The Freedom Agenda. How do you know Larry Wilkes is gay?"

"Rumors."

"While you were in high school?"

"No one was gay in high school. It was afterward. And you know it makes sense. I remember Anne Whittemore. It never made sense that someone would kill over her."

Rude. I decided it was best ignored. I looked to her sister Kelly and asked, "Do you remember Sammy Blanchard?"

"Um, yeah."

"Were you ever friendly with her?"

"Of course she wasn't. Our parents would never have allowed it. I mean, she was being abused by the health teacher."

"She married him," Kelly said.

"He was an old man. He's dead by now, isn't he?"

"He's in a home," I said. I didn't elaborate.

"Really gross," Sharon said.

"I'm asking about before all that happened. Did you know Sammy at all?"

"No," Kelly said. "I mean, I knew things about her. Her parents were never around so some of the kids would go over and drink out of their bar. They never noticed so Sammy never got in trouble."

"Kelly was a good girl in high school."

Kelly blushed again. Maybe not as true as Sharon thought.

"She had a car too. It was small and she used to pack kids into it, eight, ten. It was kind of crazy."

"Do you remember what kind of car it was?"

Kelly shrugged.

"A sedan or a fastback?"

"It was two doors, definitely. I don't think it was a fastback."

"It was a Chevy Pinto," Sharon said. "I remember her driving it into the parking lot. Even the seniors were jealous."

"Ford Pinto or Chevy Vega?" I asked.

"Vega," Kelly said.

"What color was it?"

"White," Sharon said.

"Yellow," Kelly said at the same time.

"It was definitely white."

I tucked that away. "What else? It sounds like Sammy was popular?"

"No. She wasn't," Kelly said quickly. "She was never popular. She just had things kids wanted. It was kind of mean, actually."

"So, I'm confused," Sharon said. "I mean, Larry Wilkes was gay. So, obviously, he had some kind of obsession with Pete Michaels and killed him. What does that have to do with Sammy Blanchard?"

"I can't really talk about that," I said. Then I asked, "What do you remember about Pete Michaels?"

"That I had a huge crush on him. A lot of girls did. He was so sweet and funny and such a good athlete. Yeah, most girls go for the football players, but... tennis players in those little white shorts. Oh my God."

"What about Andy Showalter? Do remember him?"

Sharon shivered. "Creepy. Now that would make sense.

If you told me he's the one who killed Pete, I'd think, 'Yeah, absolutely.'"

"He killed himself."

"I guess he did the world a favor."

Cold, even under the circumstances.

"What about you, Kelly? Do you remember Pete?"

"Yeah, my sister wouldn't shut up about him."

That was all I had. Even though I was only part way through my coffee, I stood up, ready to leave. "Well, thank you. I appreciate you talking to me."

Ignoring that I was trying to say good-bye, Sharon said, "You know, the gays are so free. I'm jealous."

"Yeah, nothing says freedom like being illegal in twenty-six states."

She smirked and said, "That's not true."

I just walked away. Sometimes people were too stupid to bother with. My car was on 2nd Street, a couple blocks east of Junipero, close enough to my house that I just walked by it. Another block and I could see my front yard. There were people standing on it. One of them was Mai, Ronnie's mother. She was a little younger than me and had probably been a beauty in her youth. It had been a while since I'd seen her. She wore impeccably pressed slacks and a bright silk blouse. Her makeup was flat in a way that made her look like a mannequin. Ronnie stood on our porch glowering at her. Next to her was a guy close to Ronnie's age. I didn't recognize him. This couldn't be good.

As I crossed Molino, Ronnie saw me. He smiled which drew Mai's attention to me. She did not smile.

"What's going on?"

"It's not your business. You're not our family," Mai told me.

I was about to say anything that happened in my front

yard was my business, but Ronnie said, "I'm not your family, so what are you doing here?" To clear up any confusion, he said to me. "She's here to tell me I'm disowned, and this is her new son."

"You're shitting me."

"Arthur is good boy. He will honor his elders. We will find him a good wife and he will be a rich man when I die."

Arthur looked mortified but held his ground. Ronnie's anger was covering the hurt I knew was there.

"Do you know the word cruel, Mai?" I said.

"My English is perfect."

"Good. You're being cruel. If you don't want Ronnie in your life, we can live with that. But don't come around here. Stay the fuck away."

Her face turned white under her makeup. People didn't speak to her like that. I walked up to the porch and Ronnie. When I turned around, she and her protégé were climbing into her BMW.

Ronnie leaned toward me and said, "You know what's funny? I know that guy. He started working for us right before I got my real estate license. I caught him in the back once sucking off a customer."

"You didn't fire him?"

He shrugged and smiled in a way that made it clear he'd done the same thing.

"Oh."

"By the way, you are so getting laid tonight."

"You won't get an argument from me."

CHAPTER TWELVE

July 27, 1996
Saturday morning

Saturdays with Ronnie were a rare treat. Most weekends he was completely booked with clients who wanted him to show them properties. Given that we had the commitment ceremony in the afternoon, he decided it was simply easier to move all his clients to Sunday.

We stayed in bed until nine, which was now late for us. My hours were much more normal since I'd quit bartending. We skipped showers, put on some old crappy shorts and T-shirts, and hopped into my Jeep. After a stop at a fast-food place for some breakfast biscuits and borderline coffee, we drove to our co-op.

He hadn't said much about the stunt his mother pulled the night before. I was curious, of course, but I didn't bring it up. As we walked up the steps to our future home, he said out of nowhere, "The joke's on her. By the time she dies, I'm going to be so much fucking richer than she is. She can give her money to whomever she wants. It won't matter to me."

"You don't need her. You'll be fine."

"Did you go through this with your parents?"

This put us into territory I didn't talk about. They, too, disowned me. And eventually I left town. I gave the simplest answer I could think of. "It was a lot cleaner."

Inside the co-op, Ronnie had already spread-out plastic in the living room. Sitting in the corner were several bottles of pigment, a can of white paint, buckets, rags and a bag of big sponges.

"Okay, this is going to be interesting," I said, mainly to get off the subject of family. "You've got it all set up."

"Yeah, I was here yesterday morning."

We ate breakfast standing up and Ronnie explained how this was going to work.

"We're going to mix up three different colors: one dark, one light and one in the middle." He pointed at three bottles: red brick, yellow and terra cotta.

"Okay."

I must have sounded dubious because he said, "You'll see."

We finished our biscuits, and he scurried around getting ready. He filled three buckets partway with water and then with white paint. He added pigment and then stirred. When he was done, he said, "You like?"

"I guess," I said. I had no idea what I was looking at.

"We should see what it looks like on the wall," he said. "Sponge or rag?" Anticipating my next question he said, "One you dab, the other you roll."

"Roll," I said, not sure what I was getting into. He handed me a rag which was folded together and bound in three places with rubber bands. He picked one for himself.

"Let's start with the dark color," he said, dipping his rag into the brick-colored paint and then squeezing it out with his hands. This was going to be messy. "We'll start with this wall."

He walked over to the north side of the living room which had one window looking into the courtyard. I watched as he rolled the rag up and down the wall. It left a mottled mess in its wake. Ronnie turned around and looked at me.

"Start at the other end."

I dipped my rag into the paint, squeezed it out and began rolling it up and down. Pretty quickly, I realized I was going to have a problem. I couldn't raise my right arm much above my head, hadn't been able to for a very long time. I stopped.

"We have to do this three times. Isn't this harder than regular painting?"

"It's about satisfaction. How satisfying it's going to be to remember that we painted this ourselves."

I had a strong feeling we'd hang pictures over the paint job and forget completely about it. I mean, sure if someone came over and said, 'Wow this is great,' it would be fun to say we did it ourselves. But I wasn't sure how likely that was to happen.

I did the best I could for a while, but it wasn't much. After a while, I looked over at Ronnie. He'd managed to do about eight feet, starting at his knees and reaching above his head by a couple of feet. Even though I was taller, he was able to reach much higher.

He looked over and saw how I was doing.

"This is bothering your shoulder, isn't it?"

"Yeah. A bit."

Okay, a lot. Of course, Ronnie knew I'd been shot. I

remembered the first time we had sex—well, not the first time. The first time we had sex without our clothes on.

"What happened there?" he'd asked, touching the scar on my chest.

"I fell on a nail."

"No, you didn't. There's a hole in the front and one in the back. Nails don't do that. Even big ones. That's a bullet hole. Someone shot you."

"I told you I used to work at Denny's. Someone tried to rob us one time and I ended up getting shot."

"You took a bullet to save the Grand Slam?"

Obviously, he didn't believe me, but he did stop asking questions about it.

There was a ladder, so when we finished the middle part of the wall, Ronnie got onto it and worked on the top part. The ceiling was about nine feet at its low point and maybe fifteen at its highest point. There were beams across the ceiling. The previous owners had painted them white to match the rest of the ceiling.

"I got to see unit 20 the other day. They have the original beams, which are brown and have symbols painted on them in different colors. I'm thinking of finding an artist who can duplicate them."

"Uh-huh," I said, hovering around the bottom of the ladder in case he started to fall.

"You don't have to stand there."

"I know."

Then he asked me what was going on with Patrick Gill. I said, "I had to spend most of yesterday working on the Larry Wilkes case. I did find out a little about Ivan Melchor. He was a set designer. His obituary mentioned that he died at his Holmby Hills home, so he was probably living with Patrick. For how long I don't know."

"He was a set designer for the movies?"

"Yeah. It mentioned *The Girl From Albany*."

"Oh my God, I love that movie. You've seen it, haven't you?"

"I don't think so."

"It has that song, 'I'm Too Blue to Be Blue'."

"That I remember. My mother used to sing it when she did the dishes."

"We should rent it. Since you know someone who worked on it... sort of."

"Yeah, it's kind of hard to actually *know* dead people."

He'd finished the top, so he climbed down from the ladder. He still needed to do the bottom around the baseboard, but he stood back and took in what we'd done.

"What do you think?" he asked.

"It's dark," I said. I didn't say it was a bit too much like the color of dried blood for my taste.

"It's going to be much lighter when we're done."

"I don't know if I'm going to be much help with this."

"That's okay. John said he'd help me."

The way he said it made me wonder if he'd known I wouldn't be much help. I grabbed a sponge and dipped it in the brick-colored paint. Then I rubbed it onto a two-by-two patch on the inner wall. I flipped the sponge over and basically rubbed it off, leaving the wall looking tea-stained with darker spots catching in the textured plaster.

Ronnie watched what I was doing.

"I actually like that," he said. Then he took another sponge and dipped it into the terra cotta. The patch I'd made was basically dry since I'd rubbed most of the paint off. He repeated what I'd done on top of it. The patch was now about the color of honey with different bits of brick and terra cotta here and there.

Ronnie stood back and took it in. "Yeah. That's it." He looked at the wall we'd already done and asked, "What do we do about that?"

"I guess we could try washing it off."

And we did.

———

The commitment ceremony was at two o'clock. We'd finished up at the co-op around noon and gone home to have lunch. Ronnie was pleased. We'd managed to wash a lot of what we'd done off the one wall and by the time we'd added the second color it looked pretty much the way he wanted it to. He added a little of the yellow tint to the terra cotta and made it all look even more like honey. I have to say I liked it, too. Though, in all honesty I liked most things that made Ronnie happy.

We were very nearly late. Ronnie changed outfits three times. Finally settling on a cute pair of cuffed linen slacks and the requisite Hawaiian shirt—his was a bright orange, green and yellow. I stuck with a pair of black 501s and the Hawaiian shirt Ronnie had bought me—sexy surfers on a blue background.

On the drive over, Ronnie said, "You need to see a doctor about your shoulder."

"As soon as I have insurance," I said. Actually, Lydia had put me on the policy she had for her and Karen in April. I had the insurance card in my wallet, but I wasn't ready to use it. I know going to the doctor was supposed to be a good idea, but it was also something that never seemed to end well.

Robert and Doug lived in California Heights on the north side of the 405. They'd bought a three-bedroom

Spanish-style house on a quiet street for a song. We'd been there once for a party and the inside looked like a Pottery Barn. I'd been tempted to check for prices.

The ceremony, though, was in the backyard. We followed signs and balloons up the driveway, through a wooden gate. There was a rented dance floor with about fifty white folding chairs arranged on it facing a small tent under which the ceremony would take place. On the other side of the yard, was a long white table. There were lumpy tablecloths hiding what was probably our dinner. At one end, sat a very large, elaborate three-tiered wedding cake with two tiny grooms standing on top.

There were nearly fifty people there, most in Hawaiian shirts, we were among the last to arrive. The moment we stepped through the gate Ronnie was off like a racehorse who'd just heard the starting gun. I walked over to the bar and picked up two glasses of champagne. One for Ronnie and one for me—I promised myself I'd just have the one. I avoided alcohol most of the time since it made it difficult to find my way through the thicket of lies my life had become. Alcohol had the effect of loosening my tongue.

When I turned to find Ronnie, it took a moment. Finally, I located him standing next to the gift table talking and waving his hands around with a couple whose names, I think, were Octavio and Phillip? Something like that. I headed over.

We hadn't brought a gift with us. Ronnie had bought them something kitchen-y at Williams and Sonoma and had it sent to them.

"It's cast iron," he'd said. "I'm not schlepping that around."

I handed him his wine. Octavio and Phillip said hello,

but there were no introductions since we knew each other. I wished I knew them well enough to remember their names.

We spent a few minutes complimenting each other's shirts and mentioning where we'd gotten them. Then, they were talking about the bombing at the Atlanta Olympics, which had happened the night before. I'd seen something about it on the eleven o'clock news the night before but hadn't had time to read the paper that morning.

"Have they caught anyone?"

"No. Not yet," Octavio said. "They're still not sure how many people were killed."

"Do you think it's another Timothy McVeigh thing?" I asked.

"Could be. Those people are crazy," Phillip said.

"And they're saying that plane that went down near Long Island, that was a bomb too."

"All right," Phillip said. "Enough of bombs. We should talk about important things. We just booked a trip to New York in November. We're going to see *Chicago* with Ann Reinking. We have second night tickets. *Almost* opening night."

"Who's in it with her?" Ronnie asked.

"Bebe Neuwirth."

"Who is that?" I asked. I only knew who Ann Reinking was because I lived with Ronnie. And even she was fuzzy.

"Lilith. Frasier's ex."

"She can sing?"

"Hopefully."

I saw our tenants, Brown and Melissa, and was about to go over and say hello when a young woman dressed as a bridesmaid came out of the house and said, "If everyone could take a seat…"

Ronnie grabbed us a couple more champagnes and we

stepped over to the chairs, taking seats about four rows back on the aisle. Phillip and Octavio sat further up. I noticed Robbie, who I'd worked with at The Hawk. He was with an older, larger guy with a beard. A bear. His type. I suspected it was the partner he rarely talked about.

People settled. Ronnie took my hand and held onto it. I couldn't help thinking of Ivan and Patrick. This was no longer the world they'd lived in. That was a good thing. It wasn't perfect. I hadn't been lying when I'd told Sharon Hawley we were still illegal in twenty-six states, but it was also getting better.

Today was an example of that. Yeah, it wasn't legal, and I didn't expect it ever would be. They'd manage to keep that from us, but slowly, incrementally, we'd take everything else. We'd live our lives the way we wanted. Sharon Hawley was jealous that we seemed so free. I wondered why she couldn't see that we'd taken it for ourselves. And why didn't she take whatever freedom she wanted for herself? Because that's what freedom was, something you took, even when they tried to keep it from you.

The wedding march started. We all turned around and watched as the attendants came out from behind the garage and down the aisle alone. First, was the girl I'd seen looking like a bridesmaid even though there was no bride. She carried a small bouquet and tried to look demure, though I was fairly certain she was anything but. Then the best man wearing a Hawaiian shirt to which he'd added some well-placed sequins.

Under my breath I asked Ronnie a question I should have asked long before, "Why Hawaiian shirts?"

"Honeymoon."

Well, that explained it.

The attendants took their place under the tent. An

actual minister in robes had snuck in while I wasn't looking. After a slight pause, Doug came down the aisle with an older woman who was obviously his mother. Doug was in his twenties, around Ronnie's age and pretty enough to be an actor, something he'd tried for a few years. He noticed that the guests were all wearing Hawaiian shirts and made a big show of shock, though I suspected he'd been in on the joke for quite some time. Robert and his mother followed. He was older, also flawlessly handsome, his mother around the same age as Doug's.

The ceremony itself was overlong. First, the minister talked about his church and how it was accepting of the LGBT community, which after a minute or two started to sound like an infomercial. He kept emphasizing the *love thy neighbor* aspect of religion, ignoring the long history of religion doing the exact opposite. Then the boys said the vows they'd written themselves, which were sweet and would be terribly embarrassing if things didn't work out. And then it was over.

The bridal party took over one corner of the yard for photos, and we were asked to step away from the dancefloor while tables were brought over and chairs spread around them. As we waited, I said to Ronnie, "I didn't know the boys knew Brown and Melissa."

"I put them together. They want to foster. Brown and Melissa know all about that. You know what, I just remembered something. Doug's mother used to work in the industry. I wonder if she knew Ivan Melchor."

Looking over at the wedding party posing for photos, Doug's mother was definitely in her early sixties. She'd have been born in the early thirties, the depth of the depression. She'd have been old enough to work after the war. That would have given her an overlap with Ivan of a couple of decades. Of course, the industry was large. Different studios. Different departments. They probably—

"Come on," Ronnie said, pulling me around the dance floor. The mothers seemed to have been dismissed. Doug's mom was hovering nearby but now separate.

Boldy, Ronnie walked up and said, "Hi. You're Doug's mom. I'm Ronnie Chen. I sold them the house, and this is my partner Dom Reilly. He's an investigator."

I could tell he desperately wanted to put 'private' in front of that. His interest in my being a P.I. didn't make much sense until I remembered him saying how much he'd lusted after Magnum P.I. when he was a teenager. I was his own personal Tom Selleck.

"Dotty Bridges."

"Someone told me you were in the industry. Do you happen to know Dwayne Whatley?"

I cringed a little. Dwayne had the same last name as the man I had killed, the man Lydia claimed she'd killed. The police had tried to make something out of that, but dropped it when they couldn't find a connection. Ronnie was continuing, "He's in development. Sony or Paramount. I can never remember which."

"I was in crafts. Costumes mostly."

"Oh. Do you remember Ivan Melchor? He was at Monumental."

"Of course, I remember him. I was in and out of Monumental during the fifties and early sixties. I didn't work as much after I had Doug."

"So, you knew him?"

"I wouldn't say that. I knew who he was. I saw him. In the commissary or around the lot. And, of course, people talked."

"What did they say?"

The surprised look on her face made me explain. "I'm looking into a murder from 1949. We think Melchor knew the victim. A woman named Vera Korenko."

"Well, he didn't kill her," she said, reflexively. "I mean... people said he hated women, but I don't think that was true. I think he only hated lesbians. I can't say why. But the woman who got me work at Monumental was named Betsy Carter— her friends called her Bob. I was a very good seamstress and I could pattern. Anyway, she talked about how much Ivan hated her. To the point where it sounded paranoid, but I saw him snub her once. Probably the coldest shoulder I ever saw."

"And there was no real reason for their feud?" I asked.

"None that I ever heard of. He just didn't like lesbians."

I couldn't help but feel that had something to do with Vera Korenko. But what could she have done that made him hate lesbians so much? While I was thinking that the subject changed.

Ronnie was saying, "You're such a wonderful mother, supporting Doug like this."

"I don't think I deserve credit for that. I knew so many gays when I worked at the studios. It was always a safe place for them. Doug came out to me when he was in high school. Not that it was a surprise really. The only thing I said, and maybe I regret this, but I told him not to tell anyone until he was through college. Fortunately, he ignored me and joined a gay fraternity in his senior year."

"I think you still deserve a lot of credit," Ronnie said. I could tell he was thinking about his own mother who deserved none.

Then it was time to sit. We got more champagne. There were a couple of toasts before we went up to the buffet. A couple of times I thought about the invitation to the Westin

I'd received. I hadn't decided if I was going or not. It was on the tip of my tongue to tell Ronnie about it, to ask his opinion. Which meant I had to stop drinking. I poured the rest of my champagne into his glass.

He gave me a sidelong look and said, "You don't have to get me drunk to take advantage of me. You know I'll volunteer."

"Down boy."

He slipped his hand into my lap, saying, "I don't think anyone here would really mind."

"I think you're probably wrong about that. But let's not find out, okay."

And then it was time to go up and get our dinner. When I picked up a plate, I noticed that I still had paint around my nails. It has been hard to get out, but I should have tried harder.

We ended up at a table with Brown and Melissa, Robbie and his boyfriend, Kyle, and another lesbian couple whose names eluded me even as they were introduced. We talked about how good the food was, how we all knew Doug and Robert, which parts of the country we were originally from, and current events. The grooms stopped by and said hello for a few minutes.

Honestly, the whole thing was a bit overwhelming. Fifteen years ago, something like this would not have happened. Certainly not like this with an actual minister and mothers walking their sons down the aisle.

I said to the table, "In seventy-eight or -nine, I don't remember which, but I went to a 'gay' wedding at a Howard Johnson's. A flight attendant was marrying his best girlfriend so she could get free trips. Halfway through the reception, he went upstairs to screw the best man while she went to her room to bang the maid of honor. That's what a gay wedding used to be."

"You're right, you've had too much champagne," Ronnie whispered to me. He was right, of course.

Later, when the tables had been cleared and it was time to dance, the DJ played a cover of "Unchained Melody," and Ronnie and I danced. As he slipped into my arms, I realized it was the first time we'd ever danced like that.

"Do you want a commitment ceremony?" I asked him.

"Oh no. I have your name on a deed. There's nothing more committed than owning real estate together."

"That's not very romantic, though."

"You want to do something romantic for me?"

"Sure, I do."

"Tell me the truth. All of it."

Well, I wasn't going to do that.

After a very long, very awkward pause he said, "That's what I thought. It's fine though. Here's what's important. I love you; you love me. That's all we need."

"And as much real estate as we can afford."

"That's a given, darling."

CHAPTER THIRTEEN

July 28, 1996
Sunday late afternoon

The lobby bar at the Westin Hotel was located two steps up onto a very large platform. Dozens of tiny pin lights hung down from the atrium ceiling three floors above. Everything was cream and beige, there were comfortable barstools surrounding the bar, and small tables and chairs surrounding them.

Brian Peerson was now in his mid-thirties, and it had been more than eleven years since I'd last seen him. I recognized him right away, though. Blond and blue-eyed, his hair was still thick and something of a wavy mop on top of his head. In the eighties his hair had curled, but that might have been a perm. People did that then. Aside from being thinner he looked healthy. That was a huge relief.

He wore a pale-blue, button-down, short-sleeve shirt with madras shorts and flip-flops. People from the Midwest always over-compensated for the warm weather. I remembered Chicago summers; it was probably hotter there than it was here.

Sitting with him was a woman whose blonde hair had such strong highlights and lowlights that it couldn't possibly be natural. When she turned and lowered her giant sunglasses, it was Sugar Pilson. The well-known Chicago socialite was now in her late forties, like me. She was well-polished but had already begun the slow drying out that rich women put themselves through. Someday she'd look like a flower pressed in a book. Of course, she'd still be fabulous. She had a heart the size of her hometown: Dallas, Texas. She wore a kaftan in a riot of colors and had a handbag sitting next to her that was large enough for a stowaway.

They both saw me at the same time and slowly stood. Sugar inhaled deeply and then said, "Oh my, Lordy Lou, it is you! Nick it's so wonderful to see you. Oh, come here—"

And then she was in my arms. Brian right behind her. We stood like that for a moment—looking ridiculous, I'm sure.

"We should sit down," I said, my voice thicker than I'd expected.

Brian and I sat. Sugar flitted over to the bar. We stared at each other for a moment, then he said, "So, who is Dominick Reilly?"

He knew that from the mail he sent me, but not much else.

"It's an alias."

"Dominick. I can still call you Nick?"

"You can. Most people call me Dom, but Nick is fine."

And I won't be staying long, I thought. I was already regretting the location. An open hotel bar in a city where I'd served most of the gay men a beer was probably a bad idea if I didn't want this getting back to Ronnie.

"I can't believe I'm sitting here with you," Brian said. "It's been so long."

"So, tell me, you're back in Springfield? Are you still with Franklin?"

"I am. He's good. He had testicular cancer last year, but he's recovered and doing well."

"And your health?"

"Surprisingly good. Yours?"

"I'm good. Stopped smoking. Don't really drink."

"Don't look now but here comes Sugar with a bottle of champagne."

I turned and there she was with three flutes hooked in one hand and a bottle of champagne in the other. Apparently, it was my weekend for champagne.

"Can you believe I had to tip the bartender so he'd let me open the bottle myself!" She set the glasses on the table. Then she set about opening the champagne. Brian and I smiled while we waited. The cork popped and she filled the glasses. Before she sat down, she leaned over close to my ear and said, "If I wasn't so happy to see you, I'd rip your hair out. How dare you disappear for a decade."

When she was seated, I said, "Sugar, you can't tell anyone you saw me."

"And that horrid book about the Chicago mob. The writer said you were dead! I grieved for you. I was absolutely distraught for weeks until Brian finally swore me to secrecy and told me you were alive."

Luckily, Brian changed the subject. "Is there someone in your life?"

"Yes, I have a partner. His name is Ronnie. He's twenty-eight."

"Oh, I love younger men," Sugar said. "The last man I dated was twenty-five."

"Things didn't work out with you and the painter?"

"Actually, they worked out just fine. We had six wonderful years, followed by two bad ones. I stopped wanting to know what came next, so I divorced him."

"I'm sorry."

"Don't be. I'm really glad I married him. I'm also really glad I divorced him. What can be better than that?"

"Tell us about Ronnie," Brian said.

"I'm monopolizing the conversation, aren't I?" Sugar said.

"Just a tad."

"Sweetheart, just slap me."

"Ronnie and I have been together about four years. He's a real estate agent. We own three properties together."

"And he calls you Dom," Brian said.

"He doesn't know anything about Nick Nowak," I said.

"Darling, that's terrible," Sugar said. "We love Nick. He would too."

This time I changed the subject. "How is Terry?"

"Still wild. I still have my condo in Chicago. We're up there for weekends twice a month. Terry lives in the condo for me. Takes care of the place."

And Brian takes care of him, which was a relief.

Sugar put her hand on mine, "You should tell your partner who you are." She didn't want to let that go.

Part of me thought, why not let them back into my life? Why not invite them to the house so they could meet Ronnie. But then I knew what a bad idea that was. I knew that Brian wouldn't mention watching his stepfather drown in Lake Michigan or the time I killed a man on a construction site. I knew that Sugar wouldn't make jokes about my connections to The Outfit. But they would slip and call me Nick. They'd talk about Chicago and not Detroit.

In no time, he'd be able to put things together. He'd seen my real birth certificate, my real ID. He thought it was my fake ID. He hadn't realized it was the other way around. But if he met Brian and Sugar, he would.

"He knows who I am. He doesn't need to know who I was," I said with as much finality as I could. "Why are you going to Mexico in the middle of summer?"

"You can't have forgotten," Sugar said. "Chicago in the heat is a nightmare, but Mexico in the heat is a delight."

"Hot is hot wherever you are."

"Yes, but one has a pool and handsome boys bringing you margaritas and the other smells bad."

I turned to Brian and asked, "Franklin didn't want to come with you?"

"He's upstairs. He's not feeling well."

"You mean he didn't think this was a good idea. It's not, you know."

"I couldn't be in the same city and not see you."

"We can't make a habit of this."

"I know," Brian said.

Sugar pursed her lips, clearly wanting to object but thinking better of it. After that, conversation became a little more challenging. I decided not to tell them about The Freedom Agenda. They already knew too much about me. Our cases were occasionally mentioned in other states. I wouldn't want them bragging about knowing me. Well, Sugar might. I didn't think Brian would.

At one point Sugar mentioned they go to the same therapist. "She's wonderful, except sometimes she complains that it's unethical to see us both since we're good friends. But I never complain to her about Brian, and I know he never complains about me—wink, wink." He probably didn't complain about her though. He had bigger things to talk about.

When we finished the bottle Sugar tried to buy another, but I put my foot down. "I'm sorry, I can't stay. You guys feel free though."

She pouted for a moment, then excused herself to go to the ladies' room. Once she was gone, Brian said, "I saw Joseph about a year ago. We both go to Dr. Macht."

"How was he?"

"He seemed good. Healthy."

"Good for him."

"He mentioned that he was upset when he heard that you'd died."

"How did he hear that? I mean, why would he be reading books about The Outfit?"

"Gloria Silver put it in her column after the book came out. Made it sound like you were one of her closest friends."

"You didn't tell Joseph I'm still alive, did you?"

"No. It felt awful, Nick. Is all this really necessary?"

"I don't know. But I do know I don't want to be wrong. If I'm wrong, people die."

A cloud passed over his face. He seemed to be remembering the time that happened to him. And in that moment, everything I'd done for the last eleven years seemed exactly right. It was hard enough to be responsible for that cloud. If I'd been responsible... I couldn't risk that.

"You're happy?" he asked when he came out of it.

"I am."

"Good. That's what I needed to know."

INTERLUDE

Winter 1948

"The Beverly Hills Brown Derby?" Vera asked as they were parking. "Wouldn't it be more impressive to eat at The Polo Lounge? It's right across the street."

"The partners made the decision, not me."

Patrick Gill was a junior partner at Webster & Steenburgen. The dinner had been planned to impress a lawyer named Hammerstein they were courting from New York. As much as Vera's question was right on the money, it annoyed Patrick. He was finding she did a lot of annoying things.

She'd come to Thanksgiving dinner; at which time they'd announced their engagement. She'd worn a green dress with a floral print, large skirt, matching belt, and a white collar. It wasn't as formal as he'd have liked. She was wearing the same dress to dinner, and he kicked himself for not insisting they buy her something more appropriate. He knew the partners were expecting evening wear.

Unlike its sister restaurant in Hollywood, the restaurant

was not shaped like a hat. There was a derby on a neon sign sitting high above them as they walked under the awning into the restaurant. Inside, the walls were covered in a light beige linen on top of which hung dozens of 8x10s of movie stars neatly arranged in rows. From the ceiling hung spider-like chandeliers with two dozen light bulbs every ten feet. The round tables were surrounded by dark green leather club chairs held together with brass tacks. Dinner was well underway, and the room was filled with chatter and cigarette smoke.

The maître d' led them to a large round table in one corner. There were already three other couples there. Seeing them, Roland Webster stood up, acting the senior partner. He was well into his fifties, balding, angry blue eyes and a phony smile. He wore a loose-fitting gray suit with a fresh white shirt and a navy blue tie with white anchors.

"Well, there you are. We've already ordered drinks. Patrick, this is Bernie Hammerstein and his wife Rachel."

Bernie was just a bit older than Patrick, though he looked younger. He seemed terrified of something. Patrick couldn't decide if it was the restaurant, Roland, or California in general. His wife looked surprised.

"It's good to meet you," Patrick said. "This is my fiancée, Vera Korenko."

Bernie stood up and shook Patrick's hand but then wasn't sure what to do with Vera. She said, "It's a pleasure to meet you both." Which allowed him to sit back down. She smiled at Rachel. Dressed in a crepe black dress with a modest décolletage, she seemed in awe of everyone and everything around her.

Harold stood, saying, "Well Patrick, you know who I am, but your fiancée doesn't. Vera, I'm Harold Steenbergen and this is my wife, Catherine."

He was tall, in his early sixties and graying, while his wife was also tall, rail thin and around the same age. They were both in black; his suit impeccably tailored, her dress fully formal going nearly to the floor.

As Patrick held out a seat for Vera, Roland said, "I've been remiss. This is my wife, Olive."

Patrick and Vera smiled and said "Hello."

Olive smiled. She wore a navy dress with a large rhinestone brooch. Hooked in her elbows was a mink stole—though it was anything but chilly.

A waiter arrived with the drinks they'd ordered. The men appeared to be having some kind of highball, while the women had ordered grasshoppers. When everyone was served, the waiter asked Patrick, "Can I get you cocktails?"

"I'll have a rye and ginger," Vera said.

"Scotch and water," Patrick said.

The menus were waiting in front of them. Patrick perused his while Roland asked Bernie, "So, how are you finding Los Angeles?"

"Everything's so far apart," Rachel answered for her husband.

"That's the American dream," Roland said. "Space."

"You've certainly got that," Bernie said. It was clear to Patrick he wouldn't be joining the firm. If he were, he and his wife would be talking about the sunshine and the constant warmth.

The overlooked Olive must have picked up on the unease, because she asked, "What's everyone having? It all looks so good."

"I'm having the calf's liver," Roland said.

"Of course, you are dear."

"Well, you won't cook it at home."

"It smells up the whole house. I'm thinking the Pompano Beatrice."

"Oh, that sounds good," Catherine said.

"Is the seafood here any good?" Rachel asked.

"Rachel went to Brandeis," Bernie said proudly. "The seafood in Boston is incredible." Then to his wife he suggested, "Maybe the chicken curry with bananas. You'd like that. I'm thinking the creamed turkey, myself."

Patrick and Vera's drinks arrived. Vera said, "Thank you."

"Ladies, save some room," Olive said. "They have fresh spinach ice cream. Nonfattening."

"That's a terrible idea," Roland said. "Don't want any of you girls turning into Popeye. Especially you Olive."

That got a chuckle from his wife.

Vera took a pack of Parliaments and a lighter out of her purse. Rachel glanced at them and asked, "Oh, what are those?"

"Parliaments. They have a filter. 'Only the flavor touches your lips,'" she said, quoting their slogan.

"So you don't get tobacco on your lips? I hate that. Can I try one?"

"Of course." She held out the pack of cigarettes. Rachel took one and Vera lit it for her.

After inhaling, Rachel said, "Oh it's very mild." She smiled at Vera and sipped her grasshopper.

"I like this fellow Nixon," Roland said. "We need politicians like that, unafraid to go after communist spies."

It was obvious to Patrick that the comment was meant for the men at the table. He could see Roland bristle when Vera replied. "Oh, but I feel sorry for Mr. Hiss. I mean, the whole thing is ridiculous. Who hides important documents in a pumpkin? I mean, it makes no sense."

"And where would you hide classified documents, young lady?"

"It depends on who I'm hiding them from."

"Imagine I'm the FBI and I'm coming to search your house."

"Oh, that's easy. I'd put them in an envelope and mail them to myself with insufficient postage. I'd get a notice from the Post Office that I owed postage due. I wouldn't pick them up until the coast was clear."

Her answer seemed to make Roland very cross. Patrick was blushing deeply.

"What did you say your last name was?" Roland asked.

"Korenko."

"And what kind of name is that?"

"Czechoslovakian."

"Are you a communist?"

Vera laughed. "Why would I be a communist? I love money too much. Ladies, don't you love money?"

That seemed to embarrass the other women at the table, and Patrick knew why. If you were rich, you tried not to talk about money. It was bad form. Vera seemed to be good at bad form.

Roland gave him a look, one that said they'd be discussing this later. His pact with Vera was meant to solve problems, not create them. But here it was again. He knew that he'd have to remove himself from this situation. But how?

CHAPTER FOURTEEN

July 29, 1996
Early morning

By Monday morning, there were a lot of loose ends. I poked my head into Lydia's office as soon as I got to The Freedom Agenda, and said, "Did you notice that one of the witness statements mentions a small yellow car stopping in front of the Michaels' house at eleven-thirty that morning and a young girl going inside?"

"Yes, of course."

"I interviewed a woman named Kelly Wallpole. She was in Sammy's same grade. She said that even though Sammy wasn't popular, kids used her to get to her parents' well-stocked bar and for rides in her yellow Chevy Vega."

"Circumstantial. I'll use it at trial if we get a new one. But it's not going help our petition."

She grew silent and thoughtful. After a moment, I asked, "What?"

"Nothing. I'm plotting. I'll let you know if I come up with an actual plan."

"Any idea when we'll have Harris in again?"

She rolled her eyes at me. I took that to mean the conversation was over. I went back to my makeshift desk. Waiting for me was the list of names I'd asked Karen to research. They were all people mentioned in *Canyon Girl*. There were phone numbers and addresses for most of the names. Three of the names were crossed out with the notation "DEAD" written next to them: Carmichael Crampton, Detective Schmidt and Betty Brooks.

Crampton was the kid who'd found Vera's body. To be honest, I couldn't think of anything he'd tell me that might have been useful. Betty Brooks was a friend of Vera's. She might have been useful. But I couldn't know how much. I folded up the note and put it in my pocket. I'd deal with it later.

Then, I called Edwin at exactly nine o'clock and arranged to have lunch with him and his brother. We had to haggle a bit before finally settling on Musso & Frank at one o'clock. The main thing I liked about the place was that it was a few blocks away from the Hollywood Freeway, meaning that popping in and out for lunch meant I'd miss most of the really bad traffic.

I decided it was a good time to go to the county clerk's office and get the skinny on the house in Holmby Hills. They were located in Norwalk, so I drove there first. Believe it or not, they have records going back to before the Civil War. It took about an hour and a half, but I was able to establish that Ivan Melchor bought the Holmby Hills house in 1943. In 1965, Patrick Gill's name was added to the deed. Then in 1972, Ivan's name was removed due to his death. Patrick's was the only name associated with the property until last year when the house was sold.

When I got done it was only eleven. I had roughly two

hours to get to Musso & Frank, so I decided to try and squeeze in another errand. I drove downtown to the big library. I parked in a garage, paying through the nose for the privilege. Walking in the door, it was noon already. I was cutting it close since I'd need at least twenty minutes to drive to Hollywood. I walked around until I found the reference desk and I told the librarian I wanted to look at the white pages starting in 1945.

"We have all that on fiche," he said. "1945 until..."

"How about we do five years at a time. So, 1950." Then I changed my mind. "Wait. Give me every other year from 1945 until 1955."

A few minutes later, he brought out five boxes of rolled fiche. "It's two years per roll, so what you have is 1946 until 1955. If you want to go back another year—"

"No, it's fine. I'll start with these."

"The fiche room is over there," he said, pointing behind me. I walked in that direction and into a long room with four fiche machines, two on each side of the room. They were all empty. I walked to the furthest one and set to work.

I've done this before, though it took a moment to remember how to correctly feed the rolls into the machine. It was quick work. I looked at 1946. I found Patrick Gill at a phone number with an address on Keystone Avenue in Culver City. He was at the same address in 1947, 1948, 1949 and 1950. Then in 1951 he had a new phone number and a new address: 410 Faring, Holmby Hills.

I looked up Ivan Melchor. He was listed at the same address, except he had a different phone number. They had separate phones. That made sense. Patrick was a lawyer. If his office called, he wouldn't want his lover answering the phone. Among other things, it was expensive to be in the closet. That was what I'd wanted to know.

I returned the boxes of fiche and hurried out of the library.

Musso & Frank is the kind of place where I feel like a real private eye. It's dark and smoky, even though it's been years since you could smoke in restaurants. Don't get me wrong, they're not breaking the rules, it's just that it somehow still seems smoky. They should hand out fedoras at the door.

I was twenty minutes late. When I found Edwin and Jan at a booth near the front, there was a nearly empty martini glass in front of Jan.

"I'm sorry I'm late."

"It's not professional," Jan snapped.

"It's also L.A. and I stopped to do some research on your uncle."

The waiter came over. He was old enough to be my father. "Can I get you a cocktail?" he asked.

"I'll have a ginger ale." Not what he was hoping for, but I'd had enough champagne over the weekend to last me six months.

"And you sir? Would you like another martini?"

"Yes, of course," Jan said in a tone that suggested anyone not having two martinis at lunch was an idiot.

Edwin waved the waiter away before he could ask if Edwin wanted a drink. He kept his eyes on me, saying, "Go ahead" as soon as the waiter was gone.

"Your uncle moved into the house on Faring Road sometime late in 1950 or early 1951. The house was owned at that time by Ivan Melchor. In 1965, your uncle's name was added to the deed. Ivan Melchor died in 1972, at which time your uncle became the sole owner of the property. There was a standing order to put flowers on Melchor's grave for years. Your uncle paid for that. I'm guessing your uncle Patrick is gay."

I decided to leave out the part about him feeling up the male nurses at his nursing home.

Edwin looked a bit surprised; Jan did not. He said, "I don't see what that has to do with anything."

"Wait," Edwin said. "Is this why you were so set on Harmon and Coyne? You thought they'd cover this up for you?"

"They're discreet." He looked at me as though I'd just planted an item in the *L.A. Times* about his uncle's sexuality.

"Given that your uncle was gay, I think it's unlikely he killed his fiancée."

"Really?" Jan said. "I think that makes it more likely. She probably threatened to expose him."

I was tempted to say that my boyfriend had the same theory. Instead, I said, "Vera Korenko was brutally beaten and raped before she was strangled."

"You don't think a gay man could rape a woman?" Jan said. "Rape isn't about sex it's about violence. Isn't that what they say?"

"I still think it's very unlikely," I said.

"Gay men lack morals. It would be just one more taboo to break. That makes it very likely."

"John, cut it out," his brother said.

That left me an opening. "I went through everything you have in storage. It's pretty obvious that someone removed things. Your uncle had no photo albums? No framed personal photographs? No letters? No diaries? Not even an address book? Did you do it alone, Jan, or was it the two of you?"

"He did it alone," Edwin said. "I didn't know Uncle Patrick was gay and I wouldn't have been party to that."

"I did it for Mother. You know she thinks the world of him."

"She can still think the world of him," Edwin said, though it wasn't a confident statement. I'm sure he knew I was gay. There seemed to be things he didn't want to say in front of me. He shifted the topic. "Where does that leave us?"

"Would you like me to continue?"

"Of course, we want you to continue," Jan said. "Mother wants to know what to say to him when he says he killed that girl. Are you suggesting she tell him, 'You couldn't have killed that girl because you're a fag?'"

"John, please—"

"Do you still have the things you removed from the house?" I asked.

"Of course not. I destroyed them."

"You had no right to do that," Edwin said.

"I had every right, and you know it."

I was siding with Edwin, but that's just me. I said, "Well in that case you've made my job much harder."

"I think you're exaggerating. Are you trying to get more money?"

"It's important to know who his friends were during that period. Photographs could have helped, address books, diaries…"

"You'll have to work without those."

My ginger ale and Jan's martini arrived. The waiter asked if we'd like to order, but Jan gruffly sent him away. I wondered if they were going to buy lunch or was I about to be tossed out.

"What do you know about the book *Canyon Girl?*"

"That it's trash," Jan said.

"Your mother said your father threatened legal action if your uncle was mentioned in the book. Do you know anything about that?"

"Not really," Jan said. "That has to be twenty, twenty-five years ago. I wasn't a lawyer then. Edwin was still in grade school."

"Patrick was a lawyer himself. Why do you think he had your father handle it?"

Now Edwin answered. "Given what you're uncovering, I imagine the whole idea of the book was terrifying for Uncle Patrick. Any legal matter is better handled by someone with a level head."

Jan added, "Our father was a fixer. He handled problems for the rich and famous. Patrick couldn't have had a better lawyer for something like that."

"Why was it such a problem? Wouldn't it have been better to tell the writer he was Vera's fiancé?"

Of course, he might have dug a little further and exposed Patrick, I thought, answering my own question. Just as well. Jan ignored me, "Is this what you're doing for us? Reading a very dubious book?"

"I called the author. He hung up on me as soon as I mentioned your uncle."

Jan smiled, saying, "Father had that effect on people." That was probably true. He'd certainly scared the bejesus out of Wallace Philburn. "What do you plan to do next?"

"The book mentions a number of Vera's friends. I'd like to talk to any of them who are still alive. Ivan Melchor's papers are at some library. I'm going to see if there's anything there that might be helpful."

"I can't imagine there would be."

"What is it you think I should be doing that I'm not doing?"

"Can't you get the original case files from the Pasadena Police Department?"

"Yes and no. I can submit a written request. It's unlikely I'll get the complete file. What I'll get will be heavily redacted and likely not include much more than what's already publicly available. And it will take months." I took a long pause, then continued, "This is why I'm trying to talk to Wallace Philburn. He's done a lot of the leg work. If he'll share the information, it will save a lot of time."

"You're doing fine," Edwin said. "Just keep going."

I could tell Jan wanted to argue, but he decided better of it and said, "Well. Thank you for coming."

From his tone, I knew I wasn't getting any lunch. I stood up and said good-bye. Next time, I'd meet them on a park bench.

CHAPTER FIFTEEN

July 29, 1996
Monday afternoon

Instead of lunch at Musso & Frank's I got McDonald's drive-through. I ate a quarter pounder with cheese while driving through downtown L.A. on my way to the 710 and Downey. I ended up with a ketchup stain on the light green Henley I was wearing. I arrived in the Michaels neighborhood about two-fifteen.

I parked at the end of Via Amorita, a few houses down from the Michaels' house. I didn't want them to be bothered by what I was doing. It might have been helpful to talk with Pete's parents to get their immediate impressions of Larry, but I knew it would be painful and possibly, probably, not have much point.

There was a ten-year-old orange Camaro sitting in the driveway, meaning Paul Michaels was there with his parents. I couldn't remember if I'd asked what he did for a living that he could spend so much time with them. I was curious, but that too didn't seem to have a point.

I walked over to the house across the street. 7816. This was where Celia Wickers had lived. There was no mailbox on the street, so I couldn't reach in and check the mail to see who lived there. There was a car in the driveway. A Chevy Citation from the early eighties. I walked up to the front door and knocked.

After a moment, the door was opened by a woman in her late forties wearing shorts and a big T-shirt. Through the screen door she asked if she could help me.

"I'm with an organization called The Freedom Agenda. We work to get wrongly convicted people out of prison."

"I'm sorry, I can't contribute."

"Oh, no, that's not... There was a murder across the street in 1976. Celia Wickers was a witness. She lived at this address and I'm wondering—"

"Celia was my mother. She passed eight years ago. She left me her house."

"I'm sorry to hear that. You are?"

"Connie Wickers."

"I'm reading through your mother's statement and there are some things I'm curious about."

She opened the screen door and came out. Standing with me on the stoop, she crossed her arms and looked at me skeptically.

"Are you a cop?"

"No, as I said, I'm an investigator with The Freedom Agenda."

"Cops say things that aren't true."

"I can't argue with that. Did your mother have a problem with the police?"

"I was in graduate school then. Fullerton."

"What did you study?"

"Political Science. Don't ask me why."

"Does that mean you were living here at the time?"

"For a while. I had an awful boyfriend I'd just broken up with."

"In her statement, your mother said she was gardening that day. She saw a yellow car at eleven-thirty. That car left while she was behind the house and then a brown car showed up at noon. Did she talk to you about that?"

"Maybe. I'm sure whatever she said is what happened."

"Yes, but I'm not certain the statement is accurate or complete, so anything you could remember would be helpful."

She shrugged. "I think I remember her saying the officer was very young and very rude."

"Rude like he didn't believe her?"

"I don't know. I just remember she said he was rude."

"Your mother was hard of hearing?"

"No. Never. Her hearing was pretty scary, actually."

That just made my visit worthwhile. I had to wonder if the police had already decided what had happened and did what they could to bend the evidence in that direction.

"Was your mother friendly with the Michaels?"

"No. Not at all. I mean, I think she made a cake for them when Pete died but, no. The boys were always outside, playing some kind of sports and making a lot of noise. We could never keep the windows open. We had to have air conditioning, so we didn't have to listen to them."

That was probably not entirely true. We were pretty far inland, so it was much hotter than Long Beach. Ronnie and I could get by without air conditioning. I doubted that was the case out here.

"Your mother saw a yellow car and a young girl who may have gone into the house. Did she ever talk about that?"

Connie thought about it for a long time. "Yes. A few

times. Before the trial. But then not after that. She felt bad she hadn't paid more attention. The guy who's in prison, what's his name?"

"Larry Wilkes."

"She heard that he said he didn't do it, but we knew that couldn't be true. It had to be him. It couldn't have been the girl in the yellow car, she was very young. My mother always felt bad because she was in the house when the murder happened, so she didn't hear the gunshot. If she'd heard the shot... well, there wouldn't have been a trial even. He'd have taken a deal, and the Michaels wouldn't have had to go through all that."

"But your mother testified she *did* hear a gunshot."

"What? No, that's not possible."

"You weren't in court when she testified?"

"No. I was probably in class."

"Do you remember your mother talking about her testimony?"

"Not really. But I was a typical twenty-something. Narcissistic. Self-involved."

"You don't like the police."

"I had a few run-ins. It was probably around that time."

I couldn't help wondering if there might be a connection. Had someone hinted to Mrs. Wickers that if she didn't remember the gunshot her daughter might be—

"My mother wouldn't lie in court," she said, stubbornly. Though from the look on her face, she was obviously thinking the same thing I was. I thanked her and stepped off the stoop to head back to my Jeep.

"Hold on," she said. "Why do you think Larry didn't do it?"

"Because I know the girl in the yellow car did."

———

I knocked on a few more doors, both on Via Amorita and Irwingrove, but no one was home. Back at my Jeep, I sat looking out at a park where some kids were playing with their mothers looking on. I dug out my cellular phone and called Ronnie.

"Hey, what's going on?"

"Busy. I got a new listing. It's a condo in a building behind The Park Pantry. Andrew and Carl. They were at the commitment ceremony."

"Oh, that's great," I said. I couldn't remember who they were or when he might have talked to them, but it didn't surprise me. He managed to get clients pretty much anywhere he went.

"Yeah, they want to buy a house, so we'll be doing that too."

That was a good thing. Two commissions. It was also a bad thing. Jumping from one property to another can sometimes be tricky. Not to mention the clients, who are generally kind of nervous can get very nervous.

"I need to go over to Palm Springs. I'm thinking I'll go over on Thursday morning and come back Friday afternoon."

"By yourself?"

"Well, I guess."

"Uh-huh. No way. I'll arrange everything. We'll go over Wednesday afternoon and come back Friday. I would stay until Saturday, but I just took last Saturday off. And these guys want to look at houses on Saturday. I can take Thursday and Friday though."

"Are you sure?"

"Absolutely. I can't wait."

After he hung up, I called The Freedom Agenda and asked Karen to give me the name of the journalist who wrote the article for *The Downey Ledger*. Grudgingly, she gave me the name.

"Andrea Grubber."

I asked her to spell it. Then I asked for the address of *The Downey Ledger*. With a sigh, she gave it to me. It was on Lakewood near the Coca-Cola plant.

Thanking her profusely only annoyed her more and she hung up on me. She'd been running hot and cold since the whole Stu Whatley thing. Though, to be fair, it wasn't her job to get me information. In a more traditional office, she'd only be asked to work with legal documents since she was actually a paralegal.

The offices for *The Downey Ledger* were located in a strip mall next to a Mercado. I walked through the door and was immediately confronted by a counter on top of which were recent editions of the paper. Behind the counter were half a dozen empty desks. On a stool was a young woman in her very early twenties. Since she refused to look up, I picked up one of the papers and flipped through. It was largely ads.

Finally, she looked up at me and pushed back her glasses, and asked, "Are you here to place an ad?"

"No, I'm not. I'm looking for a reporter who used to write for you."

"We don't really have reporters. We have a few free-lancers, but most of what we publish we buy from the AP."

"Okay. Would you have records for someone who was writing for you in nineteen seventy-six?"

She looked at me like I was the most annoying person on the planet. She and Karen ought to form a club. Finally, she said, "Hold on a minute."

Walking to the back of the open area she knocked on a door, and after a moment went in. I waited. The place felt like a morgue, without the horrible smell. Finally, the girl came out of the office. Behind her, a man in his fifties. He wore a white shirt, navy tie and khaki pants. His sleeves were rolled up. He was overweight and his clothes were bunchy. There was something not very authentic about him, like he was dressed as a newspaper editor for Halloween.

"What do you want?" he asked when he reached the counter.

I figured a full explanation was in order. "I'm with The Freedom Agenda. We work on getting innocent men out of prison. We're looking into the Pete Michaels murder from nineteen seventy-six. You had a reporter named Andrea Grubber who wrote about it. Do you have any idea how I can find her?"

"She really can't tell you anything that wasn't in the paper," he said, gruffly. "She can't reveal her sources."

"That doesn't mean she wouldn't be able to give me more information."

"Last I heard she was out in Riverside. That was ten, twelve years ago."

"She worked for you for a while?"

"Five, six years. Not full-time. She mainly wrote newsletters for a pharmaceutical company down in Orange County."

"Do you think her name is still Grubber?"

"Yeah. She got married but didn't change her name."

"All right, thanks."

I walked out to the parking lot and climbed into my Jeep. I immediately dialed information and asked for the area code to Riverside. 909. Then, I dialed 909-555-1212 to get information. While it rang, I realized this was perfect. If we were going to Palm Springs, we could easily stop in Riverside. The operator answered. I asked for a number. She found three A. Grubbers. I wrote them all down and asked for the addresses that went with.

Then, I called the first number. A woman answered.

"Hi," I said. "Is this Andrea Grubber?"

"You have the wrong number," she said, barely waiting to hang up on me.

I lucked out on the second call. "Hi, is this Andrea Grubber?"

"It is. Who's this?"

"I'm hoping you like magazines, because I have an amazing offer for you."

She hung up. But it was just as well. I had the information I needed. Or at least, I thought I did. Just in case there were two Andrea Grubbers in Riverside I called the third number. "Hi, is there an Andrea Grubber there?"

"No! And stop calling!"

Okay. I guess I wasn't the only one looking for Andrea. Now that I knew she lived on Granada Avenue, we could stop there on the way to Palm Springs. I could have asked my questions over the phone, but it was easier to brush people off over the phone than it was in person. What I really wanted was for her to tell me who it was that gave her the tip about Pete's supposed engagement. She wouldn't want to reveal her source, but maybe once I explained that it was probably the murderer who tipped her off, maybe then she'd give me the information. Off the record. You never know.

It was after three. I wouldn't get home until nearly four. I decided it was time to call it a day.

CHAPTER SIXTEEN

July 30, 1996
Tuesday morning

Busy work. I'd kept myself busy all day Monday, and then when I got home I kept it up. I did two loads of laundry and then vacuumed the whole downstairs before I mopped the kitchen floor. When he got home at seven, Ronnie looked at me like I'd gone mad.

But I hadn't gone mad. I was just trying not to think too much about Sunday afternoon. It had been wonderful to see my old friends, but it made me nervous. What if they'd been followed? Ridiculous, I know. I was sure they'd traveled in the last decade. Probably quite a lot. If someone had been following them, they'd have given up long ago.

No, the bigger thing to worry about was whether I'd been seen there by someone who knew Ronnie. Someone who'd mention it to him. If he did find out, I'd tell him I was visiting two old friends. He wouldn't want to leave it at that, but I could say they were from Detroit. I could give them different names and make up stories about who they were. And no matter how good I was... he wouldn't buy it.

After a fitful night, I got to The Freedom Agenda around eighty-thirty. Lydia was already in her office with the door closed. That was fine. I'd decided I needed to spend the morning tackling the list of names Karen had given me for the Patrick Gill case. Several of the numbers were long distance. It was just easier to call them from the office, I wouldn't need to be reimbursed.

I made a fresh pot of coffee, poured myself a cup, then sat down and dialed the first number. Vera's friends, Harper and Georgia Dawson. They had a 602 number and an address in Scottsdale, Arizona. I was pretty sure that was a tony suburb. They'd done well for themselves.

A man said hello when the phone was answered.

"Is this Harper Dawson?" I asked.

"It is. You're not selling something are you? 'Cause I'm not buying."

"No. I'm not. I wonder if I can talk to you about Vera Korenko?"

"There's nothing to talk about."

I could hear a woman in the background asking, "Who is that? Who are you talking to? Harp, what's going on?"

I forged on. "You were mentioned in a book about Vera's murder. Your photo is in there."

"We didn't really know her, though. Georgia worked with her at the bank. The writer made things up. That's all."

"Vera? Are you talking about Vera?" The woman must be Georgia.

I asked, "Could I talk to your wife?"

He set the phone down, which made a clunking noise. A moment later the woman came on the phone, "Hello?"

"Is this Georgia?"

"It is. I'm Georgia. Do you know something about Vera?"

"I was hoping you could tell me about her. You worked together?"

She left a pause, took a long, ragged breath, then: "Vera was a wonderful girl. So, so smart. And pretty. But the boys... Well, she was too smart for them. I told her she had to pretend she didn't understand things or she'd never get a husband, but she didn't listen. Always had to let the boys know how smart she was."

"Did the boys get angry at her?"

"Some did, I suppose."

"Do you remember anyone in particular?"

"Oh, no... I'm sorry, I don't. I was already married to Harp. I didn't pay any attention to other boys."

"Do you remember the last time you saw Vera?"

"I do. I mean, I wouldn't normally, not after all these years... but the police came to the bank and interviewed all of us. It was very exciting. The last day Vera worked was September 30th. I remember it was hot that day. We didn't have air conditioning in those days. All the windows would have been open and the fans blowing. All of us, we couldn't wait to leave."

"What was it you and Vera did at Security First National?"

"We did mortgage settlements. They were complicated and they had to be right. The tiniest typo and you've screwed up someone's life for twenty years."

"Was there anything unusual about her last day?"

"The police asked me that when they came to the bank. They came about a week later. It had cooled down by then. I remember I was wearing a cute little sweater set."

That wasn't an answer. "What did you tell them?"

"No. I told them no. There wasn't anything strange about her last day. She was her normal self. Happy. Busy. She was so good at her job. I was sure she'd be promoted, but then—"

"What about that last week, did you notice anything?"

"No. She seemed happy. Maybe even happier. I don't remember why though."

"Did she talk to you about her engagement?"

"She did. But I don't think it was real. She didn't have a ring. I mean, it would only come up if one of the managers started to mash on her. I think she got tired of being asked out all the time, so she made up a fiancé. And it wasn't in the book, so I don't think..."

"You don't know the name Patrick Gill?"

"No. Who was that? Is that the person who killed her?"

"You don't remember the name of Vera's fiancé?"

"Well, she didn't use his name much. She'd say 'my fiancé' this or 'my fiancé' that.' But she wouldn't say a name. She might have said he was in the Marines. It wasn't that long after the war and all of us girls were just crazy about servicemen. I mean, I was married; I wasn't crazy about anyone."

"Well thank you. You've been very helpful. If I have more questions, do you mind if I call you back?"

"Oh no, you can call me. I don't mind."

Then I gave her my number in case she remembered anything she thought might help. After I hung up, I sat back and thought over what she'd said. It did sound like her husband was right. Philburn had exaggerated their friendship for his book. But why would he do that?

The bell rang at the front, and someone walked into the office. I walked out that way and found Karen settling in at her desk. I decided to take the opportunity to say, "Listen, I'm sorry about yesterday. I know you don't work for me."

"It's fine. I'll let you know when you have to apologize to me. All right?"

"Okay."

Then she actually smiled at me. A rare event. Particularly in the past few months.

"You're in a good mood."

"Of course, I'm in a good mood. Carl Lewis won a gold medal last night. That makes me happy."

I'd noticed this before. Karen was always happy when Black people did well. For a moment, I wondered if that was weird. But then I thought, I'm actually pretty happy when gay people did well. Though there weren't a ton who were honest about who they were. Other than Elton John you didn't hear much about gay men unless they died of AIDS. So, yeah, more power to her.

Of course, there was a long discussion of whether or not Lewis was gay at our dinner table. But I decided not to mention that to Karen. It didn't seem like a good idea.

"Anyway, thanks for the phone numbers. I'm calling them now. Has Lydia's door been closed since you got here?"

"Yeah."

She nodded and turned on her computer. After that I walked to the back. Manny and Virginia Marker lived in Eagle Rock. I called the number Karen had found and got an answering machine. I decided it was too complicated to leave a message; I'd call back later. Before answering machines, if you didn't get an answer you could call back to your heart's content. Now that everyone had an answering machine it seemed rude to call back if you'd already left a message. That's the main reason I didn't.

Rocky Havoc had a number in Long Beach. That shouldn't surprise me. Long Beach had a pretty large lesbian population. Unfortunately, when I called the number it had been disconnected. There was a street address, and it took me a few moments to realize it was around the corner from us. 243 Lime Avenue.

As I walked through the lobby again, I said to Karen, "One of these addresses you got is right around the corner."

"It took you four days to figure that out?"

"It took me four days to look. I figured it out pretty fast."

"Tell her I said 'hello'."

I decided to ignore that and just walked out the door. It was over eighty degrees and expected to hit ninety sometime in the afternoon. The sky was clear and there was a barely there breeze. Lime Avenue was two blocks down. When I reached it, I turned north and walked almost the whole block. Right before 3rd Street there was a small, clapboard, one-story courtyard complex made of five small buildings. It was painted light green with cream-colored trim. Between the two buildings at the front was a black iron gate that had been added at some point. It wasn't a great part of town.

The two buildings at the front were 239 and 247. That meant the other buildings had the numbers in-between. There was a call box attached to the fence. I pushed the button for 243 and waited. And waited. Nothing happened.

I could see 243 from where I stood. It was the back building. I couldn't tell if it looked lived in or not. Taking a chance, I pressed all the buttons to see if anyone in the complex was at home.

While I waited, I moved my shoulder around to loosen it up. Ronnie was right, I should go to a doctor. It had gotten worse over the years. When I was a bartender, I managed to avoid lifting cases of beer and wine whenever possible. I wasn't a dick about it, I'd tip the other bartenders if there wasn't a barback around. Lifting a single bottle of vodka was well within my abilities.

A screen door flopped, and a short, squat little woman in her late twenties came out of 245. Her hair was cropped except for a patch above her forehead, and she wore a T-shirt that said QUEER NATION. She looked at me and said, "Yeah?"

"I'm trying to find Rocky Havoc. Do you know if she's around?"

"Who the fuck are you?"

"My name's Dom Reilly. I used to be a bartender at the Hawk. Now I'm looking into the murder of a lesbian in 1949. Vera Korenko. She and Rocky were friends."

I put as many bona fides into my response as possible, and still she stared at me like I was a Christian minister ready to cart her off to a conversion camp.

"She told me all about Vera. What do you want to know?"

"Well, I'd like to know where Rocky is."

"Yeah, I get that. I'm not sure I want to tell you. Do you get that?" She was jutting out her chin ready to keep fighting.

"It's coming across," I admitted. "So, you're close to Rocky? You watch out for her?"

"Everyone watches out for Rocky. You don't know who she is? You said you worked at the Hawk. You should know who she is."

"I worked there for about three years."

Doing some quick math, Rocky had to be at least in her mid-70s and was probably more like 80. That made it less likely I'd know who she was even if she was locally famous.

"Do you want to know what she told me about Vera or not?"

"Okay."

It would have been nice if she'd open the gate and at least sit on the stoop with me, but that didn't seem likely. I said, "She and Vera were friends. How close?"

"Close. Rocky's a bull dyke. I don't like that expression, but she calls herself that. To each their own, you know? Vera was femme. Rocky was crazy about her, but she wasn't Vera's type. Vera had a thing for straight girls, mostly married."

"Did she mention any straight girls in particular?"

"A lot actually. She wasn't a U-Haul kind of girl."

I smiled at that. She was referencing a joke that has made the rounds a hundred times. What does a lesbian do on a second date? Rent a U-Haul. But that wasn't Vera. She liked to get around, and she chose women who'd have trouble maintaining a relationship.

"Does she remember anything specific around the time of Vera's murder?"

She took a moment. I could tell she was having a little trouble remembering. Then, "I think she said once that she had an idea about who murdered her, but she didn't say who it was. We were probably drinking. She was a bartender at Que Sera until about five years ago."

"Okay, if she thinks she knows who killed Vera then I really do need to talk to her. She's not here now, is she?"

She didn't answer, so I took that as a no.

"Do you know why her phone's disconnected?"

"Someone forgot to pay the bill."

That was vague.

"So, what's a good time to catch her?"

"Do you have a card or something?" she said. Then added, "It's the best I'm going to do."

I wasn't happy about that. Even so, I took a business card out of my wallet – Ronnie had made it for me on his printer – and held it through the gate. She snatched it like my fingers might burn.

"I'm not going to hurt her," I said.

"You don't know what's going to hurt her." Then she turned and walked away from me. I stood there watching as she disappeared. That had been helpful and not helpful at the same time. Rocky thought she knew who might have killed Vera. That mattered.

I started walking back to The Freedom Agenda and decided I'd pick up coffee for everyone. There was a little shop right on the edge of the East Village. I stopped in and ordered two regular lattes and one vanilla soy. They gave me a little cardboard carrier, and I walked the three blocks back to the office trying to think of other ways I could get to Rocky Havoc.

It was after ten when I got back to the office. When I set Karen's coffee in front of her, she raised an eyebrow. Then I stepped around the corner so I could see if Lydia's door was still shut.

"Has she been out at all?"

"Not yet."

I looked down at the coffee I was holding and said, "Wish me luck."

"You may need it."

I knocked on Lydia's door. I heard her say yes, so I opened the door. She was dressed casually and had a very glum look on her face. Several thick legal books were open on her desk.

"I brought you a coffee."

"Thank you."

"Is everything okay?"

"I'm ruminating."

"Anything I can help with?"

"No. Legal questions. I have a few calls out."

I nodded. "I have to drive over to be in Palm Springs Thursday and Friday for the Karpinski thing."

"Really? You're getting a vacation out of that?"

"Looks like. It's actually only half them. I'm also going to stop in Riverside to talk to the journalist who wrote the first story about the Michaels murder. That piece first mentioned the idea of an engagement."

"Don't mention that to Edmund. I don't want to pay for half your trip."

"Got it."

I left her alone and went back to my area to enjoy my coffee. I tried the Markers again and didn't get an answer. I wondered if they were screening their calls. If they were twenty years younger, I'd be sure of it. But then, if they were twenty years younger they might be at work.

I thought about what Rocky's friend said about Vera liking married women. Had she liked Georgia? Did Georgia even know it? Or was she hiding something? And what about Virginia Marker? Had she been one of Vera's married girlfriends?

I ruminated for a few minutes, just like Lydia, then I called Junior and invited him to lunch.

CHAPTER SEVENTEEN

July 30, 1996
Tuesday noon

Junior and I met at the Coffee Cup, which was east of Redondo so I didn't get there much. It was a breakfast and lunch place, kind of like the Park Pantry, which meant I'd usually just go to the Park Pantry since it was closer. Inside, the place was rustic and beaten up, with old menus pasted to the walls instead of wallpaper. Junior was already sitting at a table in the back.

I sat down and said, "So you like this place?"

"You haven't lived until you've had their mashed potato omelet."

Somehow, I doubted that. Honestly it sounded like a mouthful of mush. The waitress set two cups on the table and offered us coffee. When we said yes, she told us there was cream and sugar right there in the basket. "Do you know what you want?"

Junior ordered the mashed potato omelet, while I chose a cheeseburger with bacon and avocado. When the waitress walked away, Junior said, "All right, I'm dying to know. Why did you ask me to lunch? Are you throwing me out?"

"No. Nothing like that."

"Oh, thank God. Homeless isn't a good look for me."

"I wanted to ask you about Rocky Havoc. Do you know who she is?"

"Of course I know who she is. I'm surprised you don't."

"I've heard that before. The thing is, I've only been in Long Beach a few years."

"Well, she isn't only about Long Beach, but, whatever. Rocky Havoc is a legend. She's been fighting for LGBT rights since the nineteen-fifties—back when it was just G and L, and not very friendly G's and L's. She did a lot up in Los Angeles before she moved to Long Beach in the seventies to bartend at Que Sera. The Center practically started in her living room."

"Do you know where she is right now?"

"She took a fall at Ghetto Vons and broke her hip. There's a nursing home on 7th. I think we drove by it. That's where she is. Why are you asking about Rocky Havoc? And by the way, I'm sure Ronnie knows about her too."

"I didn't know she was connected to The Center, so I didn't think to ask him."

"You might want to repeat this conversation with him. So he's not offended."

"I think he'll be okay," I said. "He doesn't offend easily."

He stared at me for a moment, and then said, "I'm waiting. Why are you asking about Rocky Havoc?"

"I've been told she was in love with Vera Korenko."

"*Really.* Now that's interesting."

"I went to her apartment earlier today and her neighbor said Rocky talks about Vera a lot."

He narrowed his eyes and asked, "Small girl, buzz cut except for a tuft in the front?" I nodded and he continued. "Her name's Jo Miller. She does everything for Rocky. Speaking of unrequited love. If Rocky was even ten years younger they'd be a match made in heaven."

"Do you think we can get in to speak to Rocky?"

"We can try. You really think she knows something about Vera's murder?"

"According to Jo, Rocky has a pretty good idea who killed her."

"Putting two and two together... Someone's husband?"

"Jo couldn't remember. But probably."

"Well, that's exciting. Don't you think?"

The waitress brought our meals and then swung around to refill our coffees. When she left, I asked, "You mentioned a murder in the late sixties. Do you remember much about that?"

"Maybe. I don't know. I do remember the sex I had in the sixties. My God! It was so amazing. There was something about it being illegal and forbidden that just made it so much better."

"I bet you could recapture that feeling if you moved to Texas."

He looked aghast for a moment, then said, "On the other hand, maybe the excitement came from the fact that I was in my twenties."

"The murder?" I prompted.

He'd taken a bite of his omelet, so he chewed for a few moments. "Let's see. She was in her early twenties; her body was dumped near a golf course in South Pasadena. I'm pretty sure she'd been beaten and raped."

"Can you narrow down the date?"

"Oh my, I'm not even sure..."

"Where would you have heard about it?"

"Well, it was years before fag rags were freely available... I suppose it must have been in *The L.A. Times*."

"And they said the woman was a lesbian?"

"They probably wouldn't have, no. But The Sisters of Artemis staged a candlelight vigil in West Hollywood. I'm pretty sure I went—though after the eighties I do tend to get my candlelight vigils confused."

"They claimed her as a lesbian?"

"She went to the meetings."

What I was looking for was something I could use to search a newspaper. A key word that might lead me to an article with the woman's name. He wasn't giving me much to go on. Then:

"Oh, wait. I think it was 1968. I remember going to something up in West Hollywood. A vigil. I was driving a two-year-old Dodge Charger I'd gotten a deal on. What a car. A fastback that was open all the way to the back bumper. The backseats folded down and there was all this space. The things I did back there. Or rather, the men I did back there."

1968. That helped. That and South Pasadena might get me somewhere.

I began eating my burger in earnest. It was pretty good, as burgers go. Hardly the pinnacle of fine dining, but tasty.

"Have you talked to Ronnie about my getting your room when you move?"

"I've been a little busy. Why don't you talk to him?"

"No offense, but I think he'll raise my rent."

"I'm sure he'll raise your rent."

And he wanted me to go to bat for him. I didn't see any reason to do that. On the other hand, there was no reason not to give Junior some good advice.

"When you moved in, you said you had a section eight voucher. If you do all the work, Ronnie will probably accept that. You might be able to work it so we get more money, you pay less, and you get the room you want."

He thought about it for a moment, then said, "You might be a genius."

"I've heard rumors to that effect," I said, facetiously.

We finished our lunch and decided we'd try to get in to see Rocky Havoc at her nursing home. As it turned out, there are two nursing homes on 4th Street. We found the one that was down near Temple first, but when we checked at the door they had no idea who we were talking about. I asked Junior if he was sure she was in a home on 4th in front of the receptionist and she sent us back down the street to a nursing home that was two blocks east of The Coffee Cup. That was where Rocky Havoc was recovering from her broken hip; and had been for months.

Oceanview Rehabilitation Center was a modest building of one story about three hundred feet wide. Aside from the absurdity of its name—it did not have anything resembling an ocean view—from the street it didn't look like it could house more than six patients at a time.

Walking through the glass double doors, we stopped at an ultra-mod reception desk and asked for Rocky. Without asking who we were the girl said, "She spends most of the day in the courtyard."

That's when I realized the interior glass wall faced out onto a large courtyard overgrown with tropical plants. I could see that the building was actually quite large and probably went through to 5th Street. Junior and I walked through another set of glass doors and followed the winding path until it brought us to a grizzled, overweight woman in her late seventies sitting in a wheelchair. In one hand she held a cigarette; in the other a plastic-coated paper cup she used as an ashtray. It was full.

I introduced myself, leaving Junior something of a mystery. "I want to ask you what you remember about Vera Korenko."

"You say you're investigating her murder? You're not police though. You would have said."

"No, I'm not."

"So, who's paying you?"

It's not always a good idea to tell people who your client is, but in this case I decided it was. "I'm working for the family of Patrick Gill. Did Vera ever talk to you about him?"

"He's still alive, then?"

"Yes, he is. You knew that they were engaged?"

She chuckled. "I'm not sure that's what you should call it."

"What would you call it?"

"A lie. A fantasy. A cover story. I doubt they planned to go through with it."

"How long were you friends with Vera?"

"The last couple years of her life."

"I've heard she liked straight girls. Do you remember any of them?"

"I remember all of them."

"There were a lot of them?"

"Four or five while I knew her. She didn't get to bed them all." She crushed her cigarette in the cup and immediately lit another.

"I'm told you think you know who killed Vera. Can you share that with me?"

She smiled. "You talked to Jo."

"I did, yes."

"Sometimes I drink too much."

"Does that mean you don't know who killed Vera?"

"At the end she was running around with a girl named Gigi. I don't know her last name. She was married. Although you wouldn't know it if everything Vera said was true. They spent a lot of time together. They double dated with Patrick and his lover, Ivan."

"Did you ever meet Gigi?"

"I never met any of them. I would see Vera at The Sisters of Artemis meetings. We'd have a few drinks afterward. That's how we became friends. Eventually, she didn't come to the meetings much, but we still talked on the phone for hours. Every few days."

"Can you tell me anything about Gigi?"

"I don't remember much. Honestly, I don't think I wanted to know much about Gigi. She was married. Her husband was awful. He'd push her around sometimes. She told Vera she was going to leave him."

"Did she?"

"I don't know. I never heard anything about her after Vera died."

"You talked to Wallace Philburn for his book."

"Asshole."

"Care to elaborate?"

"Nothing he wrote in that book was true. He made it sound like she was just another girl who came to Hollywood wanting to be a star and ended up getting chewed up and spit out. That's not what happened. She didn't want to be in the movie industry. I don't even think she liked movies. She liked sunshine. That's why she was here. She didn't die for a dream. She died because men are evil." She looked from me to Junior, then added, "No offense."

I shrugged and said, "A lot of men are evil. Some days I'd say most."

She looked me up and down and said, "You've been around."

Then Junior, who'd been suspiciously quiet said, "Rocky, I want to thank you for everything you've done for gays and lesbians everywhere. You're a real hero."

"Want to know a secret?"

"Oh I love secrets. I promise I'll never tell."

I was sure it would take him less than an hour to break that promise.

"Being in all those groups in the fifties and sixties... best way to get laid. Better than a bar."

I had to laugh. "So, you did it to get laid?"

"You bet your ass."

"Well, you're still a hero in my book," Junior said. "I have to admit the things I did to get laid weren't always as noble."

I turned the conversation back to business. "There was another murder in nineteen sixty-eight. Do you remember that?"

"Yeah. I knew that girl, too."

"What was her name?"

"Shirley Kessler."

"How did you know her?"

"I was bartending at a place in Studio City. We met there."

"And you became friends."

"I was never as close to her as I was to Vera. But when she was killed, well, it struck a chord, you know? I did get involved in trying to get the police to do more to find her killer. Didn't work."

"Do you think there was a connection between the murders?"

"There were similar, we all knew that. But I don't know

what the connection would be. There was almost twenty years between them."

"Maybe there was no connection," I said.

"A serial killer, is that your guess?"

I shrugged. "It's possible."

"Then you'll probably never know, will you?"

We left shortly after that. As I dropped Junior off at the house, he said, "That was amazing. Thank you so much. I can't believe I got to meet Rocky Havoc."

I wasn't sure what to say to that. *I'm glad you had a good time?* I mean, I was there to interview her about a murder, it shouldn't be a good time. It shouldn't be so easy to forget why we were there.

I drove back to the office. There were only a few hours left. I spent most of that time catching up on the letters we get from prisoners. There weren't a lot, but I did take the time to really consider them. None were particularly compelling, though. Mostly, we looked for prisoners who could be exonerated by DNA testing. One of the letters was from a gentleman who'd been recently convicted using DNA. He wanted advice on how to prove it fallible. I was tempted to toss it, but then I went ahead and put it in the next box. The way he asked the question intrigued me. Maybe it would intrigue Lydia as well.

I tried the Markers again before I left. There was still no answer. Eventually I was going to have to drive out to Eagle Rock. It was about a forty-minute drive. Obviously, I wasn't doing it before Monday. We'd be in Palm Springs until Friday night. I could do it over the weekend, but I should really put in some time working on the co-op. I didn't want Ronnie to feel like he was doing everything himself, even though he basically was.

When I got home just before six, I found John and

Junior in the living room reading take-out menus. After a bit of haggling, we agreed on pizza. We ordered two large pizzas, a meat-lovers and a mushroom and black olive. They'd arrive in forty minutes.

"I have a surprise," Junior said. "I went to the video store."

"That's surprising?"

"You were talking about Ivan Melchor, so I rented *The Girl From Albany*. Ronnie said you haven't seen it. We have to watch it."

John rolled his eyes and said, "That calls for a cocktail."

"Me too, me too," Junior said.

We went into the kitchen. They made cosmopolitans, while I got a Calistoga out of the fridge. Of course, they made the drinks all wrong. A cosmopolitan is basically a kamikaze with a generous splash of cranberry juice. Theirs were really just Absolut Citron, Rose's and cranberry juice shaken and strained into martini glasses.

"Should we make popcorn?" Junior asked.

"We're having pizza."

"As an appetizer. I'll throw some in the microwave," he scooted over to the pantry and pulled out the Orville Redenbacher. "It's just not a movie without popcorn."

"Shouldn't we wait for Ronnie?"

"Oh, he's seen it already. Besides, there's no law that says we can't run it twice."

I wasn't sure I wanted to see it once. As it turned out, it was just okay. *The Girl From Albany* was basically the story of a sweet girl from upstate New York who wants to be a Broadway star. She moves to New York City, and through a series of implausible coincidences makes her debut on Broadway. In many ways it was the same story Wallace Philburn was trying to tell, except this one ended in an extravagant sequined production number while that one ended in a beautiful girl being beaten and broken and left in an arroyo.

Junior couldn't help singing along to all the musical numbers. After a second cosmopolitan, John joined in—though he didn't know the words as well as Junior.

Ronnie arrived home about ten minutes after the pizza came. We were in an intermission, the titled girl, played by Wilma Wanderly, had just arrived in New York and met a Broadway producer when his car splashed mud on her only good dress.

Ronnie kissed me, grabbed a slice of pizza then went upstairs to change. I tagged along.

"What are you doing? You should eat your dinner," he said through a mouthful of pizza.

"I already had two pieces."

"Okay," he said, skeptically. He set his half-eaten piece on our dresser then stripped off his clothes. To be honest, it was a much more interesting show than the movie. "Everything's set for Palm Springs. I got us a room in a little hotel with a pool. It's off season, so it was scandalously cheap."

"I'm charging it to the Karpinski brothers. It doesn't matter what it costs."

"I'm excited about this place though. They give you breakfast."

"Okay. Just letting you know that cost is not important.

He was putting on a tiny pair of shorts that were out of style anywhere but a gay bar.

"Junior and I met Rocky Havoc this afternoon. I didn't realize you knew her."

"I don't know her, I know who she is. And I've heard things about her. She hasn't been active at The Center for years."

"She knew Vera Korenko."

"Do you think she killed her?"

"Why would you say that?"

"I heard she could be rough on her partners."

"Rough as in violent?"

"It's a rumor. I don't know that it's true."

"It's a terrible thing to say about an old lady."

"Not if it's true," he replied.

"Are you going to say terrible things about me when I'm old?"

"Are you going to do terrible things?"

"I'm not making any guarantees."

He shook his head and picked up his pizza. We went downstairs to watch the movie. We ended up starting it again, mainly because Junior loved Wilma Wanderly's number "I Love the White Way," which pretends to be an innocent ditty about the lights of Broadway but could also be interpreted in a very racist vein.

The world is always changing and yet somehow is always the same.

CHAPTER EIGHTEEN

July 31, 1996
Wednesday morning

I only worked a half day that Wednesday. Mostly I did paperwork, making sure all my notes were in good shape for the Larry Wilkes case. Lydia was still ruminating. About what, I had no idea. I'd brought some leftover pizza for my lunch. Around noon, I took out a slice and was about to take a bite, when Lydia came out of her office and said, "Go. Have a great time."

"It's business. I'm not going—"

"It's a couple hours of business and you're going for two days. Have fun."

Before I got all the way out of the office, I heard her send Karen home, too. She was planning something. I wished I knew what it was.

Ronnie was already at home when I got there. We packed up his two-year old Legend because it got better gas mileage than my Jeep. Not to mention it had comfy leather seats and an air conditioner that turned the car arctic in seconds. Our bags went into the backseat since Ronnie had a traveling office in the trunk. All the forms he needed were in accordion files. Documents pertaining to several million dollars in real estate deals had been signed on his trunk.

We left around one-thirty. I was driving. Ronnie suggested we take 7th Street until it became the 22, stay on that past Garden Grove, the north on the 57 up to the 91, and stick with that until we get to Riverside. With traffic, that leg should take about an hour and a half.

I'd brought *Canyon Girl* with me and had it in the front seat. I was only about halfway through and really should try to finish before I interviewed Wallace Philburn. On the one hand, I didn't think it mattered; on the other, I didn't want to end up feeling like a kid who didn't do his homework if he figured out I hadn't read the whole book.

I caught Ronnie up on the chapters I'd read and then asked him to start reading with chapter nine. At first, I wasn't sure he was reading the right book. The chapter was about corruption in the Los Angeles police department in the late forties. Eventually, I started to catch on. He was making the case that if the LAPD was corrupt then the Pasadena Police Department probably was too. Corruption by association.

What wasn't clear was what that had to do with Vera Korenko's death. Was he suggesting a police officer killed her? Or the mob? Or basically anyone willing to pay off the police? He wasn't making himself clear.

Ronnie got to the next chapter about the time we were merging onto the 57. This chapter tracked Vera's move-ments during the last week of her life. Starting with Monday, she worked every day that week. Security National Bank was on Hollywood Boulevard and Ivar. There was a cafeteria nearby where the girls all ate their lunches. According to Georgia Dawson, she and Vera ate there on Mondays and Fridays. The other days they brought their lunches because they couldn't afford to eat out every day.

Georgia couldn't remember whether it was Monday or Friday when Vera told her she was going to Malibu for the weekend with friends. Philburn implied these were friends in the movie business.

"I don't think that's true," I told Ronnie. "Rocky said Vera wasn't much interested in the movies."

"It was true though, if she was going with Patrick and his boyfriend. Ivan was in the movie business. Besides, you don't have to like movies to like movie people."

"Do you like Dwayne?"

"He's not the only person I know in the industry," Ronnie said. "I do actually know some I like."

I asked him to continue reading. At the time, Vera was living a few blocks from where she worked in the rundown Hollywood Hotel. Philburn claimed she'd walk further down the boulevard to either Grauman's Chinese Theatre or The Egyptian most nights.

"Do you think there were any lesbian bars on Hollywood Boulevard?"

"No," Ronnie said. "The bars were in West Hollywood. As Junior has explained a million times, it was unincorporated, so the LAPD didn't patrol there. It was the county sheriff. They were less likely to raid bars, that's how they all ended up there."

"Of course, Rocky said she liked straight girls. There must have been some straight bars on Hollywood Boulevard."

"There was probably a bar in her hotel. But it wasn't okay for women to go into bars by themselves."

"Not nice girls, no. But girls who were in a little trouble. Girls who might have been relieved to find Vera there."

Ronnie frowned at me and went back to reading. Thursday evening, she had dinner with Betty Brooks at a drugstore and read fan magazines they didn't pay for. Betty didn't think anything was wrong with Vera, she seemed pretty normal.

"Do we have to keep doing this?" Ronnie asked. "It's not getting you anywhere."

"No, you're probably right."

"Good," he said, and then popped the soundtrack to *The Adventures of Priscilla, Queen of the Desert* into the CD player.

Before he could say anything, I said, "No, I am not strapping you to the roof of this car sitting in a giant high heel."

"Spoil sport."

We got to Riverside just after three o'clock. Ronnie had found something on the Internet called MapQuest and had printed out directions to Andrea Grubber's house on Granada Avenue. When we found her house, it was beige with a low façade of phony brick. There was an old-growth tree in the front and a row of scrunchy-looking shrubs along the concrete driveway.

"She's not home," Ronnie said.

"How do you know?"

There was a garage. It was shut so who knew if there was a car inside.

"I'm a real estate agent, I can tell when someone's home."

"That's a telepathic gift that came with your license?"

"Okay, don't believe me."

I opened the car door and went into shock. It had been

in the mid-seventies when we left Long Beach; in Riverside it was at least a hundred. There wasn't much humidity though, so it felt more like being dropped into a basket of just-out-of-the-dryer laundry than the strangled, underwater feeling you got in Chicago when the temperature went that high with humidity.

I knocked on the door. Waited. Nothing. After a minute or so, I stepped into the bushes and looked through the front window. There were kids toys all around the living room. Various ages from the look of the toys, from toddlers to grade-schoolers. At least one boy and one girl.

She wasn't home. If she were, the kids would be in the middle of the mess they'd made of the living room. I walked back to the car and climbed in. I started it up immediately so we could run the air. Even after just a few minutes it had gotten noticeably warmer.

"Go ahead, say it. You told me so."

"I wasn't going to say anything." That was clearly a lie.

"She's got at least two kids. I'd say she was picking at least one of them up from school. Do you think we should wait?"

"Hell, no. It's going to be a hundred and twenty in Palm Springs and close to that here."

Someone had been listening to the weather report.

"Should we be doing this?"

"Absolutely. As long as the air conditioner is running. But we shouldn't sit for an hour waiting. We can stop on the way back," he suggested.

I pulled away from the curb and we were on our way to Palm Springs. Once you're out of Riverside, the scenery gets increasingly barren. There's not much to look at but scrubby plants and sandy hills, until you get to Cabazon where there's an outlet mall smack dab in the middle of nothing.

"No," I said, even before Ronnie could ask. He liked buying things at a discount and we did have an entire new co-op to fill.

"Maybe on the way back. If it's under a hundred," he said, agreeing with me.

Hotel El Caliente was located off Palm Canyon on a side street with a dead end. It didn't look like much from the front. There was a strip of parking lot in front that held about ten cars. Through a bougainvillea-covered entrance you went into the courtyard hotel.

We grabbed our bags from the backseat, nearly burning our hands on the door handle. Going through the entrance, we found the registration desk, or rather room, to the left. It was open. There were a couple of chairs and an empty desk. Ronnie rang the bell.

An older man of about sixty came out wearing a pair of too-tight pink shorts and a Hawaiian shirt. He could have been at the commitment ceremony we'd just attended.

Ronnie explained that we had a reservation, and the man said, "Yes, of course. I'm Bart. You are an adorable couple."

"Thank you," Ronnie said, seeming quite pleased. "We think so."

Did we think so? Mostly I felt incredibly lucky, which was not the same as adorable.

"It's fairly quiet right now," Bart said. "You'll want to be on the first floor."

"We do?" I asked.

"Absolutely. There's a mister that makes it possible to sit outside the room. I'm putting you in room five."

I glanced into the courtyard, which was almost entirely

pool. The building was two floors, roughly Spanish style—though not as interesting as our co-op. You could reach the second floor via a stairway roughly in the middle. He was right, that floor felt much more exposed to the sun. Room 5 was under the walkway for the second floor and just after the stairs.

"Sounds perfect," Ronnie said. He held out a credit card, Bart poked a few buttons on his computer, and a receipt popped out a printer.

As he stapled a copy of the charge to the receipt, Bart said, "Breakfast is between eight and ten. There will be coffee and Pop Tarts if you're an early riser. Do save some room though, tomorrow I'm doing a chilaquiles casserole. You'll want to try that."

"Thank you," Ronnie said.

"If you want anything just ring the bell. I have a little apartment in the back."

We picked up our bags and walked across the sizzling courtyard to room 5. The mister was going full steam, and we got under the overhang as soon as we could. The water from the mister evaporated so quickly you never felt wet.

I hadn't noticed before, but there was an overweight man sitting outside room 6. When we got close he said, "Hello neighbors." He was completely naked. His legs were crossed, and his belly covered the family jewels. He'd had a couple of abdominal surgeries, which made it look like his belly was winking. Or maybe it was just his attitude.

"Hi," Ronnie said, pushing open the door.

"I hope I'll see more of you later," he said, his eyes glued to Ronnie.

Inside the room, it was neat: the bed queen-sized and well-made, the artwork stereotypically Southwestern. There was a small table and two chairs, nightstands and a dresser. In the back was a decent bathroom. The air-conditioning was on full blast, and I'd guess it was in the mid-seventies.

"This is a clothing optional place, isn't it?"

"Of course," Ronnie said. "Isn't that more fun?"

He opened his suitcase and began putting things into the dresser.

"So, we're going to run around naked?"

"Maybe later. You're not a prude, are you?"

"I'm not sure I like the audience. The way that guy looked at you was first-degree sexual assault."

"Oh, he's harmless. There's not much point going in the pool until it cools down tonight. What do you want to do until dinner?"

It was around four. We didn't really need to eat until sixish. I was still full of leftover pizza and some cookies Ronnie had bought for the ride over. Before I could answer the question, he said, "I think we should go find this Wallace Philburn person and then have dinner after."

"Or..." I said. I'd noticed the bowl of condoms and tiny packets of lube sitting on top of the dresser. We didn't use condoms; we trusted each other enough not to. I suppose that was foolish on Ronnie's part given all the things he didn't know about me—but I knew I'd never hurt him, so I let him be foolish.

He caught my drift and said, "Quickly. I still want to get things done."

CHAPTER NINETEEN

July 31, 1996
Late Wednesday afternoon

A hundred and twenty-degree heat made me think summer in Palm Springs was a lot like winter in Chicago: You stayed indoors, did your best not to go outside, and when you did it was just to run to and from your car. Scalding heat and frigid wind chill were distinctly different experiences, but the results were the same.

When we got into the Legend, I turned the car on and the air conditioning came right on, full blast. I touched the steering wheel and immediately pulled my hands back. It was scorching.

"I'm not going to be able to drive for a few minutes."

"Hold on," Ronnie said and jumped out of the car. I watched him go back into the hotel wondering what exactly he was doing.

While he was gone, I flipped through the radio channels until I got one that sounded local, giving a news report. Yes, it was a hundred and twenty-degrees, which was something of a record.

Then Ronnie was back, coming out of the hotel with a large plastic bag of ice. He got into the car and instead of handing it to me, placed it on top of the steering wheel.

"How are we going to find this place?" I asked while we waited. "Tramview Road."

"I could go back in and ask Bart?"

"No, it's fine. It's in north Palm Springs. It's not a big place. We should be able to find it."

"Okay. I'm up for sightseeing."

Once the steering wheel had cooled off a bit, we drove north on Palm Canyon until we reached the city limits. We turned east onto Gateway Drive and started zig zagging around. Fifteen minutes later, we hadn't found it. I would have rolled down the window and asked someone for directions, but there was no one around. Apparently, it wasn't a good idea to walk your dog when the pavement was melting.

"Should we find a gas station and ask?"

"Go a little further north," Ronnie suggested. "The tram is up that way." He pointed at one of the mountains above us.

"You've been here before?"

"Of course, I've been here before. You didn't think I was a virgin, did you?"

That gave me a very good idea what he'd done on his last trip. I would need to make sure I didn't disappoint in that department.

And then we found it. It was the very last street before the desert began again. Parts of Tramview Road had recently planted trees that were meant to cut the wind coming in off the desert, and they probably would sometime in the next century.

When we found Philburn's house there weren't any fledgling trees across the road, just a pile of rocks. The brown house was flat-roofed with a metal box sitting on top like a cupola. It wasn't a cupola; I was fairly certain it was a swamp cooler. Something people bought when they couldn't afford central air-conditioning.

The yard was nearly dust, and the driveway was cracked and crumbling. A fence circled the property as though there was something to protect. We walked up the driveway to the front door. I knocked.

Sophia Hadley answered the door. She was about fifteen years older than I was, making her in her early sixties. She'd been the fantasy of a lot of the teenaged boys I'd grown up with. She'd spent much of the early sixties making movies that required her to wear a bikini. I'm not sure I ever saw her on screen fully dressed.

Ironically, or coincidentally, or something like that, she was wearing a bikini top, and a light shawl wrapped around her waist. Out of character for an actress her age, she looked exactly as old as she was. Which made me wonder if plastic surgery wasn't allowed outside of Los Angeles County.

"Yeah?"

"I'm looking for Wallace Philburn."

"Are you from the bank?"

"No, I'm not. I want to talk to him about his book, *Canyon Girl*."

"A fan? Jesus. He'll come in his pants."

She swung the door open, and we walked in as she called out, "Wally, you've got company."

The living room was filled with the cheesy kind of furniture you bought in a set after seeing an ad for it on the back page of the newspaper. A leg on the sofa had broken, making it sag in the middle. It looked sad and unhappy. The room was twenty degrees cooler than it was outside but by no means cool. It was also damp.

Wallace Philburn came down a hallway that probably led to several bedrooms. He wore a wife-beater and a pair of shorts that had once been slacks until they got cut off at the knees. On his feet were black socks and brown slippers. He was around seventy and looked every minute of it.

"Who the fuck are you?"

"Manners Wally," Sophia said. "Don't cuss people out until you know why you're doing it."

"As I told you on the phone, Mr. Philburn, I'm investigating the Vera Korenko murder for the family of Patrick Gill. I'm Dom Reilly."

"Okay, yeah, I remember. I don't remember inviting you here."

Ignoring that part, I continued, "This is my partner, Ronnie Chen."

"Reilly and Chen. Sounds like a goddamn TV show. A pair of mismatched private eyes." He'd totally missed that I meant partner in another way. I glanced at Ronnie and saw the delight in his eyes. He'd love it if we were a TV show. Then Philburn added, "Not a successful TV show. One that would get canceled mid-season."

That dampened Ronnie's enthusiasm. Sophia asked, "You want some water? It's all we got. I'm not sure we've got any ice cubes left."

Ronnie and I said we were fine.

I said, "I want to ask you some questions about the people you interviewed for your book."

"Why do they want to dig all this up again?"

I explained Patrick's condition and what he'd been saying.

"It's distressed his sister quite a lot."

"Have you found any proof he did it? That he murdered Vera?" He asked excitedly. "You'll have to let me interview you. If you've found the murderer my publisher might put out a new edition of the book... with a brand-new final chapter."

Like an old-fashioned cartoon his eyeballs turned to dollar signs. I tried to let him down easy. "I haven't found the killer yet. But I'm hoping you can help with that."

"You're sure Gill didn't do it?"

"I'm sure."

"It would make sense. They went to great lengths to make sure I didn't mention any of the family in the book. Why else would they be so worried?"

"He's gay. So was Vera. Their engagement was a kind of misdirection."

He didn't look surprised. "Yes, well, that wasn't the story my publisher wanted, so that's not what I wrote. You see, Gill's family freaked out for nothing. I couldn't include him in the book. Not truthfully."

That seemed off. Patrick's sister didn't know he was gay. Did her husband?

"When they threatened to sue you, did it come up that he was gay?"

"No, of course not. People didn't talk about that then."

"Why didn't your publisher want you to tell the truth?" Ronnie asked. "Wouldn't that be the point of the book? The truth? If she was killed for being a lesbian?"

"The point of any book is to sell books. There had been a very popular book about the Black Dahlia a few years prior. That's what they wanted. The same story. Beautiful young girl comes to Hollywood to become a star and her dreams end in tragedy. It doesn't work if she's a lesbian and got what she deserved."

Knowing Ronnie, I placed a hand on his shoulder to keep him quiet. Philburn took it in, but continued, "The audience is women all over the country who thought about a life in Hollywood but were too scared to leave home. Stories like Elizabeth Short and Vera Korenko tell these girls they made the right decision. But for the grace of God... you know? They pay money for that."

"But you did interview people; you did actually investigate Vera's murder," I said.

"Of course, I did. Just because I gave my publisher what they wanted doesn't mean I don't have integrity."

Actually, it meant exactly that, but I had to let it pass. I asked, "I've heard that Vera liked straight women. Is that what you heard?"

"I did, yeah, but you see that made it even worse. Who wants to read a story about a predatory lesbian? Like I said, she got what she deserved, didn't she?"

This time, I let Ronnie off the leash. "She didn't deserve to be murdered. And so what if she liked straight girls? She didn't rape anyone."

"That we know of," Philburn said.

Before Ronnie could continue, I cleared my throat. The international code for shut the fuck up.

"Do you know the names of any of the women she chased after?" I asked.

"If I'd known you were coming, I would have gotten out my notes."

"If you'd known we were coming you'd have left town."

Sophia laughed. I hadn't realized she was still there. She

said, "It's a hundred and twenty degrees, you don't think we'd leave town if we could afford to?"

She had a point.

"I've talked to Harper and Georgia Dawson. He says they weren't that friendly. But you wrote that they were very close. You even included a picture of them."

"People lie. Georgia gave me that picture. She was excited about being in the book. She said that Vera was one of the best friends she ever had. Maybe that didn't make her husband happy."

"Was he considered a suspect? You made it sound—"

"You'd have to ask Detective Schmidt that question."

"He's dead. I can't ask him much of anything. When you talked to him, did you get the impression Harper Dawson was a suspect?"

"I did get that impression. But I got that impression about a lot of the people I asked about."

"Manny and Virginia Marker?"

"Manny Marker was a suspect for a while, but his wife gave him an alibi."

"What do you remember about Betty Brooks?"

"Now *she* was a predatory dyke. I was convinced it was her for a while."

"Your book says Vera was raped," Ronnie said. "That they found semen inside of her."

"Maybe Brooks found her having sex with a guy and killed her out of jealousy."

That seemed like a stretch. So far, I hadn't heard anything about Vera being in a relationship with Betty Brooks. I also hadn't heard anything about her being bisexual. It felt like the kind of overlay straight people put on things.

"Do you have any proof that Betty Brooks was in a relationship with Vera?" I asked. "Didn't you write she had a husband and three kids?"

"Yeah, I wouldn't say that was completely true. My editor added that because too many single women in the book made it sound like they were all lesbians."

"They *were* all lesbians," Ronnie said.

"Who was Betty Brooks really then?"

"She'd been married after the war until around fifty-two. Had a kid. Her ex-husband had two more by another woman that she raised for a while."

"So, you could defend what you wrote as an honest mistake."

"That's the nature of journalism."

"How do you know about the rape and the semen? Were you able to get access to Vera's autopsy?"

"Not exactly. Detective Schmidt told me about it."

"You didn't have access to any of the official files?"

"Only through Detective Schmidt."

"So, indirectly."

"That's the best I was able to do."

"In your investigation..." I nearly choked calling it that. "Did you run across the name Gigi?"

"No. Jesus, is this another lesbian? I blame the war, that's why there were so many of them."

"Oh Wally, you think the minute you leave the room women are eating pussy," his wife said.

"That's what I would do."

"You haven't eaten a pussy in decades."

Okay—that was a happy marriage. I had one more question. I asked it so we could get out of there.

"Tell me... *Wally,*" I said. "Who do you think killed Vera?"

"You didn't read the end of my book, did you?"
"No, I haven't gotten there yet."
"Well, I don't want to spoil the surprise."

CHAPTER TWENTY

July 31-August 1, 1996
Wednesday evening/Thursday morning

We drove back down Palm Canyon looking for a place to have dinner, settling on Danny's Hideout, which was very old-school. A small, one-story pink adobe building with a giant awning out front, it looked like it had been there since the sixties. When we walked in it was dark, the light barely on. For a moment I thought they might be closed, but then a waiter appeared and led us to a red leather booth.

It wasn't crowded, and the people who were there were all older. Locals. A grand piano was shoved into one corner with a little sign on top that said someone named Eddie Varone would be there at seven.

Ronnie was instantly in love with the place and ordered an Absolut martini straight up with a twist.

"This is totally a martini kind of place." He lowered his voice and asked, "Do you think any of these people are mobsters?"

I didn't bother looking around the room before I said, "No. They're not." A mobster would have the good sense to leave Palm Springs in the summer.

We'd brought *Canyon Girl* in with us and while Ronnie sipped his martini we read the last chapter, holding the book sideways so we could each read.

The final chapter of the book was all about a suspect Philburn was calling Mr. Fish. The man was in his early thirties at the time and already a prominent attorney. He had many notorious clients, including a few who were believed to be involved in organized crime. He spent little time in court and eschewed publicity. Detective Schmidt had learned that he knew Vera Korenko and that she'd attended several of his family functions. He could not determine whether she'd actually been invited or not.

I looked up at Ronnie and said, "He's talking about Jack Karpinski."

"How do you know that?"

"Well... the description of his law practice matches what his sons and his wife said. Also, Karp... Carp. A fish."

"So, it's really just revenge for silencing him?"

"Yeah. It skirts libel by not directly identifying him and by calling him a suspect and nothing more."

"Do you think he was a suspect?"

"Philburn seemed very excited by the possibility I might have proof that Patrick did it. Which suggests he doesn't know who did it at all."

"Isn't it weird that none of the Karpinskis mentioned it to you?"

"Yes. No. I don't know," I said. "They're weird.

We both ordered steak and potatoes. It seemed like a good call in a place like that. Ronnie had a second martini.

"Why would a police detective give any information to someone like Wallace Philburn?"

"Maybe he was hoping a book might shake something loose."

"It didn't though, did it?"

"Not that I can see. There's never been an arrest."

"Vera liked straight girls, or really girls who appeared straight."

"Yes. I think that's probably true."

"And you think that got her killed."

"That's my working theory."

"Of the women mentioned in the book, that leaves three possibilities: Betty Brooks, Virginia Marker and Georgia Dawson."

"But we're looking for a girl named Gigi."

He started singing "Thank Heaven for Little Girls" with a French accent. Off my confused look, he said, "*Gigi*. The musical."

I felt another night of musical viewing coming on. I changed the subject. "Of course, the only connection to Gigi is Rocky Havoc. She could be wrong. It could be a dead end."

"Did you notice, when you were asking Wally questions he said something about his publisher not wanting too many single women in the book? But other than Vera, there aren't *any* single women in the book."

"And he likes to think he's ethical."

Ronnie shrugged and took a long sip of his martini. "He doesn't have any idea who killed Vera."

"You're right. He doesn't."

The piano player started and wasn't half bad. We had key lime pie for dessert with coffee. Ronnie ordered some cognac. After the waiter left, he looked at me and said, "What? I'm on vacation."

Over dessert we chatted about the co-op and Ronnie's clients. I raised the issue of Junior getting our bedroom and the possibility of his obtaining a section 8 housing voucher. Ronnie didn't say much about the whole thing except, "If he can get the money, then of course he can have the room."

More money from Junior and the ability to rent the room he was in for more would make everything work out well. If the 2nd Street house and the Bennett house paid for themselves, and the co-op cost very, very little, then Ronnie and I would be in excellent shape and well on our way to a down payment for property number four.

We stayed and listened to the piano player for a bit. Ronnie tipped him and asked for show tunes. He got through "If Ever I Should Leave You" and then Ronnie started to sing along. It was time to go.

By the time we got back to the hotel, the temperature was in the low nineties. It was barely ten, so we went for a naked swim in the pool. No one else was around. We floated back and forth staring up at the starry sky. The water was bathtub warm, close to the temperature of the air, which meant the moment you stood up or even let part of your body out of the water it evaporated and had a cooling effect.

Eventually, Ronnie cornered me in the shallow end for a kiss. The alcohol had made him soft and pliable, fuzzy even. Happiness swelled in my chest. I suppose we could have had sex right there. Even if someone showed up, they wouldn't complain. Still, I led Ronnie back to our room, where it was guaranteed to be just us.

****

The next morning, after having breakfast poolside. Ronnie got naked again and jumped into the pool. I went into the room and moved the phone over to the table. Through the window I could watch my lover swim. I called Edwin's office and got through to him.

The first thing he said was, "I've got a meeting in fifteen. Will this take long?"

"Five minutes, tops."

"Great. Go ahead."

"You didn't tell me that your father was a suspect in Vera's murder."

"Okay, well..." He was obviously not expecting that. "It's only in that stupid book. The police never thought he was a suspect."

"What did your father think about that?"

"He thought it was funny. What else could he think of it?"

"He let Philburn have the last word," I said, implying that was very unlawyerly.

"That's not how he looked at it. Philburn was deliberately trying to provoke him. He *wanted* to get sued. The publicity would have sold thousands of copies of his book. Not to mention, the suit would have failed. Defamation cases are hard enough to win without having to prove it's you the author is talking about."

Not bad points. I moved on to the next big question, "Did your father know your uncle was gay?"

"That's a tough one. I didn't know. So I don't really know what anyone else knew. I will say that one of my dad's favorite sayings was 'Don't know what you don't want to know.'"

"That sounds like lawyer speak."

"Definitely. Given the circumstances he would have

considered my uncle's sexuality a legal problem, so he wouldn't have asked. In fact, he'd probably have discouraged Uncle Patrick from telling him."

Through the window, I watched as two new guests arrived at the pool. Both were young and attractive. Both were impressively naked.

"Is that it?" Edwin asked.

"Ah, yeah, I think so..." my attention was elsewhere.

Edwin said goodbye and hung up. I put the phone back where it belonged and went out to the pool. Ronnie was already talking to the new guests. Seeing me, he swam over.

"Hey," he said.

"I'm thinking we should drive over to Riverside and try to catch Andrea Grubber. We'll be back by lunch."

"Okay, sounds *very* interesting," he said. Then climbed out of the pool.

I followed him back to the room, appreciating his ass every step of the way. Before I went in, I glanced over my shoulder and noticed that I had not been alone in my appreciation.

By the time we got to Riverside it was after ten. The temperature was a frigid hundred and ten. When we found Andrea Grubber's house for the second time, there was a minivan in the driveway. She was home. I pulled the Legend up behind the minivan, Ronnie and I got out.

Normally, I wouldn't involve him in a case I was working on for The Freedom Agenda. Those cases were likely to go to court and no one wanted to explain what my real estate boyfriend was doing at an interview. It didn't matter much with the Patrick Gill thing because that would never go to court, and even it were to spawn a trial for some reason I'm not under any professional strictures and couldn't be criticized.

For obvious reasons, I shouldn't have let him come with me to talk to Andrea Grubber, but I wasn't going to leave him in Palm Springs in a pool full of naked men, and I certainly wasn't going to leave him in a hot car.

We knocked on the front door and a moment later it was opened by a frazzled looking woman of about forty-five.

"I work for The Freedom Agenda. You wrote an article about Pete Michaels about twenty years ago—"

"For God's sake come inside. I can't afford to refrigerate my entire front yard."

We stepped into the house. There were two toddlers in the living room. Andrea had constructed a kind of corral out of the furniture and a couple of gates. It looked kind of clever.

"So, as you were saying..."

"Yes. We represent Larry Wilkes. We feel that he's innocent. I'd like to ask you a few questions about an article you wrote for *The Downey Ledger.*"

"Would you like some iced tea? I made it fresh this morning."

"Um, sure."

We followed her into the kitchen/dining room. Everything was messy but clean. There was a desk in a corner of the eating area with a computer and printer on it. She caught me taking it all in and said, "No one should have children after thirty-five. It's just a terrible idea."

"I wouldn't know," I said.

She pulled three mis-matched glasses out of a cupboard, took a plastic pitcher out of the well-stocked fridge, and poured us each a glass of tea.

As she did all that she said, "So, I wrote an article about Pete Michaels' murder."

"You did. Do you remember?"

"Of course. I was only an intern there for a year and it was the biggest thing I got to work on."

"You wrote an article about two days after the murder in which you referred to a source saying that Pete Michaels was engaged. I'm trying to track down your source for that."

"Hold on," she said, then put her tea down and walked out of the room. She disappeared into one of the bedrooms. A few minutes later she came back carrying a cardboard box. She pushed the breakfast dishes aside and set the box on the dining table. She began digging through the box.

I must have been gawking at her, because she asked, "What? Are you surprised I'm going to give you my source?"

"Very. I thought I'd have to beg."

"Number one, an innocent man is in prison. That's what you said, right?"

"I did."

"More importantly, number two, does it look like I'll be returning to journalism any time soon?"

"You do have a computer right there."

"I write a newsletter for the Inland Orange Growers Association and one for Kaiser Permanente. Doesn't sound like much, but with the kids it keeps me busy. I'm officially done with journalism."

She found what she was looking for. "Here we go." She pulled out a small, girly, notebook and flipped through it. Found the right page and said, "Kelly Hawley."

"Really?"

"You know the name?"

"I do," I said. "Do you remember the conversation?"

"Yes. But not well."

"She didn't tell you who Pete Michaels was engaged to, did she?"

After double-checking her notebook, she said, "No."

"So, you can print something like that without corroboration?" Ronnie asked.

"That's why you add things like, 'according to a source.' That means we're not sure. Our source could be lying."

"Which they were in this case," I said.

"If I'm remembering correctly, the engagement came up at trial."

"Another lie. Do you remember anything else about the murder that might be helpful?"

"I doubt it. The narrative formed quickly. I was surprised it even went to trial."

CHAPTER TWENTY-ONE

August 1-2, 1996
Thursday afternoon/Friday morning

We were back in Palm Springs by noon. We found a Mexican restaurant with take-out, got a giant chicken burrito and a small order of beef tacos and took it back to the hotel. I had some long-distance calls to make.

After we split the burrito in half and divvied up the tacos, Ronnie said, "You're not supposed to talk to me about this one, are you?"

"No."

"Fine. I'll eat outside. You make your calls."

On the one hand, he was being considerate; on the other, those cute boys were lying naked by the pool scorching themselves. I decided not to think too much about that and took a big bite of the burrito.

While I chewed, I wondered what would be the best way to get ahold of Kelly Wallpole. I didn't want to call her sister for the phone number. She wouldn't want to give it to me, not without being told why I needed it. I took a chance and called information in Los Angeles. I asked for Dr. Wallpole. Bingo. Got a number.

I reached her nurse, who didn't want to let me talk to the doctor.

"It's a personal matter. Could you let her know I'm on the phone."

"I'll tell her you called. Could you give me a number, Mr. Reilly."

"No. I'll wait."

"That won't do you any good."

"Then I'll call back. In five minutes. And then five minutes after that. Until she comes to the phone."

After a long pause she said, "Hold on."

I waited. And waited. And waited. Finally, Kelly came on the line. "What do you think you're doing?"

"Did you call in a tip to *The Downey Legend* about Pete being engaged?"

After a moment's pause, she said, "No. I didn't. And you can't call here like—"

"Why does the reporter say you did?"

Another pause before she said, "Hold on. I'm going to pick you up on another line."

I waited. Again. Finally, she picked up. "I did not make that call."

"Are you saying Sammy Blanchard used your name?"

"Yes, that's what I'm saying."

"Were you there when she made the phone call?"

"I was. I was horrified when she gave my name."

"Did she tell you why she made the call?"

"She said it was a joke."

"It was murder. Why would she joke about murder?"

"I ask that question now. But I was just a kid then."

"You were better friends with her than you told me, weren't you?"

"My sister didn't know. I don't want her to think badly of me."

Interesting dynamic, I thought. She was a doctor but her sister's opinion of her mattered enough for her to lie.

"We'll need you to do a deposition. This information could help Larry Wilkes get a new trial."

She didn't want to, but she said, "Yes, of course."

As soon as we hung up, I took a bite of my burrito, then called The Freedom Agenda.

"Karen, it's Dom," I said, through a mouthful of food.

"How's your vacation?"

"Hot."

"You want Lydia?"

"Please."

She put me on hold, and I managed to swallow before Lydia came on the line. I explained that we could prove that Sammy Blanchard phoned in the tip about the fake engagement.

"That's great. That gives us enough to petition the court."

"Is that what you've been ruminating about?"

"No. I'm considering going in a different direction."

That was surprising.

"You want to elaborate?'"

"No. I'll let you know when I decide. We'll talk when you get back."

Mysterious. Annoyingly so.

After we hung up, I paid more attention to my lunch while watching Ronnie through the window. He was on his cellular. I realized that was something we had in common. We liked to work. Most of the time, I didn't think we had much in common and I worried about that. Couples were supposed to have things in common.

Then I wondered, was that part of why Ronnie wanted me to work for Lydia? Had he sensed I'd get addicted to my work the way he was to his? It's hard to get addicted to being a bartender—unless you're an alcoholic—so I could see why he'd want to edge me in a different direction. A more challenging one.

I stopped pondering and called the Markers again. The answering machine picked up. I waited for the message to end, just to give them a chance to pick up, and then I hung up. I knew that would cause the machine to record a hang up. I'd probably caused a lot of those in the last few days. Then I was at loose ends. We'd done everything I needed to do over this way and a big part of me was ready to go home.

Ronnie came back inside. "Okay. It's ridiculously hot out there. Even with the mister."

We turned the AC up, closed the drapes, and spent the afternoon in bed. Around dinner time, we found a Chinese restaurant and then went to have a cocktail at Streetbar, which was crowded even on a Thursday night.

"We should buy a place over here," Ronnie said.

"I'm not sure I want to spend much time here. I'm not that enamored of melting parking lots."

Seriously, we'd stopped at Gelson's to pick up some sodas and snacks, and when I got out of the car my foot sank a good quarter inch into the blacktop.

"Not to live in. To rent." He had a look on his face I'd seen before. He was planning his takeover of the world. "Gay men aren't dying as much. These new meds are working. That means more of them are going to live long enough to retire." He opened up his hands and said, "And this is where they'll retire to."

I glanced around the bar and saw that the average age was nearly a decade older than I was. He might have a point.

"What are prices like?" I asked.

"Low compared to what we're used to."

"Let's talk about it after we move into the co-op," I said, knowing full well that wasn't going to work. If he found something he wanted next week, we'd be buying it.

———

The next morning, we were up by seven and checked out by eight. We skipped the breakfast they offered and went to Elmer's for a traditional breakfast. We were heading out of town by nine-thirty.

Ronnie had a lot of calls to return, so I was driving. We'd agreed I could stop in Eagle Rock on the way back and try the Markers in person. Using a gas station map, I'd plotted the route: the 111 to the 60 then cut up to the 210. The *Thomas Guide* would take us the rest of the way.

I needed to find Gigi—or at very least find out who she was. It had already occurred to me that the murders of Vera Korenko and Shirley Kessler were connected. At some point, I needed to look into the Kessler murder to see if there was anyone named Gigi involved. I was beginning to worry that was the only way I'd find her.

The drive was easy. Most of the traffic was going in the other direction. Very few people drove into the Los Angeles area for the weekend. Most wanted to escape.

On the way, in between phone calls, I asked Ronnie, "What can you tell me about Eagle Rock?"

"People are discovering it again. It's still relatively affordable. It started out mostly white but then a lot of

Filipinos and Mexicans moved in. Now you're getting a lot of artsy types. Rich white kids, mainly. You want to buy up there?"

"No. I just want to know what I'm facing."

Like most of the neighborhood, the Marker house looked to have been built postwar. It was gray stucco, plain and unadorned. Most of the houses around it had started out the same but had since gone through numerous upgrades: brick fences, carports, additions, facades, radical landscaping, wrought iron gates.

It wasn't even eighty degrees—a relief after two days in Palm Springs, otherwise known as Dante's Gay Inferno. Ronnie rolled down the window and kept making calls. I walked up to the front door and knocked. Nothing. I waited. Knocked again. Still nothing.

Next door, they had a lush front yard that probably required more water in a day than a family of five needed to shower for a week. We weren't currently in a drought to my knowledge, but it looked like these people were trying to drive us there all on their own. A woman of about fifty came out and picked up the hose. It wasn't the right time of day to water, so I figured she came out to talk to me.

I walked over to the brick and wrought iron fence, and said, "Hello."

She dropped the hose and came right over.

"They're not here," she said. "They're in San Diego. Their daughter's going through a bad divorce. They're helping out. Not that they can do much. They're in their late seventies and he's got terrible emphysema. I think helping out means they're going to pay for things."

Before I had a chance to answer her, a police cruiser floated down the street and stopped in front of a house kiddy-corner to the Markers. We watched as an officer got out and walked up to the front door. After he was let into the house, I asked the woman in front of me, "Do you know what that's about?"

"The Rabines. Their son, probably. He's a drug addict. Steals from them all the time. Usually, they don't report it, but this time he stole a pistol. They're terrified he'll use it on himself."

She seemed to know a lot more than she should. "This happened this morning?"

"Oh no, it happened a week or so ago. I don't know why they're back today. Maybe they found the gun."

"What else can you tell me about the Markers?"

"I don't like to gossip," she said, putting on a prudish face. Of course, she'd already gossiped about the Markers *and* her neighbors across the street. But that didn't seem to sink in.

"How long have you lived next door to them?"

"About ten years."

"Do you socialize with them?"

"No. We're not friends. They're not friendly with anyone."

"So it wouldn't be worth my time to talk to the other neighbors?"

"I wouldn't say so."

"Do you know how long they've lived in the house?"

"I think since it was built."

"Do you know when that was?"

"Most of the houses were built right after the war."

"Did you ever hear anything about a woman named Vera Korenko?"

She crinkled her face. "No. Why would I?"

"She was a friend of the Markers. Murdered in 1949."

She got very quiet. "There are rumors that Mr. Marker

used to beat his wife. Obviously, that doesn't make him a murderer, but it does make him violent. *If* the rumors are true. I've never seen anything to suggest that. Even before he ended up on oxygen."

I asked a rather obvious question. "If you don't really talk to them, how do you know so much about them?"

"The Rabines have lived here longer than I have. Much longer. Elsie Rabine talks to Virginia from time to time. Elsie talks to me." She seemed to hear herself and then felt compelled to say, "None of this is gossip. It's just... factual. And you did mention murder."

"I'm not here to criticize," I said.

"Well, I should hope not. I'm only trying to help."

CHAPTER TWENTY-TWO

August 2, 1996
Early Friday Evening

On the drive home, Ronnie managed to schedule two showings for that evening. Almost as soon as we got home, he was out the door. The house was empty. John was probably at work and Junior was likely doing something at The Center. I'd unpacked our bags into the laundry basket and was poking around in the refrigerator looking for something to eat when I heard the doorbell. I walked through the house to answer it. Lydia.

"Come on in."

She walked in. She was wearing a well-tailored pair of slacks and a white blouse with a built-in bow. I asked if I could get her anything, and she said, "I won't take up much of your time."

"Please, take up my time. Ronnie is showing houses for the next few hours and for once the house is empty. It feels a little weird."

"Don't get too excited for my company, I'm going to ask

you to do some work this weekend." She gave me a guilty look.

"What do you need?"

"I want you to convince Sammy Blanchard to come in for a deposition next week."

I stared at her for a moment, then said, "I'm going to get you a glass of wine. Meet me in the dining room."

What the—how did she think I was going to convince Sammy to do that? Sammy had made it crystal clear when I'd spoken to her before that she had a lawyer, a lawyer who didn't want her talking to anyone. When I got back to the kitchen, I found a bottle of red wine, opened it, and poured Lydia a glass. I went through the swinging door into the dining room.

Setting the glass down in front of her, I said, "I have no idea how to get her to sit for a deposition."

"At one point, she told you that Pete Michaels was blackmailing her husband, so he killed him."

"That was a lie, though. You know that."

"I'd like her to say that in a deposition."

"Isn't that suborning perjury?" I asked. I'd probably picked up just enough law to be dangerous.

She took a sip of her wine. And said, "Not bad." Taking a deep breath she said, "Yes. It could be considered suborning perjury. That's what I wanted legal advice on. It's defensible. For one thing, she's not my client. For another, we *think* she's lying, but we don't know for certain. We don't know anything for certain. She never confessed to killing Pete. That's just what we think."

"I doubt that she'll confess."

"It doesn't matter. Whatever story she tells under oath is likely to be good for us."

"You're planning to ask questions that show her up as a liar, aren't you?"

"Well, that's always a possibility."

"I don't think she'll do it."

"Explain to her that if she swears her husband killed Pete, then Larry will get out of prison and there won't be a second trial. If the district attorney believes her, it will all be over. She'll be off the hook."

"She's already off the hook. She's been off the hook for two decades. Isn't she better off staying silent?"

"If we get Larry a new trial, we'll need an alternate suspect. That would be her."

"Which she'll want to avoid," I admitted. I took a long moment. Then said, "I don't know if I can get this to happen."

"It's worth trying. A second trial could be risky. We don't want him convicted twice."

"God, no."

I really didn't have a choice. I was going to have to try this. I tried to decide if I had everything I needed. I shouldn't approach her until I had my ducks in a row.

"The car is important," I said. "She was a teenager, so it was probably registered to her parents."

"We have witnesses who can tie her to the car, though."

"Yes. Sharon Hawley and Kelly Walpole confirm that she had a white or yellow Chevrolet Vega."

"Do you need more than that to talk to her?"

"I need as much as I can get."

"I can put Karen on it Monday, but I'd like to move this along..."

I shrugged. "I'll lie. I'll tell her we've got the registration in her parents' name."

"And then we can work on it Monday. What else?"

"John Hazeltine."

"Remind me who that is."

"He confirmed that people suspected a relationship between Pete Michaels and Coach Carrier."

"How can that help you with Sammy? We can't prove she knew."

"I'm not sure. I mean, at trial you'd certainly be making it look like she should have known."

"True. Do whatever you need to do to get her in. Okay?"

"Okay."

She only stayed a few more minutes. I did the polite thing and asked about her husband, though I really didn't care. He lived in a world I didn't care about and didn't understand. Honestly, I didn't think Lydia cared much about that world either. She told me his career was taking off without much enthusiasm. After she left, I ate a sandwich, grabbed a few things, and went out to find my Jeep.

Sammy Blanchard lived in a stepped condominium complex in Signal Hill. One side ran along Cherry Avenue, another along Hill Street. Because of the staggered nature of the building, there was a parking lot below each section. It made sense that the spaces were assigned to the units above.

Sammy's condo was in the topmost section. I found a parking place that had a decent angle on the gate to the garage. I was about two and a half car lengths above it. There was about forty-five minutes before the sun set completely.

The walls of the garage only came halfway up. There were columns that supported the building, but the walls themselves didn't reach the first floor. I imagined the benefit of that was that you didn't have to heat or cool the garage since it was open to the elements. It also meant I had a good view of anyone leaving or going to their car. The garage lights came on and I could see even better.

If you'd asked me, I couldn't have told you why I thought it a good idea to sit outside Sammy's condo. It was just a gut thing. I needed to make sure I had as much information as I could get my hands on before I tried to convince her to come in for a deposition.

Since it was a Friday night, it wouldn't be too much to expect Sammy would leave her apartment. Go to a movie, dinner, drinks with friends. *Did she have friends?* If she was anything like she was in high school, the answer was no. But then, the worst people had friends. It wasn't that hard to find someone desperate enough to be your friend.

People came and went. There was a light over the gate that would slide back and forth so the cars could get into the garage. It was like a spotlight highlighting the drivers for me. None of them were Sammy.

About nine o'clock, a recent model Mercedes station wagon came up the hill, then did a three-point-turn and parked across the street from me about four car lengths away. A woman got out and I thought, *Holy shit!* It was Kelly Wallpole. Not only were she and Sammy friendlier than she'd originally let on; they were *still* friends.

She stopped at the intercom and buzzed Sammy. A moment later, the buzzer went off and she entered the condo. I glanced at my cellular phone and checked the time. 9:40. Late for a friendly visit. The station wagon suggested she had kids. Did she go home and put the kids to bed before she came out? Why didn't she come earlier? Couldn't her husband have put the kids to bed? Or a babysitter?

Maybe it wasn't such a friendly visit. Maybe her

husband thought she was somewhere else. This visit could have been tacked on to a visit to another friend or even her sister. Her husband wouldn't even know she was here. Lots of possibilities, very few answers.

I waited. And then waited some more. Kelly came out of the condo at 10:22. She wasn't even in there an hour. Yeah, it might not have been a friendly visit. She got into her Mercedes and then started down the hill. As soon as she was a block behind me, I turned my lights on and made a U-Turn. My Wrangler has a short wheelbase, so it turns on a dime.

It can be challenging to tail someone in Los Angeles. A couple things I had going for me though: It wasn't rush hour, and when she left, Kelly drove directly up Cherry Avenue to the 405. I followed her for about ten minutes and then we turned north onto the 605. Fifteen minutes later she was going east on the 91. We got off at Bloomfield and then zig-zagged over to La Mirada.

I lost track of where we were exactly, but I didn't lose her. We were in a suburban neighborhood where the houses all looked to have been built in the seventies. They were wide, single-story ranch houses on small plots. Anywhere else they would have been very boring pieces of property. In Southern California they were very expensive, and the wealth showed. They were nicely landscaped and well-kept.

The Mercedes pulled into a driveway and stopped. I pulled up to the curb across the street. There were no other cars on the street. I hopped out of the Jeep as quickly as I could. Kelly hadn't noticed me. She got out the Mercedes and started up the driveway. I was about ten feet behind her when I said, "Kelly. Do you have a moment?"

She jumped, and said, "Oh my God, you scared me."

Then she focused and saw that it was me. Fear returned to her face. "I don't have time to talk right now."

"I think you do. You were just at Sammy Blanchard's place. I'm guessing you told her I found out about the two of you making that crank call twenty years ago."

"I thought she had a right to know. I really need—"

"Yesterday you agreed to give us a deposition. I'm guessing Sammy talked you out of it?"

"It's not a good idea."

"Does she have something on you? Was it blackmail or just simple coercion?"

"I can't talk to you."

"This is how this works... We are going to get a new trial for Larry Wilkes. When we do, you'll be subpoenaed. If you lie on the stand that's perjury. Perjury means prison. Maybe you'll be prosecuted, maybe you won't. You can take that chance if you want to. What will definitely happen is that when we put Andrea Grubber on the stand, she'll say you're the one who gave the tip about Pete Michaels. You know what that will make you? A suspect. Do you want to be a murder suspect?"

"My husband and kids are in the house."

"I'm not doing anything to you. I'm just telling you how your life might go and what you can do to avoid making things worse."

I took out my wallet and picked out a business card. I held it out for her. "Call Monday morning. Schedule a deposition. Tell the truth. All of this will go away."

The door to the house opened and a man's voice said, "Kel? What's going on?"

"Nothing," she called out.

"Monday," I said, still holding out the card.

She took it.

CHAPTER TWENTY-THREE

August 3, 1996
Saturday morning

The next morning, I was sitting in front of Sammy's condo by seven. I had two large coffees from Hot Times and two lemon poppy seed muffins. I left the radio on for the first few minutes since it was in the middle of the news. Starbucks had opened its first store in Japan, that was important. The national minimum wage was raised to four dollars and seventy cents, which meant the members of Congress really believed people could live on less than two hundred dollars a week. And Congress wanted to declare English the national language. That probably made the go-back-where-you-came-from types really happy, though I doubt they had any idea where they themselves had come from.

I watched as Sammy's neighbors came down in their workout clothes and drove to their gyms. It was a cloudy morning and cool, below seventy. I had on a thick corduroy shirt over a white tee. It was damp too. My shoulder hurt, which is the only reason I knew that. My personal barometer. I wondered if it might rain.

A few minutes after eight I got a call on my cellular. Ronnie.

"Where are you?"

"I'm sitting in front of a condo in Signal Hill."

"Why?"

"I'm waiting to see if Sammy Blanchard comes out."

"You're on a stake out? And you didn't invite me?"

"Your idea of fun is very strange. Tell me about your showings last night."

I'd actually fallen asleep the minute I got home from La Mirada. Ronnie hadn't gotten home yet. That was later than usual for him, so it must have gone well.

"I showed Andrew and Carl six houses last night and then they put an offer in on the first one."

"That happens a lot with you."

"Well... I always show the best choice first and then show the lesser ones next. It solidifies people's choices."

"Congratulations."

"It does mean another commitment ceremony. They're tying the knot next month."

"That seems to be going around."

Honestly, I wasn't sure how I felt about commitment ceremonies. They were either a radical political act or a slavish devotion to straight culture. Not that I personally cared as long as I got to wake up next to Ronnie every morning.

"Buying property together is enough commitment for me," he said, again. I wondered if that was true or whether he was just picking up on my ambivalence about commitment ceremonies.

It seemed a good time to say, "I love you, Ronnie Chen."

"Wow, stakeouts must be really boring."

That made me laugh. Then he added, "I love you, too. But I have to go. If you're going to disappear tomorrow morning, leave me a note."

I worried my way through another two hours. I spent the time thinking about what I might say to Sammy whenever I decided to confront her and make my pitch for a deposition. At one point, I slipped out of the Jeep and took a piss behind one of the larger bushes next to her garage.

It was nearly ten when I saw her walking across the garage toward her car. I started up the Jeep and waited. A couple of minutes later, a nearly new, white Camaro convertible came out of the garage. Despite the glumness of the day, she had the top down. She turned south. I gave her a good lead and then followed.

When she reached the bottom of the hill, she turned right. I scooted up a little, just in time to see her turn right again. She was going north on Cherry Avenue. I relaxed. A few moments later I made the same turn. I could easily see her several car lengths ahead of me, heading up the hill.

I tried to anticipate where she might be going. We were going to pass The Home Depot, but I doubted she was a fix-it kind of girl. It was easy to stay a ways behind her, the white convertible made her stand out. We crossed the 405, drove by a dozen or so car dealerships, went through an industrial area. I didn't know where she was going until we turned right on Del Amo.

We were heading to the Lakewood Mall. Things turned residential on Del Amo, a decent neighborhood if you wanted to live in the suburbs while still being close to everything. Traffic thinned out a bit, which meant Sammy could speed up. I was fairly certain it wasn't because she'd noticed me. She had a sports car. Making it go fast was part of the point.

The mall was sprawling. We turned north on Lakewood and then about a couple blocks later, turned into the parking lot. The mall was popular, particularly on a Saturday morning. In the lot across from Macy's she cruised around looking for a space. She was one of those people who kept driving around to find the closest spot possible. I chose a spot on the furthest side of the lot next to Lakewood Boulevard. I sat in the Jeep for a bit, trying to catch sight of her in my rearview mirror. She drove past me once. Then I got out of the car and watched as she waited for a car to pull out just a few spots from the entrance to the store.

I walked over to the next row so I wouldn't look like I was following her, and walked slowly down it as she got out of her car and then went into Macy's. I was in the store just a few moments after her. This entrance put you in bedding. Kitchenware was to the left. I caught sight of Sammy just as she turned toward women's wear. I didn't follow her.

Instead, I worked my way through men's. Parts of it bordered on the women's department. I made my way to the edge. Just to make myself a little less suspicious, I picked up a folded sweater and carried it around with me.

I found Sammy looking through a rack of tops. I could tell she was going to be a while. I turned my back on her. She had no idea I was following her. She wouldn't. It can be hard for people to figure it out even if they suspect someone might want to follow them.

When I turned around again, she was still at the same rack. She'd placed several tops onto the rack. It looked like she might be about to try them on. I was a few feet from the shoe department. I went over and sat in a chair. I could wait, but she wouldn't see me.

After a few minutes, a cute, young salesman came over and asked if he could help me. I said, "No, I'm just taking a little rest."

"If there's anything I can do for you, please let me know."

Then he stayed nearby moving things around. He was trying to look like he was straightening things up, but honestly, they looked just fine. I don't know whether he was trying to pick me up or he'd pegged me as a shoplifter. Either way, I decided I needed to move on.

Standing up, I glanced over at the women's section. I didn't see Sammy anywhere. My first thought was that she'd gone to try on the tops she'd picked out. But then I noticed that two of the tops were still there. Had she gone and come back? What was happening?

I stepped into the main aisle and walked the store, skirting the women's department as best I could. I didn't see her for quite a while, but then I picked her out at a cashier. She was checking out. The clerk was putting her selections into a white shopping bag with a red star on the side.

I continued walking as though there was somewhere I wanted to be. I set the sweater I was carrying down on a display of football shirts. It was too warm for a sweater anyway. I guessed that she'd be going out into the mall rather than heading back to her car, so I started studying a case of perfumes and cosmetics near the front of the store.

A clerk came right over.

"Something special for the lady in your life?"

"Just browsing."

Sammy walked by on the other side of the counter, out into the mall. She turned to the left. I walked away from the counter and went out into the mall. I followed her the length of the mall until she went into Sears. I decided not to follow her.

There was a ninety percent chance she'd be coming back out to the mall proper. She could leave via one of the outer doors and walk through the parking lot to her car, but that didn't really make sense. I was sure she'd come back through this entrance.

I walked back down and looked at the food at Sbarro and Panda Express. I was getting hungry. I'd like to buy some lunch, but it didn't seem like a good idea. Sammy could be walking by at any moment. I bought a Mrs. Fields chocolate chip cookie. That didn't seem like much of a risk.

I ate half the cookie then put it back in its bag. I went into LensCrafters. I didn't wear glasses, but you could see the entrance to Sears from there. I'd be able to spot Sammy when she came out.

I'd very nearly agreed to an eye exam when Sammy came out of Sears. Well, hallelujah. I walked out of Lens-Crafters and was twenty feet behind Sammy. She'd bought a piece of luggage with wheels. It was trailing behind her.

We hadn't gone very far when she got in line at Sbarro. I drifted on, stopping to look into the windows of the Warner Brothers Store. They had lots of Bugs Bunny merchandise, Elmer Fudd coffee cups, tables full of videos.

I kept an eye on Sammy. She had a tray in front of her and was ordering, pointing at one of the premade pizzas in the glass case. I left the Warner Brothers Store, crossed the way, and stopped at Panda Express. I skipped ahead in line and bought a Coke. I turned around and checked out the tables to find Sammy sitting at one in front of Mrs. Fields. I walked over and sat down across from her.

Holding a piece of pizza in mid-air, she stopped and set it back down. She looked much the same as she had that spring. Blonde hair cut very short, her blue eyes a bit sunken. She was in her mid-thirties, not even a decade older than Ronnie. She gave me a very sour look.

"You bought a suitcase. Are you planning a trip?"

"I'm going to call my attorney and tell him you're harassing me."

"And what? He'll ground me? Give me detention?"

"I'll have him file a restraining order."

"And my boss would file a response. I think you might want to avoid that."

"What do you want?"

"I'm here to make you an offer."

"Go ahead," she said. Then she took a bite of her pizza.

I had a sip of my pop before I started. "You told me that Pete Michaels was trying to blackmail your husband and that's why your husband killed him. Do you remember that?"

"Of course, I remember that."

"My boss would like you to sit for a deposition."

"And tell you that my husband killed Pete Michaels?"

"Yes. Exactly."

"You're trying to trick me."

"I'm not a cop. I don't care who really killed Pete Michaels. All I care about is getting my client out of prison. If you say your husband killed Pete, then all of this will be over."

She thought about it. Chewed on another bite of pizza. She was checking out the angles, spinning it around in her head. I thought it might be a good idea to give her a business card. I picked out one with my cellular number on the back.

"Talk to your lawyer if you want. If you do the deposition, you can return the suitcase."

CHAPTER TWENTY-FOUR

August 3-4, 1996
Late Saturday Afternoon/Sunday morning

"Is this Virginia Marker?" I asked when she picked up the phone. I'd called as soon I walked into the house.

"It is. Who is calling, please?" she asked. She had a very faint accent, really only a hint of one. Once it might have been Italian or Greek. There wasn't enough left to be sure.

As I explained who I was and why I was calling, I tried to make myself comfortable on the couch. But as tired as I was, from almost two days sitting in my car I couldn't get comfortable.

"I have not thought of Vera in many years," I heard her say.

"Did you see her much around the time she was murdered?"

"No. No I did not."

"You were close friends, though?"

"For a time, perhaps."

"Did something happen to your friendship?"

"Oh no. People wander apart." She waited a moment and then asked, "Was that you? Have you been calling our telephone and hanging up?"

"Maybe once," I lied. "Do you know anyone from that period named Gigi?"

"That is a name short for Georgette, is it not?"

"I wouldn't know."

"I cannot think of anyone with that name."

John came in through the front door. I waved at him, and he waved back. He went through the living room and then upstairs.

"Can you tell me more about Vera?" I asked Virginia. "How did you meet her?"

"I am not even certain. Hmmm... Well... maybe she was dating a friend of my husband, Manny. That might have been it."

I had the feeling she was lying. In fact, I was pretty sure of it.

"You don't remember this friend's name?"

"Oh no, I do not."

"Was it at a party or in a bar? A double date?"

"It was fifty years ago. I do not remember."

"Did you belong to a group called The Sisters of Artemis?"

"No."

"Do you remember hearing about them?"

"Is this a group for women who hunt? I do not like hunting."

"What about a woman named Shirley Kessler? Did you know her?"

"No."

"You're certain."

"It was fifty years ago. I do not know. If I met her, I do not remember."

"Is your husband available? I'd like to speak to him as well."

"I am so sorry. Manny is not well. Because of the oxygen he does not talk well on the telephone."

"Can I set up a time to come and see you?"

"I am sorry. We will be traveling to San Diego. Our daughter is having a very bad divorce. We must help."

"Do you know when you'll be back in Eagle Rock?"

"I'm sorry. I do not."

"I could drive down to San Diego," I said. I really didn't want to do that, but I didn't want to let this go.

"My husband needs me. I must hang up."

And then she did.

I sat back on the sofa, finally relaxing a bit, and tried to absorb what I'd just heard. Clearly, Mrs. Marker didn't want me talking to her husband. She barely wanted me talking to her. Did that mean something? I had the strong feeling she and her husband knew something about Vera's death. But what? Did they know Gigi? Did she also know Shirley Kessler? Her answers weren't satisfying.

John came back down, and said, "I'm going to make a hamburger. Do you want one?"

"Sure. Thanks."

Ronnie was probably the best cook in the house, but he almost never had time. John could do basic things like spaghetti and hamburgers. I wasn't going to look a gift horse in the mouth, as they say. I followed him into the kitchen.

Taking a seat at the breakfast bar, I asked, "What do you know about abusive husbands?"

"I've dated some jerks, but I don't know that I'd call them abusive."

"I meant in your capacity as a nurse. Vera Korenko knew a woman named Gigi. I've been told her husband was abusing her. It's possible he killed Vera. He might also have killed another woman named Shirley Kessler. I guess my question is, why didn't Gigi just leave her husband after the first murder? Why didn't she turn him in?"

"Wow, um…" He chewed his lip as he thought. "You have to remember that none of this is happening now. How people thought about things in the forties was different. A lot of people at the time thought it was okay to hit your wife. And by people, I mean men *and* women. They wouldn't have known what you meant by abusing."

"Right. We're talking about murder though."

"True. But the murder might have actually made it harder for Gigi to leave. The thing about physical abuse is that it doesn't happen in a vacuum. Physical abusers are also emotionally abusive. They're controlling. They isolate their victims from friends and family, they tear down their victim's self-esteem. If you don't believe you have value, if there's no one to help you, if you think you deserve it, it's very hard to escape."

As he said that, he was making hamburger patties out of ground chuck. He dropped them into a frying pan.

"Do we have potato chips?" he asked.

"I'll check," I said, turning to the pantry behind me. I found a bag of corn chips and asked if they would work. He thought they might.

"If I want to figure out if a woman is being abused, what am I looking for?"

"When she—or for that matter he, it does happen to men. When someone comes into the ER with injuries that don't match their story, you want to separate them from their spouse or partner." He got out a couple of plates while he continued. "Let's say Ronnie hurt himself and you're in the ER, the doctor says he wants to talk with Ronnie alone. What do you say?"

"Actually, I think Ronnie would say I could stay before I said anything."

"And if he didn't."

"I'd ask Ronnie if he wanted me to stay, I guess."

"An abuser insists that he has to stay. And the abused person is too afraid to contradict them. Even if the doctor asks directly, they'll say they want him to stay."

"How do you get them away?"

"You don't. Pushing too hard can escalate things. If a doctor is absolutely certain there's been physical abuse they can report it. We have a form for that, but it's not required like it is for kids. Legally we have to report child abuse. And that's only goes back to the sixties. The time period you're talking about? There was nothing."

"Thanks. I guess I really just want to know what to look for. I think you answered that."

"I would say the longer it goes on, the harder it is to escape."

"Can abuse last a lifetime?"

"Oh yes. But it isn't always a long lifetime."

That made me wonder. Was Gigi out there somewhere still being abused? Had Vera and Shirley been attempts at escape? After her husband killed them, did she stop trying?

I had to find her.

We usually charged our cellular phones on the windowsill in our bedroom. There's a plug beneath the window so it's easy. One of them started to ring at nine Sunday morning. Usually, it's Ronnie getting early morning calls, so he got out of bed, took a couple of steps, and said, "No. It's yours."

"Shit," I said, just because.

Getting out of bed, I stretched a little to even out my back. It didn't really work. I picked up the phone and said, "Yeah?"

"This is Wesley Colcott. I represent Sammy Blanchard. She'd like to come in and talk to Ms. Gonzalez about her husband's involvement in Pete Michaels' murder."

"Okay, that's great. I'll have someone call you. Can you give me your number?"

Behind me Ronnie said, "It's on the screen."

Holding my phone away from me I saw that it was. "Never mind, I've got it. We'll get back to you to set something up, ASAP."

He hung up on me without saying goodbye. I poked around looking for a pad and pencil. There was one on the dresser, another on the nightstand next to Ronnie. I grabbed the one on the dresser and copied Colcott's phone number.

Then I called Lydia. As it rang, I said to Ronnie, "Sorry, I should have gone downstairs and used the real phone. This is costing money."

"Don't worry. I'm enjoying the view."

This was a reference to the fact that I was standing there in nothing but a pair of white Calvin Kleins he'd picked up for me at Marshalls. Lydia answered.

"Hi, sorry to bother you. Sammy's attorney called. She's ready to schedule a depo."

"He called now? On Sunday morning?"

"Yes."

"Okay. I guess they're eager. You must have done a good sales job."

"I think it was more like a sales *threat*."

"Well, it worked. I'll let you know what we decide on. You need to be there."

Then she hung up on me. I pulled on a pair of sweatpants and a T-shirt. "I'll make coffee."

"Come here."

I leaned over the bed and kissed him. "That what you wanted?"

"Yes. That and coffee."

"Coming up."

I went downstairs, grabbing the *L.A. Times* off the front stoop and then to the kitchen to make the coffee. We had some pancake mix in the cupboard which I'd put together before. Just add water. If it looked like I was 'making' breakfast I might be able to get Ronnie to fry some bacon to go with them.

I was getting out a bowl and a measuring cup when the house phone rang. I grabbed it. Not surprising, it was Lydia.

"Tuesday 9 a.m."

CHAPTER TWENTY-FIVE

August 5, 1996
Late Monday morning

The rest of Sunday was a wash. I got it in my head that I should take a day off. Not something I'm good at. Ronnie went off to meet with clients. Junior tried to talk me into walking over to see *Stonewall* at The Art. That sounded intense and a little challenging. Well, maybe more than a little.

We ended up watching a couple of Cary Grant movies on the American Movie Channel. Well, I didn't watch either of them entirely, I slept through long chunks. But, not to worry, Junior caught me up on the plots. He was sipping wine the whole time and started to gush about how sorry he was that Ronnie and I were moving out. I assured him we'd be by to collect his rent. That made him laugh.

Monday morning, I was out the door right after breakfast. It was around nine-thirty. I'd decided it was time to go to the Motion Picture Academy's library up in L.A. I tried to wait out rush hour but still caught the tail end of it.

Beverly Hills is the worst part of L.A. to get to from Long Beach. There are no major freeways nearby— nice for them, sucks for everyone else. I took the 405 to the 10 and went up La Cienega. The library was just north of Olympic. I'd driven by it a hundred times but never knew what it was.

Sitting in the middle of an increasingly valuable green space, the library was a cream-colored Spanish-style building that looked a bit like a church—it had a tower and a circular window over the door that called out for stained-glass but was just clear—and had two very long wings.

There was parking at the tennis center next door, so I paid to leave the Jeep there—otherwise I would have been circling the neighborhood until the apocalypse.

Walking into the library, I found myself in a marble foyer. I followed the signs up a flight of stairs to a reception desk. Behind it was a very young volunteer, squeaky-clean and overly enthusiastic. After he greeted me, I said, "I understand you have Ivan Melchor's papers here."

"I believe we do, yes. Do you have an appointment?"

"No. I don't. I just took a chance and drove up from Long Beach."

"You really need to have an appointment."

"Do you have anything today?"

He pursed his lips. I could tell he was unhappy about this. He looked through his book, and said, "We have an opening at two this afternoon."

Okay, well that sucked. I could drive home, eat a sandwich, then drive back; or I could spend almost three hours floating around Los Angeles.

"Your name?" he asked.

"Dominick Reilly."

"And what school are you affiliated with?"

I was tempted to name the Catholic High School in Bridgeport that I'd graduated from, but decided I'd have more luck with the truth. "I'm not affiliated with a school."

"This is a research library. We support scholars from all over the country doing research on the film industry. You can't just look at things because you want to."

I actually thought that was the whole point of any library, but okay.

"I've been hired by the family of Patrick Gill. Mr. Gill lived with Ivan Melchor for decades. I believe he's the one who donated the papers to the library. I've been asked to look into the murder of a woman named Vera Korenko, who was a friend of Misters Melchor and Gill during the forties. I'm looking for diaries of any kind, appointment books, address books, things like that."

He stood up, saying, "Why don't I go talk to one of the librarians. I want to make sure it's worth your while to come back this afternoon."

I stood there staring at the room beyond. The ceiling was... I guess you'd call it coved. It was like the inside of a barrel. As though the books and the scholars were some kind of fine wine being aged. There were rows of shelves with reference books and long tables in between.

I wondered how long this would take. Part of me wished I still smoked. If I did, I'd walk back down the steps and stand outside in their well-manicured grounds to have a cigarette. It was a beautiful day, and now that I was a non-smoker I often forgot to enjoy things like that.

Then the receptionist was back with a woman about my age. Her hair was graying. She wore a heavy-rimmed pair of glasses and a rather severe suit.

"I'm Mrs. Brewster. Your name is…"

"Dom Reilly."

"You're some kind of investigator, I believe."

"Yes. As I said, I'm working for the Gill family."

"Yes, I remember Mr. Gill. I've been with the library for nearly fifteen years. The donation came in around nineteen eighty-five. Why don't you come with me."

Okay, I thought, *I'm lucking out.* I followed her. As we walked, she explained, "We have a warehouse. Much of our collection is there. That's why you normally need an appointment. You request what you want, and it's brought over in the morning. You may have gotten lucky though." *Had she just read my mind?* "A professor from UCLA is writing an article about set designers in the postwar period, so we have quite a lot of Mr. Melchor's papers on site at the moment. Can you tell me exactly what you're looking for?"

"Appointment books, desk calendars, diaries of any sort, personal or professional, address books."

"What years?"

"Oh, of course… nineteen-forty-eight and nineteen-forty-nine."

"All right. Why don't you have a seat and I'll see what we have."

There were plenty of seats. There were no more than ten people in the library at that particular moment. Given that appointments were needed, I doubted it ever got crowded. The room was very, very quiet. So, this was the exciting life of a scholar.

About ten minutes later, Mrs. Brewster returned. In her hands, she carried a shallow blue plastic tub. She now wore a pair of white cotton gloves. When she set the tub down, I saw that there were two identical red clothbound books that said DESK PRIVATE on top. Beneath that was the year.

One said 1948 and the other 1949. Also in the tub was another pair of white cotton gloves—for me.

"The Melchor papers are things he kept at his home. Monumental Studios also has a significant collection of his work in their archives. They have not relinquished rights or ownership of materials he generated related to his employment. You cannot publish or profit from your research without their permission. I know that probably has nothing to do with what you're doing, but I have to say it."

"Is that as strict as it sounds?"

"Yes and no. If you're publishing an academic paper in a journal, they're accommodating. If you wanted to put together a coffee table book of his designs, they'd be a lot stricter."

"Sorry, just curious."

"Of course. It's all fascinating. These desk calendars have been examined by staff. They are business appointments for the most part. Presumably, he brought these home from the studio. We didn't note any personal appointments, but that doesn't mean they're not there. When I say 'examined' that doesn't mean read fully cover to cover."

"I understand."

"There weren't any address books for those years. These appointment books each have a section for addresses. Presumably that's why there are no separate address books. Though, they might also be in the Monumental archives."

I nodded.

"We ask that you only use pencil in the library. Did you bring anything for note taking?"

"I left my notebook in the car." And didn't have a pencil.

"You could go out and get it if you like. We have pencils

if you need one. Or we offer copying if you find something of interest."

"Thank you. I'll use the copier if I find something."

"We do it for you. If you find something you want copied just come to the desk. Please wear the gloves when handling the calendars."

"I will," I said, reaching into the tub for them. I slipped them on as she walked away.

I sat and thought for a moment. How did I want to approach this? I knew the day Vera Korenko died. October 1, 1949. A Saturday. I could have gone right to that date. Instead, I picked up 1948 and began flipping through it. I wanted a sense of who Melchor was before I zeroed in on the period surrounding the murder.

Flipping through, I noticed a couple of things right off. First, there were two sets of handwriting in the book. One was square, boxy and printed. The other was curling and steeply slanted to the right. They were so different, it seemed unlikely they belonged to the same person. That told me Melchor had had a secretary—as they called them in the forties—who recorded some of his appointments into the book.

The other thing that was immediately obvious was that he liked to doodle. Quite a few of the pages had doodles in the corner. Cubes, spheres, cones, thatching, the occasional word in three-dimensional lettering. On a few pages, there would be a tree with a branch that crossed the top of the page and roots that ran across the bottom.

There were very few meetings in the mornings, but many in the afternoon. I suspected that meant he did his creative work in the morning. Most of the meetings had a person's name, while others said things like PRODUC-

TION MEETING, BUDGET MEETING with the title of a film, like *Ladies Night Out* or *Pinch Hitter*.

I was flipping through the summer of 1948 when I noticed that he'd sometimes put a P in the corner of a page. He'd often draw a box around the letter and then turn the box into a cube. Was the P for Patrick? As I turned through the pages, as summer became fall, there were more P's. And then, P&V. Also in a cube. In October, there was the first IP & VG. Ivan and Patrick; Vera and Gigi.

That told me something I hadn't known. Vera's relationship with Gigi began in the fall of 1948. Did it continue right up to her death a year later?

Before moving on to 1949, I looked through Melchor's appointments again. A lot of meetings were crossed out, as though were canceled. I wondered if he was having problems because he was gay? That didn't seem right, though. People always acted like Hollywood accepted gays in background creative positions like set director. As long as he didn't get arrested or announce he was gay in the newspaper, Ivan would have been fine.

Of course, there could have been other reasons he was having trouble at work. Not to mention, the cancellations might have had nothing to do with him. It could be that the movies were cancelled and not his working on them. I didn't know enough about film history to be sure.

I zeroed in on the holidays. Thanksgiving, the twenty-fifth, was blank. But on the following day, the twenty-sixth, there was a list of names. The first three were Patrick, Vera and Gigi. There were eight other names. All first names. Six men, two women. There was a note written on a pink pad that said WHILE YOU WERE AWAY at the top. In the same handwriting that appeared often in the diary it said, *Caterer called to confirm Friday. Will arrive at ten.*

It was likely, Patrick and Vera were with his family that Thursday. His sister had said it was possible she met Vera that day. That's why there was nothing on Melchor's calendar for the holiday and why he gave his Thanksgiving dinner the day after.

Turning to December, I noticed there were several days on which he'd written IP & VG. They'd double-dated many times. On Christmas Day there was a note that said, '*Portrait of Jennie* – Skip.' I knew that movie from when I was a kid. It played on WGN all the time. There was a P on Christmas Eve. They'd gotten to spend that part of the holiday together and it looked like Patrick had Christmas dinner with his family while his boyfriend went to a movie with a friend—Skip. On New Year's Eve there was a notation that said 'Cinegrill' along with 'IP & VG.' Had the two couples gone dancing? It made sense. Ivan and Patrick wouldn't have been able to go alone.

I turned to 1949. It was more of the same. The two couples continued to go out with each other. That made me wonder... Rocky Havoc said that Gigi was married. Why was she so available? Were she and her husband separated? Or was she actually not married at all?

I turned to the end of September, September thirtieth. A Friday. At the top of the page there was a notation in the corner: 'IP & VG Malibu.' Melchor had no meetings that afternoon. I understood exactly what that meant. The two couples had planned to spend the weekend in Malibu somewhere. Except, they didn't. Vera was found dead in Pasadena on Sunday morning October 2, 1949, having been killed sometime the day or night before. If she went to Malibu on Friday afternoon, she'd have needed to leave that night or the next morning.

I thought back to my conversation with Georgia

Dawson. She'd talked about Vera's last day at work. She said they couldn't wait to leave. If Vera had left early, she would have mentioned that—wouldn't she? I might need to talk to her again.

I decided to assume that Vera and Gigi did not go to Malibu. So, did Patrick and Ivan? There were no notations for October first and second. On the third and the fourth, all of the appointments after Monday at noon had been canceled by Melchor's secretary, crossed out and the word 'cancelled' written beneath. Flipping through the following week, I saw that the secretary had rescheduled many of the meetings.

Melchor must have heard about Vera's murder around noon on the third. He'd taken the rest of that day and the following day off, presumably to be with Patrick, and possibly Gigi if they were true friends. I flipped forward a couple of months. I didn't see any G's though. But then, there weren't any P's either. The alphabet soup appeared to have disappeared.

I sat there for a few minutes attempting to look at this from every angle. If Melchor and Patrick were involved in Vera's murder, they could have killed her in Malibu and dumped her body in Pasadena.

But that didn't make sense for a lot of reasons. If you kill someone in Malibu there are dozens of places to dump the body much closer than Pasadena. And... in 1949 there would have been dozens more since the city wasn't as built up.

Also, there was Gigi. If Melchor and Patrick did kill Vera, where was Gigi? Did she watch? Did she run away? Why did she never tell? And how does any of this fit with Rocky Havoc's belief that it was Gigi's husband who killed Vera?

What *did* make sense was that Vera and Gigi either didn't go or left early because of Gigi's husband. That then resulted in Vera's death somehow.

I went back to 1948 and flipped to the address section in the back. Quickly, I saw that it was not meant to be a complete address book. In fact, there were just four pages, each with the word 'telephone' at the top of the page.

It was easy to see that most of the names were professional contacts. Neither Vera nor Gigi nor even Patrick were there. I scanned through and found Skip Harkness. TR2-7998. I figured this was the Skip who Melchor spent Christmas Day at the movies with. I wondered if he might work with Melchor. Quickly, I flipped through the pages and eventually found a meeting: 'Properties, *Suspect the Night*, Skip H.' That answered that. Skip did props on a movie they did together.

I went back to the day after Thanksgiving dinner and checked to see if any of the names appeared in the back. I found another: 'Annette Kohler SY5-7987.' Skimming through, I saw that she had costume meetings with Melchor on several films.

It was after one and my stomach was growling like a circus animal. I took the tub up to the desk and asked Mrs. Brewster if they could copy all of November and December of 1948, September 30 through October 4, 1949, and the complete address sections from the back of each book.

"That's probably fifty or sixty pages. It's a dollar a page," she told me.

"Do you take credit cards?"

"We do."

"Then there's no problem."

I'd be passing the cost onto the Karpinski brothers. Both of whom charged around two hundred and fifty an hour.

"You mentioned a professor at UCLA who's researching Melchor, can you give me his name?"

"Oh," she said, seeming surprised. "I'm not sure. I've not been asked a question like that before. I'm going to say no, just to be safe."

"Okay," I said. I was already sure I could find him on my own.

CHAPTER TWENTY-SIX

August 5-6, 1996
Monday afternoon/Early Tuesday morning

I had a rough idea how to get to UCLA, so I stubbornly refused to consult my *Thomas Guide*. After several wrong turns, I found myself at the south end of the campus. I parked in visitor parking, then walked a couple blocks south, and had lunch at California Pizza Kitchen – a barbeque salad with an Arnold Palmer.

Finished with that, I then took the longest walk I'd been on in a very long time. Once I was back on campus, I asked a couple of students to direct me to the film department. The one didn't know, the second just pointed north. So I kept walking north.

The campus was lovely, lots of interesting architecture and old growth trees. The kind you don't often see in Los Angeles. I kept asking for the film department and continued to be sent north. Finally, a third student said, "You want Melnitz. It's in the northeast corner." That's when I realized I'd parked in the completely wrong place.

Even before I found the film department, I began to dread the walk back to my car.

The Melnitz Building was brick with large metal-framed glass windows at the front. Very sixties. Immediately, you walked into a two-story lobby with paneled walls decorated with movie posters. To my right was a box office which was shuttered, in front of me double doors that must have led to a theater. They were also locked. To my left was another set of doors that was open to a hallway.

A long hallway, presumably running the length of the building. It was a typical public building: shiny linoleum floor, acoustical tiles on the ceiling, faded pastel colors on the walls. Doors off the hallway went to recording rooms, editing rooms, screening rooms. I doubted any of that was what I was looking for.

About halfway down there was an open space with some vinyl seats bolted to the floor. It looked straight out of an airport terminal. A couple of students—one guy and one girl—sat there, talking.

"Hi. I'm looking for a professor of film history. He's working on a project about postwar set designers."

They looked at each other. The guy shrugged like he had no idea, but the girl said, "You're probably looking for Aletti. I took his class on neorealism after World War Two. It sounds like something he'd be into."

"Okay, do you know where I could find him?"

"The offices are in East Melnitz. You just go down the hall, out of the building and right into the next one. He's probably not there, but his office hours will be posted."

I said thanks and walked away. A few minutes later, I found myself walking the halls of a largely empty building. I read the professors' names as I went. No luck on the first floor. I climbed the stairs to the second floor and kept looking. Halfway down there was an open door. Someone I could ask, was my first thought. But when I got there, I saw that Louis Aletti was one of three professors who occupied the office.

Inside, I found a young man in his early to mid-twenties. He was sorting some papers on a distressed and distressing sofa.

"Hi, you're not Professor Aletti, are you?"

He chuckled. "I'm his research assistant. Who are you?"

"My name's Dom Reilly. I was at the Academy Library this morning and they said Professor Aletti was doing research on set designers after the war."

Not exactly true, but whatever.

"Um, actually, he's researching gay *set* designers." He said the words 'gay set designers' very clearly. I assumed people often heard 'gay sex designers,' which was something else entirely. Having navigated the difficult part, he continued, "We're examining the impact of sexuality on the film arts. The school is finally putting together a queer studies program. Professor Aletti is hoping to teach a class in both departments and also publish a paper on the subject."

"I see," I said. "And you are?"

"Eldridge Hall. I got a B.A. in Women's Studies last year. My focus, though, was sexuality. That's how I ended up here. Can I ask why you're interested?"

"I'm working for the family of Patrick Gill. I believe he was Ivan Melchor's lover."

"He was, yes. What are you doing for them?"

"I'm looking into the murder of a woman named Vera Korenko. She was Patrick Gill's fiancée for less than a year before her death in 1949."

"I'm pretty familiar with Ivan Melchor. I know that he

and Patrick Gill were together from sometime in the late forties until his death."

"They met in 1948."

"Really?"

I explained to him the coding in Melchor's appointment books.

"Thanks. I'll take a look at that. Are you saying that Patrick was engaged to a woman while he was seeing Ivan?"

"I think it was a relationship of convenience. Most of the time they spent together a women named Gigi was also with them."

"Beards."

"Yes. Lesbian beards."

"The best kind."

"Can you tell me anything else about Ivan and Patrick?"

"They lived very quietly. They weren't active politically. They socialized mainly at home with a small circle of friends."

"Was Skip Harkness one of those friends?"

"Yes."

"Did you talk to him?"

"He passed away four years ago. I did talk to his partner though... So, Patrick Gill is dead, right?"

"No. He's not."

"The house he shared with Ivan was sold last year. We thought it was because he passed—though, I couldn't find an obituary."

"He's in a home. He's senile... has dementia... whatever they're calling it now."

"Oh, I see. Would it be worth our time to try to talk to him?"

"That's tricky. His sister doesn't know he's gay."

"Um... he lived with a man for more than two decades."

"I know. He's much older and they weren't really close during that time. She's romanticized his relationship with Vera. Thinks her death is the reason he never married."

"But..." he stopped. He was clearly angry that a gay relationship could be so invisible.

"Explain to me how you're going to connect Melchor's sexuality to his design work?"

"He and Skip Harkness, and a number of other designers, were very influenced by Greek and Roman architecture and sculpture, and then the renaissance artists Michelangelo and DaVinci who themselves were influenced by the Greek and Romans. You see the influence clearly in the films *Venus de Memphis*, *New York in Twilight* and *The Langley Boys*. All of which were directed by Cecil Ryland, who placed coded gay references into the story and action."

I could imagine him having long and confusing conversations with Junior.

"Is Ryland still alive?" I asked. He would be someone else to talk with.

"No, he was one of the early victims of AIDS. They didn't even realize what had happened to him until years later."

"In your research you didn't run into a woman named Gigi? Like the musical?" He seemed like the kind of gay guy who'd benefit from a musical theater reference.

"No, we'd only have run across her if she worked in the industry. We're not looking at all of Melchor's friends, just the ones who were involved in moviemaking."

This was feeling like a dead end. Still, I gave the kid my card and thanked him for his time. Before I was able to leave the office, he said, "My boyfriend and I are totally into mysteries."

Not wanting to get into a conversation about Sherlock

Holmes and Agatha Christie, I nodded awkwardly and said good-bye.

It took forever to get back to my Jeep. It had to have been at least a mile. Probably much more. By the time I turned over the engine it was around four. Rush hour had already begun. Having learned my lesson, I got out my *Thomas Guide* and looked up Faring Road. Looking at the map I noted that the UCLA Film Department was nearly in Holmby Hills.

Roughly five minutes later I sat in front of 401 N. Faring Road. Ronnie had said it was a tear-down and he'd been right. The house was gone. Even the foundation had been ripped out. All that remained there on that particular afternoon was a giant hole in the ground.

This was where Ivan and Patrick had lived happily for decades. All of that was gone now, knocked down and ripped away. I couldn't help feeling that's what would eventually happen to the property Ronnie and I owned. It would change, disappear, become something else, forgetting we were ever there.

I drove away trying to forget I'd ever had that thought.

The next morning, I walked into The Freedom Agenda around eight-thirty. I was planning to make a pot of coffee the minute I got to the back, but as soon as stepped into the area I was stopped cold. Tacked to the walls were Andy Showalter's drawings. Not the ones he'd drawn of the Nazis invading Poland, but the ones he'd drawn of Sammy Blanchard. The ones that told the story of his buying a gun for her. There were only five sheets, but they clearly told the story of what happened.

Not only the story of Andy buying Sammy the gun, but the story of Sammy going to Pete Michaels' house and shooting him.

Lydia and Karen had hung the drawings on one wall—actually, copies of the drawings Karen had made at a place that did oversized copying for architects—but still, they sent a message. Otherwise, the conference table was set up just as it had been for Anne Michaels.

I was still gawking at the artwork when Lydia came out of her office. She'd beaten me there. She wore her most professional suit, the one she wore to court when she wasn't sure of the outcome. Navy blue and sharply tailored—the way generals had their uniforms cut—she paired it with a bright white silk blouse underneath. She didn't wear any kind of tie or bow with it, just left it open at the collar so that you could clearly see the gold crucifix she wore around her neck. One that wasn't simply a gold cross; it was one that had a small, suffering Christ tacked to it, as though to remind everyone that injustice had been happening for a very long time.

"What are you up to?" I asked.

She simply smiled. "How was yesterday? Are you making progress for the Karpinski boys?"

"I'm finding things out. Not necessarily what I need to find out, but I'm definitely getting a complete picture of Patrick's life and how Vera might have fit into it."

The bell rang over the front door. It was Karen. I'd never seen her arrive this early before. She was often late and ran on what she called CP time—Colored People time. I'd noticed two things about that. One: Lydia never said anything about her being late. And two: When it mattered, Karen was there. Which probably explained number one.

I was telling Lydia some of the things I'd learned about

Patrick Gill, when Karen came back with three notebooks that held anything we might need for this deposition.

"Karen, could you call Eyes on Justice? They should be here by now."

"I'll try, but they don't pick up the phone until nine."

I wondered how she knew that since I never saw her before nine, but... that might be another reason Lydia never cared about CP time. Just because Karen wasn't at her desk didn't mean she wasn't doing her job.

The bell over the door rang again. We walked out to the lobby. It wasn't Eyes on Justice, it was Sammy Blanchard and her attorney, Wesley Colcott. The show was about to begin.

CHAPTER TWENTY-SEVEN

August 6, 1996
Tuesday morning

One look at Wesley Colcott and I knew he and Lydia would have a lot of friction. He was a dinosaur from another era. In his late sixties, he wore a charcoal gray suit and had oiled his thinning hair. Sammy looked small and waifish, wearing a pink blouse with a lacy collar and a matching skirt. She was trying to look like a church-y teenager. She'd put a lot of thought into it.

Introductions were made and Karen offered coffee or water.

"This shouldn't take long," Colcott said, more a command than a reason not to have a cup of coffee.

"The videographer is late," Lydia said. "We're trying to reach them, but their office isn't open yet. If need be, I have a decent tape recorder."

"I prefer a written transcript anyway," Colcott said.

"Facial expression can be distracting. Just because we can do things doesn't always mean we should."

As he said that, we walked into the back. Sammy took one look at the drawings on the wall, and said, "What the fuck is that?"

Colcott took them in. He leaned over and said something into Sammy's ear. Then to Lydia, "What are you playing at?"

"You mean the drawings? We put those up weeks ago. I didn't want them getting all curled or wrinkled in case I have to bring them into court."

"Artwork is not admissible."

"Artwork is *usually* not admissible. It's up to a judge. Andy Showalter is dead so we can't reexamine his testimony. If there's a new trial and the prosecution attempts to enter his testimony, I'll provide these to refute it. They speak to his state of mind."

"They won't be allowed in."

Lydia shrugged. "I'd agree if we were talking about direct evidence. I would never want to see someone convicted on the basis of his artwork. However, I would be using these drawings to impeach prior testimony. The images create reasonable doubt; the bedrock of our legal system. I'd say I have a fifty-fifty shot." Smiling, she suggested, "Why don't we sit down."

Colcott led Sammy to a seat where the images were behind her back. I could see that she was seething—jaw tight, eyes narrowed. Exactly where Lydia wanted her.

Karen came out of Lydia's office with a tape recorder and set it in the middle of the table. After Lydia turned on the tape, she made the same sort of introduction she'd made with Anne Michaels. That took two or three minutes.

When she was done, she asked Sammy, "Are you ready to begin?"

"Yes," her voice was terse, sharp. It could have cut glass.

"You told my investigator, Dominick Reilly." She gestured toward me. "That Pete Michaels attempted to extort ten thousand dollars out of your husband, Bernie Carrier. And that because of this your husband killed him. Is that true?"

"Yes."

"How did you become aware of this?"

"Bernie told me."

"When was that?"

"When did he tell me about it?"

"Yes."

"Sometime after Pete's murder."

"Before you married? Or after?"

"It was well after."

"Can you estimate the date?"

"I suppose, five or six years ago."

"Some time in nineteen-ninety or ninety-one?"

"Yes. I guess."

"When did you learn that your husband liked to have sex with teenaged boys?"

"It was around the same time."

"Can't you be more specific? That seems like the kind of thing a person would remember exactly when they heard it."

Lydia got a sharp look from Sammy. Colcott said, "Tone, Miss Gonzalez."

She responded to Colcott, "It's a reasonable question. People remember things that are traumatic. It would have been a traumatic thing to hear. Don't you agree?"

"Assumptions you make about how my client should or should not respond are not relevant."

"I think my question would be allowed in court. We can agree to disagree. Now, Miss Blanchard, I want to be very clear on one point. At the time of Pete Michaels' murder, you had no idea he'd had a sexual relationship with your eventual husband?"

"None."

"Were you friendly with Pete Michaels or Larry Wilkes?"

"No. They were two grades ahead of me. Two years makes a big difference in high school."

"At the time of Pete Michaels' murder, you were already in a relationship with Bernie Carrier?"

"When was the murder?" she asked, as though she wasn't sure. We all knew she knew.

"September 18, 1976. Were you in a relationship with Bernie Carrier at that time?"

"I don't remember exactly when things began."

"Can you tell us *how* your relationship with Bernie Carrier began?"

"He was my health teacher."

"Can you elaborate? Not every high school sophomore marries her health teacher."

"Again, would you watch your tone," Colcott said. "Ms. Blanchard was sexually abused by her teacher. She's a victim."

"She later married the man who abused her."

"While she was still a child."

To Sammy she said, "Bernie Carrier was your health teacher. When did that class begin?"

"I was a sophomore."

"What year were you a sophomore?"

"Nineteen seventy-five."

"The class began in the fall of nineteen seventy-five and ended in the spring of seventy-six. Several months prior to the murder. That would mean your relationship with Bernie Carrier began prior to Pete Michaels' murder."

"I suppose that's right."

"Miss Gonzalez should stop referring to sexual abuse as a relationship. My client was a child. Bernie Carrier sexually abused her."

Lydia nodded, seeming to concede the point. "Miss Blanchard. Can you tell us when your ex-husband began abusing you?"

"He's not my ex-husband."

"You're still married to your abuser almost twenty years later?"

"I was very young. I didn't necessarily understand what was happening."

"Can you elaborate on that? Starting with how the abuse began."

Sammy glanced at her attorney. Clearly, she did not want to tell this story. But her attorney couldn't save her, so she began: "I started staying after class. Thinking up questions to ask. I played dumb. I already knew men liked that."

"Are you saying you were the aggressor?"

"She was fifteen. He was fifty-six," Colcott said. "The abuse was illegal regardless of how it came about."

"I'm not blaming Mrs. Carrier," Lydia said, voice as sweet as maple syrup. "I'm just trying to establish what happened."

"Blanchard, please," Sammy said.

"If you like. Coach Carrier was married when the abuse began. You lived with your parents. How did the two of you manage to meet?"

Colcott reached out and turned off the tape. "My client was led to believe this deposition was about her husband admitting to killing Pete Michaels. Which you've already established. At this point, you've strayed too far."

"I don't think so," Lydia said. "A judge will want these questions answered. Not to mention the DA." She reached out and turned the tape recorder back on. "Tape was paused by Mr. Colcott resulting in a thirty-second lapse."

After an awkwardly long pause, Lydia repeated, "How did you and Coach Carrier arrange your meetings?"

Sammy glanced at her attorney. He showed her an open palm, meaning there wasn't much he could do.

"My parents were alcoholics. They left me alone. A lot. When they did, I would call Bernie's house and let the phone ring twice and then hang up. He'd know to come over."

She'd told me that before, but now we had it in a deposition. Better. Much better. It also matched the way that Pete and Larry met each other. And the way the killer lured Larry to Pete's house.

"When did you learn that Mr. Carrier was also abusing teenage boys?"

"Not until the Tamayo boy."

"Which was when?"

"Three years ago. Four."

"That would be ninety-two, ninety-three?"

"Yes. Somewhere in there."

"You're sure it wasn't earlier?"

"My client has answered the question."

"Your husband was severely beaten by Alfonse Tamayo on the fifth of March in nineteen-ninety-one. Would you like to adjust your answer to my question concerning when you learned your husband was abusing teenage boys?"

"It was before he was beaten, yes."

"Sometime in nineteen-ninety or ninety-one?"

"Yes."

"Around the same time he told you he killed Pete Michaels?"

"Yes. I told you, he wanted to frighten me."

"You said Pete Michaels attempted to extort money from him. Blackmail. Did he tell you what information Pete was using to do that?"

"That they'd had a relationship."

"You became aware that Coach Carrier and Pete Michaels had a sexual relation no earlier than nineteen-ninety?"

"Yes. Around that time."

"Did you have a car as a teenager?"

"Yes."

"What kind was it?"

"A Chevrolet Vega."

"What color?"

"Yellow."

"I want to object to this," Colcott said. "Once again you're straying into territory that has no relevance."

"Your objection is noted," she said, smiling in a reassuring way. "In one of the original statements taken by the Downey police, the woman across the street claims she saw a small yellow car arrive at the Michaels house at around eleven thirty that morning. A young woman matching your description got out of the car and went into the house."

"It wasn't me."

Lydia glanced over Sammy's shoulders at the drawings.

"You sure it wasn't?"

"My client answered your question. She's sure."

"I want to ask again: You were *not* friends with Pete Michaels?"

"No. I was not."

"You did not know of his relationship with your husband until nineteen-ninety?"

"No. I did not know."

"There's no reason to ask questions twice, Miss Gonzalez."

"How did your husband obtain the gun that killed Pete Michaels?"

"From Andy Showalter."

"He told you that?"

"Yes."

"When did he tell you that?"

"When he threatened me."

"So, the two of you had a much longer conversation than you've indicated."

"It might have been."

"Is there anything else you haven't mentioned?"

She shook her head.

Lydia asked, "Since we're on tape, would you please say no."

"No."

"Did he tell you why Andy Showalter got him a gun?"

"No."

"Do you know why he didn't get a gun himself?"

"No."

"Did you know Andy Showalter well?"

"I didn't know him at all."

"Can you tell me why he'd make drawings of you?"

"Because he was a freak. Everyone knows that."

"How did your husband convince Andy to perjure himself at Larry Wilkes trial?"

"I don't know."

"What leverage did he have over Mr. Showalter?"

"She just said she doesn't know," Colcott said.

Again, Lydia looked over Sammy's shoulder at the artwork.

I thought this an interesting angle. In the original trial there was no real reason for Andy Showalter to obtain the gun for Larry Wilkes, but his counsel didn't follow up on it. That wouldn't be happening this time. The only logical reason for Showalter to get a gun for anyone would be to get it for a sixteen-year-girl. Sammy.

"A woman named Andrea Grubber wrote an article for *The Downey Legend* in which she said she'd received a tip that Pete Michaels had a fiancée. That tip came from someone who claimed to be Kelly Hawley. But Miss Hawley, now Dr. Wallpole, claims to have been in the room when you made the call impersonating her."

"She doesn't claim that," Sammy said. "You're wrong."

"We know you attempted to coerce Dr. Wallpole into not speaking with us—"

"Wait just a moment," Colcott said. "You're making accusations about things you couldn't possibly know."

"We've spoken to Dr. Wallpole. We know exactly what was said. We know what your client was trying to do."

That was not exactly true, we hadn't yet deposed Dr. Wallpole, but it had the desired effect. Sammy was terrified. Lydia was circling close to what had actually happened.

"You planted the item about Pete having a fiancée," Lydia said. "That led the police to think his murder had to do with a love triangle. Which I think it did. Just not *that* love triangle. Sometime in 1976, you found out about Coach Carrier and Pete Michaels. You wanted to get rid of your competition, so you killed Pete."

"That's enough," Colcott said. "This deposition is over."

Sammy was glaring at me. She seemed to have taken the phrase 'if looks could kill' to heart and was trying to figure out how to remove the 'if'. I checked to make sure there weren't any sharp items within her reach.

Colcott was standing, pulling her up by the arm.

"You completely misrepresented what this deposition was about," Colcott was saying. "I'll be filing a complaint with the bar."

"Go ahead. I did nothing wrong and it's all on tape. If you want to waste your time, be my guest."

We were all up by that point and following Sammy and her attorney out of the office. In the lobby, Elaine Joy was struggling with her equipment, trying to come fully inside. Colcott shoved her out of the way as he dragged Sammy outside. Elaine Joy landed on her ass.

Sammy and Colcott were gone. It was silent for a moment, and then Lydia looked down at Elaine Joy and said, "You're late."

———

Naturally, the rest of the morning was anticlimactic. We listened to the tape twice, then Karen started working on the transcript. Lydia was chomping at the bit to write her motion.

"Do we have enough?" I asked Lydia before she went into her office.

"Yes, yes. We have enough. We can challenge every aspect of the original case."

"Do you think the DA will accept that or will they go for a retrial?"

"All they really have is Larry being found with the

body. And we have two witness reports that says the gunshot was twenty minutes earlier. Before he even arrived at the house."

"So, they have nothing."

"Not a thing."

"She's a flight risk," I said. "She was buying a suitcase at the mall on Saturday."

She raised an eyebrow at me. Making me say, "Yes, I know. Catching murderers is not our job. Our job is to get Larry out of prison. It would be nice if part of that was sending the right person to prison."

"If the police in Downey have any sense, they'll be looking at her closely."

"If they can find her."

At lunchtime, I suggested pizza. We ordered a large chicken pesto pizza from The Pizza Place. They didn't deliver, so I offered to go and get it. Karen was deep into the transcript and Lydia was absorbed by her Writ of Habeas Corpus. They barely noticed my leaving. My Jeep was across the street. As I crossed, my cellular phone rang. It was Ronnie. I stood next to the driver's door and answered, "Hey."

"Do you remember what today is?"

"Oh God. It's an anniversary?"

"Yes."

To be fair, we had a half a dozen anniversaries he wanted to celebrate. The first time we met, which was also the first time we had sex; our first date, which came later; the first time I said I loved him; the day we bought the Bennett house; and then the day we bought the house on 2nd Street. I could never keep straight which happened when.

"Which one?"

"We met four years ago."

"Dinner?"

"Absolutely."

"Fancy or casual."

"Fancy."

"You sure? You don't want to save that for next year. Five seems like a bigger deal."

"It's all a big deal."

"Okay. La Boheme or Nectar? Or what about that place you like in Seal Beach?"

Before he could answer, I heard the screeching of tires. I turned in time to see a white Camaro fishtailing out of a parking spot a half a block away—and then it was bearing down on me. I had it in mind to get in front of my Jeep, but in a split second realized I wouldn't have time. A flash of Sammy's angry face behind the wheel and I jumped onto the hood of the Jeep—my phone flying, the Camaro side-swiping the Jeep and then nicking my foot, spinning me round, tossing me through the air over the Jeep, and onto the sidewalk beyond. I landed on my right side and heard my shoulder blade snap. And then, mercifully, everything was gone.

CHAPTER TWENTY-EIGHT

August 6-11, 1996

The next week was a kaleidoscope of images and snippets as I was drugged into various states of semiconsciousness. Ronnie fighting his way into the emergency room, arguing with a nurse about the definition of family, a doctor trying to explain my injuries to me. John showing up and putting them into English: broken bones in my shoulder, mostly the ones that had been shattered years ago, I'd need surgery—old screws out, new screws in. Much less important, a sprained wrist, a badly bruised ankle and foot, general bruising and abrasions, a possible—probable concussion.

After hours in the ER, I was moved to a room. That first evening—or maybe the next, I have a sliver of a memory—Lydia showing up in a red satin evening dress, her hair swooped over one eye. The movie premiere she'd mentioned ages ago was that night. I never realized before, but she looked like Ava Gardner. I can't tell you if we talked about that or not. In fact, I don't remember anything we talked about. There was concern on her face, though. I remember that.

The surgery happened, early in the morning the second day I was in the hospital and things became even more disjointed. I spent a good portion of that day uncomfortably, lying face down. Eventually, back in my hospital room I was allowed to gingerly lie on my side. It wasn't much better.

Ronnie was there whenever I woke up. One time Junior was there too, with a gigantic bouquet that made me wonder how he afforded it. A uniformed police officer showed up, traffic, but I was too out of it to talk to him. They got me up the day after surgery and made me walk up and down the hallway.

I was still being given a lot of morphine on Thursday when two detectives from the Long Beach Police Department showed up. Old school White guys, older than me. One fat and one skinny, they both looked like they needed a cigarette just to get through a conversation. The fat one was Swanson and the skinny one Forsyth. I was struggling to understand why we'd gone from a traffic cop to detectives without my saying anything.

"We need a statement from you, as much as you can remember," Swanson said with over-practiced kindness.

I went with the obvious, "Sammy Blanchard tried to kill me."

"Yeah, that's what your boss says. Your coworker, Karen Addison saw the crash happen. She ran out and got the first two numbers off the plate."

"What do you remember?" Forsyth asked.

"I was on my cellular phone talking with my partner, and then she was coming at me."

"You saw her behind the wheel?"

"I did."

They looked at each other.

"Is she trying to say her car was stolen?" I asked.

A couple of nods, then Swanson said, "She reported it stolen about an hour later."

"We accused her of murder that morning. I'd say it's quite a coincidence that someone stole her car and then ran me down with it."

"How about you answer the questions and we'll draw the conclusions," Swanson said.

"Is there something else you need to know?"

"Why you?"

"She doesn't like me."

"And why would that be?"

"Because I figured out she killed someone twenty years ago. It tends to turn people against you."

"All right, thank you," Forsyth said.

They looked like they were about to leave. "Are you arresting her? Or do I have to look over my shoulder forever?"

"She's already in custody."

"Thank you."

Without another word, they left. Then it was time for another pill and I forgot about them altogether. I forgot about everything altogether.

Around dinner time, Ronnie showed up with *The Press-Telegram*. He set it on the moveable tray with my dinner. "You're a star."

"What? I'm in the newspaper?"

"'Long Beach Man Mowed Down In Hit And Run.'"

"They don't use my name?"

"Not in the headline. The lede is, 'An investigator for The Freedom Agenda, Dominick Reilly (44), was struck in a hit-and-run accident by a late model Chevrolet Camaro across the street from their offices. A suspect is in custody.'"

"Fuck," I said.

"It'll be fine," Ronnie said. But he had no idea. I didn't like the attention. I didn't want anyone looking too closely at Dominick Reilly. Yes, I had a story I told people about my life. What I didn't have was documentation. What little documentation there was only went back to around eighty-nine.

The real Dom Reilly disappeared in 1982. I imagine there was documentation on his life. Given that he was peripheral to organized crime in Detroit he might have an arrest record. All I had was a Michigan Certificate of Live Birth that gave me date of birth, the names of his parents and their ages.

I'd once gone there for a long weekend and learned a few things about him—me. The real Dom Reilly dropped out of Murray-Wright high school at sixteen. He worked as a dishwasher in an Italian restaurant called Louisa's, working his way up the ladder until he was running the place in the mid-seventies. Word on the street was there was gambling in the basement and money laundered through the till.

Given that I was trying to go unnoticed, I didn't ask too many questions about what it was he might have done wrong to get himself killed. Perhaps disappeared is a better word since he was never found.

Of course, I'd never explained any of that to Ronnie who was under the impression Nick Nowak was my fake identity and Dom Reilly my real one.

"You're right. It'll be fine," I said. It probably would be

fine. Dom Reilly disappeared several years before Nick Nowak. Logically, I didn't think anyone was looking for either one of them. I was safe. I just had to make myself believe it.

On Friday, Edwin Karpinski showed up. Alone, which was not surprising. His brother didn't seem like the empathetic type. And it was a long drive.

We spent a nearly impolite amount of time talking about my health before he asked, "When do you think you'll be able to get back to work?"

"Soon," I said. The doctor had said I'd be recovering for six weeks, but I wasn't going to tell Karpinski—or anyone—that. And, in the scheme of things, six weeks *was* soon, right?

"Is your mother anxious?"

"Yes. That makes John anxious, which is more troublesome."

"Is anyone going to tell your mother that her brother is gay?"

"We don't have any plans to do that."

That struck me as odd, Sheila seemed reasonable enough. I didn't see what possible difference it could make at this point. But then, I had no idea what went on in the background. For all I really knew Sheila was a rabid homophobe addicted to talk radio.

"I'm going to need to see Patrick again. Without your mother."

"We can arrange that when you're better."

"I'm fairly certain that Vera had a girlfriend named Gigi who was married. I think it was Gigi's husband who killed her. It's possible Patrick might be able to tell us who Gigi was."

"I'll leave your name at the front desk at the home. You can go whenever you're ready."

He stood up, as though he was about to leave, so I said, "Oh, yeah... My partner is interested in purchasing Patrick's things you have in storage. He's offering ten thousand dollars."

Edwin stared at me a minute. He nodded, "I'll talk to my brother about that."

"Let me give you Ronnie's number. If you decide to do it, just call him directly."

If he called me after they'd given me a pill, I'd never remember. He felt through his pockets and found a pen and an old receipt. I gave him Ronnie's number. I imagined he must have a cellular phone somewhere. He must have forgotten it. Or maybe he still had a car phone.

Saturday morning they put me in a wheelchair, gave me a prescription for another three days of pain medication with the instruction to take Tylenol afterward, and wheeled me downstairs where Ronnie and Junior were waiting with the Legend. The orderly helped me get in. It was only a little painful. They had to hook the seatbelt up for me. I couldn't make that kind of move.

I was taking very focused, deep breaths. All we had to do was drive home, which would take about ten minutes, maybe fifteen, and once we got there all I had to do was limp into the house and then go straight to the couch.

"I'm going to be on the couch, right? I don't have to go upstairs, do I?" I asked once we'd closed all the doors.

"We'll start you on the couch," Ronnie said. "You'll need to go upstairs eventually. The bathroom's up there."

"Okay."

Junior was in the backseat. As we pulled out of the parking lot, he said, "I rented a stack of videos for you.

You're going to be thoroughly entertained. There's nothing on television though... I can't wait until they start the new season of *Melrose Place*. Just a suggestion dear, but next time get run over in September."

"Premature attempted murder," I mumbled, loud enough for Ronnie to hear. He chuckled as he pulled into traffic.

Junior ignored us and kept chattering, "John had us get you prune juice and bran flakes."

"Am I ninety?"

"No darling," Junior said. "The pain medication you're on acts like a cork."

"I don't want to be having this conversation." I decided to change the subject. "What's going on in the world? What have I missed."

"Your newspapers are stacked by the front door. Nobody touched them. Today's headline said Dole picked his running mate, someone named Kemp. It's like *Dull and Duller*. Who wants to see that?"

"I'm glad you're taking an interest in politics."

"I like Clinton. A man who can't keep his dick in his pants is always fascinating."

"I doubt Hillary shares your enthusiasm."

"I have the feeling, while the cat's away the mice are running everything."

"Maybe you could get a job as a political commentator."

Before Junior could answer, Ronnie said, "I'm going to drop you off and go show a house. I'll be back by five and we'll walk around the block."

"Yeah, not today," I said. Somehow sitting there in the passenger's seat felt like too much exertion.

"Doctor's orders," Ronnie said.

"Doctor or John?"

"Same thing."

Sunday morning, Lydia came by with some fabulous donuts and a latte for me. I was cocooned on the sofa, and she sat in one of the orange chairs.

"I have news. Larry Wilkes will be out of prison by the end of the week."

"You finished your writ and got it filed?"

"No, I was a little distracted last week. There was a proffer. Sammy Blanchard has offered to confess to Pete Michaels' murder in exchange for a lighter sentence."

"How light?"

"Manslaughter."

"What is that, ten years?"

"Yes."

"She'll be out in five."

"Probably."

"And the attempted murder... Which would be first degree by the way. She sat there for hours waiting for me to come out."

"She'll plead guilty to that as well." The way she said it I knew it wasn't as good as it sounded. "Sentence to be served concurrently."

"So, five years for two class A felonies."

"She was an abused teenager when she killed Pete Michaels. Nobody wants to put that in front of a jury."

"Do they have to be lumped together? Do I have anything to say about it?"

"You'll be able express an opinion."

"Which they won't listen to."

"Dom, it's not a bad thing if there's no trial. Is it? Do you want to testify? Do you want the scrutiny?"

That was the real issue; I knew it, and she knew it. Scrutiny was the last thing I wanted. Now I wondered if she had a hand in this. Was she protecting me?

"You're right," I said. "I don't want the scrutiny. They can do what they want as long we get Larry out of prison."

"It's a win for our side," she said. Though, honestly, it didn't feel that way.

CHAPTER TWENTY-NINE

August 12-13, 1996

On Monday, I stopped taking the pills. There was pain, but I wanted to be able to think. There was still a lot I had to do on the Vera Korenko murder and I needed to have my wits about me. I'd spent much of Sunday attempting to make a list of what I'd need to do, and between the Percocet and everyone coming and going I hadn't gotten far.

The first useful thing I did was send Junior to the library for me. "Get me whatever you can find on the Shirley Kessler murder. You said you remembered it. Ask the librarian to help you and then copy everything."

I gave him forty dollars and didn't expect to see any of it back. Once he was gone, I got up and brought the phone over to the couch, carefully sat down again, and called Georgia Dawson.

"Hi Georgia, this is Dom Reilly again."

"Oh, hello."

"I have some additional questions for you."

"I don't know. I'm not sure about this."

"Why are you not sure?"

"Harp and I got into a terrible fight after the last time you called."

"Was there a reason for that?"

"Harp doesn't think we should dredge up the past, that's how he says it, 'dredge up the past'. I don't see the harm, though. I mean, it's nice to think about how things were."

"When you were friends with Vera, did she talk about her other friends?"

"Oh, she did. She was very popular."

"Did she mention a woman named Gigi?"

She was quiet for a long time. So long in fact that I asked, "Are you still there?"

"Yes, I'm here. I'm sorry, I was thinking. I don't think she ever talked about anyone named Gigi, but now that you're asking me, I don't remember a lot of names. I just remember she mentioned different people. But now... I couldn't tell you anyone's name."

"What about Manny and Virginia Marker?"

"They were in the book, weren't they? I'd never heard of them before. Who are they?"

"Did Vera ever talk about a girlfriend whose husband beat her?"

"Heavens no. I think I would remember that. But then, well... people didn't talk about that kind of thing then. It was considered impolite."

"What about your husband? Would he remember?"

"Oh no, he's useless when it comes to people's names."

"In Philburn's book, he said you knew about the trip to Malibu. You don't remember who Vera was going with?"

"I don't remember... I think Mr. Philburn made that up. Not everything he wrote was true."

That raised an interesting question. If she was telling the truth, then how did Philburn know about the trip to Malibu? I doubt that he went to the Academy Library. That would suggest an ambition I didn't think he had. Georgia was lying to me.

"Maybe you didn't really know Vera that well."

"What? Why would you say that to me? Why are you being cruel?"

"I'm just trying to get to the truth. And I think you're lying to me."

I heard the phone crash into its cradle as she hung up on me. Yeah, she was lying to me. But why? What was the point?

After I got hung up on, I flipped through the TV channels and settled on an old episode of Andy Griffith's show. I fell asleep before I could figure out what kind of trouble Barney Fife had gotten himself into this time.

The front door flew open and Junior blew in. I sprung awake, having no idea how long I'd slept.

"Well, that was traumatic. You didn't tell me I'd have to operate machinery," Junior said, flopping into one of the orange chairs. "I nearly lost a finger when those frightening pieces of glass crashed together."

Just a bit of an exaggeration. He dropped a stack of copies onto the coffee table. "I've read every word. I'm now an expert on the Shirley Kessler murder. Ask me anything."

"Is there a woman named Gigi mentioned?"

"No. There is not."

"Who was the investigating officer?"

"Gunner Olavson."

"Who was he with?"

"Highland Park Division."

"That's LAPD?"

"Yes. The girl's body was found at Elyria Canyon."

"Where is that?"

"Mount Washington."

"Nineteen-sixty-eight is twenty-eight years ago. You think he's still a cop?"

"Absolutely," Junior said.

"We need to find him."

He said, "On it," then switched orange chairs to the one that was next to the phone. Ronnie and I had a ridiculous number of phones. Not counting our cellular, there was a phone in the living room, another in the kitchen, one in his office and one in our bedroom. Actually, there were two lines in his office, one was dedicated to the fax machine. It would have been kind of crazy if Ronnie hadn't been able to take them off his taxes.

Junior dialed 411 and asked for the LAPD general line, then he agreed to be connected (for an extra charge). When he got through, he said, "Yes, can you connect me to Highland Park Division? Oh, oh, I see... Can you connect me? No? All right, hold a moment."

He grabbed a pen off the coffee table. I'd collected a ridiculous number of things there while recuperating.

"Go ahead... uh-huh... uh-huh... thank you."

Hanging up, he said, "Highland Park Division is now Northeast Division." He immediately began to dial. "Yes, hello. Could you connect me with Gunner Olavson? Oh. Oh my. You couldn't... I see. I understand."

Apparently, whoever he was speaking with hung up because he looked at me and said, "Retired."

Then he dialed 411 again. "Yes. Gunner Olavson." A moment later he said, "I'm not sure, could be an F or a V.

Uh-huh. Okay. Yes, that sounds like it. Can you connect me?" He waited. "Gunner Olavson? Fabulous. Hold please."

Junior brought the phone to me, holding it well in front of him. I took it, saying, "Hello, Gunnar Olavson?"

"Yeah, it's still me."

I explained a bit about who I was and what I wanted to know, then said, "I'm surprised you're not still on the job."

"I've been retired less than a year. This is about Shirley Kessler?"

"Well, that's not completely right. I'm trying to get information. I've been looking into the death of Vera Korenko. I think there might be a connection."

"Yeah, I've heard of that case before."

"Do you remember if there was a woman named Gigi mentioned anywhere in your case?"

He was silent for a long time. "Yeah. We could never find her. Did you find her?"

"Not yet. She was married but sometimes went with women. It's that what you know?"

"Shirley was crazy about her. That's all I know, except that her husband beat the crap out of her now and then. At least, according to Shirley's friends."

"Yeah, I heard that too. Can I run some other names by you?"

"Yeah, go ahead."

"Harper and Georgia Dawson?"

"Not sure."

"Rocky Havoc."

"Yeah, we interviewed her. Bartender. Kind of political."

"Not a suspect, though?"

"No."

"I didn't think so."

"Betty Brooks?"

"No."

"Manny and Virginia Marker?"

"No. My mother's name was Virginia, Ginny, I'd have remembered that."

"Anyway, could I look at your murder book?"

He was silent.

"The case is archived."

"You didn't bring home a copy?"

"My wife would kill me if I did something like that."

That wasn't exactly a 'no'. I left a long silence.

"There's someone I can talk to, though. Let me see what I can do."

"Thank you."

I gave him my number and Ronnie's fax. After I hung up, Junior caught me up on his difficulties with the Section 8 people. I barely paid attention. Basically, they wanted to come and look at the house. Or more specifically, my bedroom.

"Talk to Ronnie."

I sat up, and then stood up. A bolt of pain ran through my right side. Taking a few deep breaths, I turned toward the kitchen.

"What do you need? I can get it for you?"

"That's fine," I said, then began walking. Ronnie had made me some lunch and left it in the fridge. Just a turkey sandwich and potato salad, but I didn't have to make it.

I was part way there when I realized I was not getting through the whole day without my pills. I called for Junior and asked him to go upstairs and get my Percocet from the bedroom. And I knew the rest of the day was about to slip away from me.

———

First thing Tuesday morning, I asked Junior if he could drive a stick.

"Of course I can."

"That's not a double entendre."

"The first three cars I owned were stick shifts."

"Good. Where's my Jeep? I need you to drive me to Eagle Rock."

"Your Jeep's in the shop. We'll take my car."

Why didn't I think he had a car? Everyone had a car. Even desperately poor people had cars in California.

After breakfast we left the house. He led me around the corner and then down the alley behind our house. We didn't have a garage—one of the reasons Ronnie had gotten the house for a song. It wasn't that difficult to park on the street in our neighborhood, so it didn't matter much to us. Halfway down the alley, Junior took out his keys and unlocked a padlock on a garage. He pushed the garage door up, and behind it was his car. He was renting a garage from one of our neighbors. Ronnie was going to kill him.

He drove a 1982 Oldsmobile Toronado, mint green with a darker green landau roof. The car was in pristine condition, looking like he'd just driven it off the showroom floor. I waited while he pulled out of the garage, then got out to lock the door.

"Get in, get in," he said.

I opened the passenger door. The seats were plush, forest green velvet. The dashboard was imitation burled wood. As carefully as possible, I folded myself and slid into the passenger's seat. I tried to pull my seatbelt around me, but I couldn't. I had to ask Junior to do it. When he was done, he said, "Well, off for a big adventure."

On the way we talked about cars. Junior told me about every car he'd ever owned. And then every car he remembered his parents owning. "The first car I remember is a 1941 Nash Ambassador. It was teal blue with a mint green top. Are you sensing a theme? When I saw this car, I simply had to have it because of the color. We kept that Nash forever. They didn't even make cars for years during the war. What was your first car?"

"I had a 1960 Valiant. It had been in an accident, so the frame was bent. It went through tires like you wouldn't believe." It also had taillights that looked like they were squinting at you.

I should have shut up then and there. But I didn't. I'd taken another pain pill before we left so my judgement was off. I told him about my baby blue '74 Duster that had gotten blown up. And the sherbet green '79 Nova with mag wheels I'd been given by a mobster.

"Okay, there are some interesting stories there... care to explain?"

"Oh, um, no... not really."

"Well, I've never had anyone give me a car, no less a mobster. And I've been blown in a car but never had a car blow up."

I was deeply regretting the conversation.

Finally, we got to Beverly Hills and Our Lady of Angels Care Home. Junior's mouth fell open even before we parked. He bent over the steering wheel to get a good look at the place.

"Oh, my Lord. If we hadn't driven here I'd think we were in heaven."

We got out of the car. He had to come around and give me a hand getting out. Stopping at the reception desk, I gave my name and they let us in. Edward had done as he'd promised. As we headed to Patrick's room, a nice-looking, young orderly walked by. Junior leaned into me and said, "Oh yes, this is heaven."

In Patrick's room, we found him sitting in a chair by the window. The television was on as it had been before. Jennie Jones was interviewing Richard Simmons. I turned the sound down.

"Patrick. Hello. I'm Dom Reilly. I was here before. This is my friend Junior."

He looked at us, seeming to attempt focusing. In a whisper he asked, "Where am I?"

"Oh darling, this is the most fabulous place," Junior gushed. "You're so lucky. I'd kill for a two-week stay."

"A hotel?"

"Exactly."

"Patrick, do you remember I asked you questions?"

"No."

"Questions about Vera?"

He looked at me blankly. That concerned me. Had he forgotten Vera? Was the whole reason for my investigation a moot point? Not that it mattered. Sheila just wanted to know what to say to him. But, well, I wanted to know. I wanted to know who'd killed Vera.

Junior said to me, "You should sit down in that chair, Dom. I don't want you falling on your face."

I must have looked more unstable than I felt. I gingerly eased myself into a chair across from Patrick.

"Now—"

"Patrick," Junior interrupted me. "Do you remember the movie *The Girl From Albany*?"

That got a smile from Patrick. He said, "I was there."

"You were there? In the movie?"

"Ivan had us to see the set. Do you know Ivan?"

"I *do*. Ivan is fabulous."

"Fabulous..."

"Patrick, who went with you to see the set?" I asked.

"It was so big. There were ten janitors to clean the floor when it got dirty. It couldn't be dirty. It would ruin the shot."

Junior began humming. That made Patrick smile. Junior stopped, and said, "That was the set for 'I'm Too Blue to Be Blue' wasn't it?"

I think that was for my benefit.

"Who was with you when you went to see it?" I asked again.

"Vera and..."

He stopped. A blank look came over his face.

"Was it Gigi? Was Gigi with you?"

Fear filled his face and then terror. "No! No, don't hit me! Stop!"

"It's okay, darling. No one's going to hit you."

"Help! Help me!"

The nurse we'd walked by before rushed into the room. Junior was thrilled.

"We haven't done anything to him. Not a thing."

"It's all right. Mr. Gill has these episodes." He raised his voice, "Patrick, everything's okay. No one here is going to hurt you."

Patrick was shaking, tears coming down his face. He looked terrorized.

"Can you tell me who hurt you, Patrick?" I asked as gently as I could.

"Vera," he whispered. "I killed Vera."

"No, dear, you didn't," Junior said.

"I *did*."

CHAPTER THIRTY

August 13-18, 1996

I n the lobby, I noticed Mrs. Carper at the reception desk. I stopped and asked, "Are things any better with Mr. Gill?"

"Yes and no. He's still up to his tricks, but Mrs. Karpinski sent the loveliest basket of muffins and that went a long way to smooth things over. Was that your idea?"

"No, no, not at all," I lied. Sheila had to deal with these people, so it was better they think the kindness a hundred percent hers.

"Patrick had an episode. He became quite frightened and began to yell. The nurse said it happens frequently?"

"I'm aware of that, yes."

"It seems like he's remembering something. Someone hurting him."

"Well, I'm not sure you should put much stock in that. Patients like Patrick can be reliving things that happened to them, that's true. However, they can also be fantasies. I know it's hard for families, but the elderly can get caught in very negative dream worlds. Losing touch with reality would be easier if it were always a lovely reality they escaped to... but I'm afraid it's not."

Driving back to Long Beach, I fell asleep. That shouldn't have come as a surprise. I'd been told to take a walk around the block every day. I'd managed it on Sunday, but it had exhausted me. As it turned out, sitting in the car for forty-five minutes then walking into a nursing home had a similar effect.

I woke up around the time we got onto the 710. Junior, noticing I was awake, asked, "What do you think? How much of that was real?"

"I think a lot of it was real."

"Even after what that woman at the desk said?"

"Gigi was married to a violent man. A couple of people have said that. I'd guess Patrick was either threatened or attacked because of his connection to Vera."

"And you think Gigi's husband killed Vera?"

"I do."

"Gigi is a nickname," he said. "Georgiana, Georgina, Georgette... almost any name with a G—"

"Georgia Dawson," I said.

"That's someone you talked to?"

"She worked with Vera. She said Vera never talked about anyone named Gigi."

"I guess we know why she'd say that." After a moment, he said excitedly, "Where do they live? We'll go there now."

"They live in Scottsdale Arizona."

"Oh my. That's a six-hour drive. You're not up for that."

And he was right. I wasn't.

Later that afternoon I tried to take a shower and wiped out the next seventy-two hours. I didn't fall down, but I did slip and slam myself against the tiled wall. As soon as he got home, Ronnie dragged me to the emergency room so they could do an X-ray. Everything was fine, thank God. The last thing I wanted was more surgery. They gave me another, stronger prescription for pain, and the instructions to stay at home for at least a week.

Seven very boring days of TV and not much else. Well, that wasn't entirely true. I knew I was going to have to go over to Scottsdale as soon as I got better. But in the meantime, I had to make sure I knew everything I could about Georgia Dawson and her husband Harper. On Thursday, I let the drugs wear off long enough to call Wallace Philburn. When he picked up, I said, "Wally, it's your old friend Dom. I've got a few more questions."

"Jesus fucking Christ."

"I knew you'd be excited."

He hung up on me. I called again. And again. The sixth time he picked up, and said, "Can't you fucking leave me alone!"

"I'm going to tell you who killed Vera."

There was a long pause, and then he said, "Go ahead. Tell me."

"No. I'm going to ask you questions. From my questions you'll be able to figure it out."

I knew that once I told him he would just hang up again.

"Go ahead. Ask your goddamn questions."

"You put a picture of Harper and Georgia Dawson in your book, but you barely mention them. Why?"

"We had to have some kind of art, and the picture was evocative of the period."

"Tell me everything you remember about the Dawsons."

"Harper Dawson? He killed Vera?"

"Tell me what you know about them. Where were they living when you interviewed them?"

"Oh God... I think they were in Glendale somewhere."

"Glendale's not far from where Vera's body was found."

"No. It's not."

"In your book, you say that Georgia Dawson told you about the trip to Malibu that Vera was planning. She told me she didn't know anything about that. She said you made it up."

"I didn't make it up. That's what she told me."

"You made it sound like Vera was going with show business types."

"They were planning to stay at some movie star's beach house. I don't remember which, I'd have to check my notes."

"Vera and Georgia worked together at Security First National Bank. Is that how you found her?"

"No. I found her through Virginia Marker. They all used to go to a bar called The Blue Fox."

"Is that a lesbian bar?"

"At this point it's a little murky what it was. It was a place on the Sunset Strip—well, before people called it the strip. Before West Hollywood was a thing. It was a dance place. Fags and dykes. Everything went, you know."

"Yeah, I know." I wanted to reach through the phone and ring his sleazy little neck, but I needed him to keep answering questions. "So, let's be clear... Vera, Georgia Dawson, Betty Brooks, Rocky Havoc and Virginia Marker, they all went to The Blue Fox. But you didn't think this had anything to do with lesbians?"

"I never said that. I said my publisher didn't want a book about a dead dyke. And frankly, neither did I. I wanted to sell books. That's what writers do. And no... Rocky Havoc didn't go there. It wasn't a place for bull dykes. It was for the normal looking ones. See, you weren't supposed to have queer dancing. So when the sheriff tried to raid the place, they switched partners. The ones like Rocky made it all little too obvious."

"Why didn't you tell me this before?"

"I don't know what it's got to do with anything."

"Vera and Georgia went to the same bar, *and* they worked together. How did that happen?"

"Georgia got her the job at the bank."

Which was something I'd started to wonder about.

"I called my publisher about the new edition. They're very excited. I'm going to want to do a detailed interview. When do think we can schedule that?"

I hung up on him. I mean, it was the least I could do. Besides, it was time for another pill, and I needed to spend a couple hours of making a concerted effort not to drool.

Two things happened on that Friday: The body shop called and told me my Jeep was all repaired and ready to be picked up; and Larry Wilkes got out of prison. The body shop called in the morning. I didn't have to pay anything; Sammy's insurance company would pay. Actually, they'd pay and then they'd go after Sammy for the money. No one covered deliberately running someone over. I got Junior to drive John there to pick it up for me.

When it arrived that afternoon, I walked out to the curb and looked it over. It looked like nothing had happened to it. I wished I could say the same about my body. I went back inside and took another pill.

On the six o'clock news there was a story about Larry Wilkes being released from prison. Edwin was right next to him at the microphone. Next to Larry was a young guy, good-looking. I guessed that might be Brysen, his prison boyfriend, who would be around until they determined if there would be a settlement and how much it would be.

He would probably get something, but I doubted it was going to be a lot. The police didn't do a great job, but Larry himself had encouraged a witness to perjure herself. The state was likely to say things would have turned out differently if he'd been honest about his relationship with Pete even though we all knew that wasn't exactly true. They wouldn't want to pay a lot of money, so they'd say whatever they could get away with.

———

Sunday, I waited until Ronnie kissed me good-bye and went off to show houses. Then I carefully got dressed and walked out to my Jeep. I climbed in and managed to get my safety belt on all by myself. Progress. I pressed the clutch down and started it. I looked at the stick shift and realized I was going to need to remove my sling.

I turned the Jeep off, undid my safety belt and started over. First taking the sling off and then repeating the steps. I put it into first gear and that only caused a tiny bit of pain, so I pulled out into the street. I told myself if I made it to 7th Street I'd go all the way. It was touch-and-go, but I knew it was mostly freeway driving on a Sunday, which wouldn't require me to shift gears often.

It still took an hour, by the end of which I was sweating even though I'd had the air conditioning on full blast. Getting out of the Jeep in front of the gray stucco house, I hoped I'd stop sweating soon. It was only in the mid-seventies.

In the Marker's driveway there was a big blue Buick

from the mid-eighties. That meant they were home. Good, the journey was not pointless.

Before I crossed the street, I put my right arm back into the sling, which helped to lower the pain to a sharp ache. I made my way slowly up their driveway and knocked on the door with my left hand. A few moments later, Virginia Marker opened the door. She was a thin, sinewy woman in her later seventies. She had on a pair of peach-colored shorts and a pale-yellow sleeveless blouse. Her skin was well-tanned and loose. From the look on her face, she had a good sense of who I was before I introduced myself.

"I have nothing more to say," she said before I got my full name out. "I have told you everything."

"You've told me very little and most of it lies. I'll be going over to Scottsdale soon to confront Harper and Georgia Dawson. I think you and your husband have information that will help me trap Vera's killer. I'm hoping you'll help me."

After studying me a long time, she said, "Come in then."

She had to hold the door open for me. I slipped by into a small living room with two large reclining chairs on opposite sides of the room. In one of them was Manny Marker. He seemed to be in his early eighties, though he could have been older or younger. He was clearly frail, attached to a tank of oxygen, and you could still hear him struggling to breathe. Like his wife, he wore a pair of shorts and a thin shirt. His arms were covered with bruises of various ages. I wondered what exactly was wrong with him.

"Manny this is Dominick Reilly. He says he knows who killed Vera Korenko."

"And Shirley Kessler," I added.

"Yes, of course, Shirley."

Manny's breathing hastened, as though the prospect of finding their killer excited him. Virginia sat down in the other recliner. There wasn't really anywhere else to sit. The small sofa was covered in newspapers.

Looking straight at Virginia, I said, "You met Vera at a bar called The Blue Fox."

"Yes. I did."

Her husband gasped, "No."

"Manny never went to The Blue Fox. It wasn't his sort of place."

He seemed to want to say something but couldn't get it out.

"Did you go there a lot?" I asked Virginia.

"Oh yes. There was not very much on television," she said, dryly. I doubted that was the reason.

"You have a slight accent. Where are you originally from?"

"France. Manny and I met there after the war. He brought me home with him. I was a war bride. Why do you think Harper Dawson killed Vera?"

"A number of people told me that Vera's girlfriend named Gigi had a violent husband. Georgia lied to me about a number of things and Gigi is a nickname..."

I had to stop. Something was becoming clear. Or at least clearer. It wasn't Georgia Dawson who was Gigi, it was Virginia Marker.

"I'm wrong though, aren't I. You're Gigi."

She just smiled. "Yes. Gigi is a pet name for Virginie, which is my name in French."

I looked at her husband. This frail, crippled creature had killed two women? It seemed impossible.

"How long has he been sick?"

"Several years. Emphysema. He won't last much longer."

"Don't—" he attempted to speak again. She stood up and spoke to him angrily in French. He looked confused. She touched his shoulder and he flinched.

"Does he speak French?" I asked.

"Not a word. He gets the gist, though."

"He beat you, he killed two women you loved, why are you taking care of him?"

"Why do you think I'm taking care of him?"

And then the bruises suddenly meant something different. They weren't there because of his illness, they were there because of his wife. She was now the abuser. It was pay back.

"Why didn't you leave him all those years ago?"

"I was trapped. I lost my family in the war. I didn't know many people in the U.S. I had my daughter to think of. I thought Vera would help me escape him. I thought the same about Shirley. He made sure I couldn't get away. He made sure no one would help me."

I started to say she could have called the police, but that was barely true today. It wouldn't have helped her in 1949. I didn't know what to say. I was out of questions and I had the answer I'd come for.

I thanked them and said good-bye. Before I was out the door Manny said something I didn't quite catch. I turned to wait for him to say it again, but Gigi said, "He says good-bye."

Walking out of the house, I crossed the street to my Jeep. I wasn't sure what to do. An elderly man was being abused. I knew I should do something about that. But then, he'd also brutally raped and murdered two women, not to mention abusing his wife for decades. I wasn't sure he deserved compassion. The only thing I was sure of was that it wasn't up to me.

I turned to go back to the house. It would be better for Gigi if I convinced her to turn him in. They'd take him away and then she wouldn't be tempted—

A gunshot rang out from inside the house. I was sure she'd just killed him. I stopped in my tracks. I was frozen. I should call—

And then there was another shot. I couldn't breathe for a moment. I was sure she'd just shot herself too. Could I be wrong? Could it have taken two shots to kill her husband? But he could barely move. She couldn't have missed... No, she'd just killed them both.

I looked around the neighborhood. It was quiet. No one was coming out of their house. No one seemed to be home. Slowly, I walked back to my Jeep. I got in, took off my sling, and drove away.

CHAPTER THIRTY-ONE

August 22, 1996
Thursday

About a week later, well after I put my invoice in the mail, I called Sheila Karpinski.

"I know who killed Vera," I said. I'd already let her sons know, but I felt I ought to talk to her myself.

"I know. I'm so glad." I could hear her lighting a cigarette as she said that.

"It was a man named Manny Marker."

"Do you know why he did it? Edwin wasn't clear."

I knew why he wasn't clear. Sheila seemed to have gone to great lengths not to see her brother's sexuality. Could I talk about his fiancée being killed over an affair she'd had with another woman? Would that tip Sheila off? Did I want to be the one who'd tipped her off? It didn't feel like my business.

I sidestepped the question by saying, "She wasn't the only woman Marker killed. He killed another woman in the sixties."

"Oh dear, Edwin didn't tell me that. How horrible. You are turning him into the police?"

Just a day after my trip to Eagle Rock there was a newspaper article about an elderly couple involved in a murder-suicide. The wife had stolen a gun from the neighbors and used it to kill her terminally ill husband and herself.

"I'm afraid he passed away."

"So that poor girl won't get any justice."

"Not in a traditional sense, no." I decided to move off this topic. "Now you have something to tell Patrick."

"Yes. Manny Marker killed Vera."

Unfortunately, I think he already knew that, and I wasn't sure saying the guy's name was going do anything but terrify him. "You know, I think Patrick will still feel responsible. You might want to just tell him it wasn't his fault. And now you know that for certain."

"Yes, we do know for certain. Thank you. I appreciate what you've done for my family."

Of course, I understood how Patrick felt. From what I'd pieced together, Vera and Gigi had meant to go away that weekend but didn't. That led to Vera's death. Patrick's guilt came from the fact that he hadn't, and probably couldn't have, saved Vera. I knew what that felt like. There were people in my life, those I'd loved, liked, even disliked, who I wish I'd been able to save. I suppose the grown-up thing to say is that we can't save others, we can barely save ourselves. But that doesn't help with the guilt.

———

Later that afternoon, Ronnie came home unexpectedly.

"What are you doing home?" I asked. "Did the bottom fall out of the real estate business?"

"You wish," he teased back. "I have something I want to show you."

That was a little nerve wracking. 'I have something I want to show you' often resulted in our spending hundreds of thousands of dollars on a piece of property.

"Are you feeling up to a walk?"

I was supposed to, doctor's orders, so I said, "Yeah, I guess."

We walked a block to 1st Street and then turned west toward our co-op. I hoped that was where we were going, it wasn't that far. We chatted a bit about this and that, then as we were walking by Bixby Park I asked, "How are you feeling about your mother?"

"Who?"

"Don't joke about it. It was an honest question."

"I don't feel much about her. It's been coming for a long time. One of us has to change and I'm not expecting to wake up heterosexual one morning, so I think it has to be her."

"Just to go on record, I would be very unhappy if you woke up heterosexual one morning."

"I should hope so."

When we got to the El Matador, we walked into the courtyard and then up the stairs to the co-op. I was healing, so I very nearly walked like a healthy person. Ronnie took out his keys and opened the front door.

Immediately, I saw that the living room was completely decorated. The paint job had gotten finished somehow and was a lovely, mottled honey color. The ceiling was a crisp white. Someone had painted the beams with a pattern I assumed was at least similar to the original.

The room was completely furnished. Without telling me, Ronnie had made the deal with the Karpinskis for the Melchor/Gill household. I recognized the sofas from storage. One of them was the tufted leather sofa—later, Ronnie explained it was called a Chesterfield. Across from it was the other, a gold sofa with swatches sitting on it. The black-and-brown plaid wingback chairs were sitting with the sofas, completing the grouping.

"There wasn't enough time to get anything covered," he said. "I haven't decided about those chairs. They almost work."

"How did you get this place painted?"

"John helped me."

There was a Deco chest between the doors to the Juliet balconies that was set up as a bar—complete with a selection of liquor and a mirrored tray. He'd even hung velvet drapes in a deep brown velvet. Pointing, I asked, "Were those in storage?"

"No. Linens 'N Things."

And there was artwork. Sketches and a couple of oils. "And the pictures?"

"Ivan's. Worth a little. More curiosity than art." He'd been doing some research.

Then I looked into the dining room. There was a gorgeous dining table with scrolled legs and six matching chairs. "I don't remember that."

"No, it was buried. Rosewood. Deco. That's worth more than the artwork."

"Did we rip these people off?"

"Maybe. I don't know. I had to go up to fifteen thousand. But I made half that back selling the piano."

The dining room had been painted by painters. The color went with the living room but wasn't mottled. The coved ceiling was a different complementary color.

The kitchen was nearly finished. The tile was on the counters. It was busy. Pretty but busy. I'd get used to it though. There were still empty places where the stove and refrigerator would go.

We walked down the hallway to the bedrooms. The smaller bedroom had been turned into an office, the walls a deep green. In the center the partners desk I'd searched through. One side for me, one for Ronnie. It was then that I realized there was no place for guests or roommates. I have to say, I was happy about that. It would be just us.

"This is basically it. We still have a lot of work in the bathroom, and I can't decide what color to paint the bedroom."

I hugged him and kissed him. Then I whispered in his ear, "It's a beautiful home."

I sat down at the desk; the chair was leather and tufted like the sofa in the living room. Remembering something, I opened the bottom drawer to my right. It hadn't been cleared out yet.

"I haven't gotten rid of everything. I was going for impact."

"That's okay. Impact was lovely."

In the drawer, the cassettes marked with the letter P were still there. I took them out and set them on top of the desk. There were thirteen of them, labeled P1-P13.

"What happened to that funky word processor thing from the seventies?"

"I took over the lease on the storage units. I've cleared out two of them and let them go. That word processor and a bunch of other stuff is in the remaining unit."

"I want to find out what's on these tapes."

———

A few days later, Ronnie, John and I drove up to the storage place near Silver Lake. There was no electricity in the storage unit itself. Ronnie had called ahead and arranged for an extension cord to be waiting for us at the front desk. We had a one-hour window. They didn't want to pay for the electricity.

Of course, we weren't even sure we could get the thing running again. The one unit left was three quarters full of things Ronnie was still trying to sell or otherwise dispose of. We moved things around so we could get to the word processor—which John called a Wang, so that's probably what it was.

Luckily, there was a handbook. John, I'd learned, had put himself through nursing school as an office temp, so he actually had some experience with typewriters and computers and all of that. He read through the computer while Ronnie and I figured out how to plug it in. There was a moment of suspense as we actually waited to see if it would come on. It did.

I had a bag filled with the tapes labeled with a P, which I assume meant Patrick, though it could also have meant personal. I'd also brought a ream of paper snagged from Ronnie's office. John put one of the cassettes into the machine, rolled a piece of paper into the typewriter part, and then hit the special key on the side that said AUTO START.

Miraculously, it began typing. It took a few hours to go through the thirteen tapes. Eventually, I had to go downstairs and give the kid at the desk forty bucks to ignore the fact that we were taking too long. Two of the tapes wouldn't play, one was actually broken. The remaining tapes only contained a page or two of broken text.

I was immediately excited because the first page contained Vera's name and a date: February 1973. Sometime shortly after Ivan's death. I imagined that Patrick had created these documents himself, without the help of a secretary. Patrick's private grief and the personal nature of his relationship with Vera almost demanded it. I imagined him in an office, waiting for his secretary to go home so he could make these tapes.

Something else became apparent quickly. Patrick didn't have a grasp of how the processor worked. The pages John printed out had long gaps, repeated lines, and multiple errors. Some lines just simply stopped, words like lemmings falling off a cliff... abrupt endings, half-thoughts. Reading through the pages John printed out, it felt like the first draft of a story that longed to end differently. In its way, it was a confession from someone who wasn't guilty.

Patrick and Vera met during a sheriff's raid of the Blue Fox. Ivan was there, so was Gigi. None of them were arrested. Afterward, they went to Ivan's home in Holmby Hills. The four of them got on well. Initially, Patrick liked Vera quite a lot.

A week or so later, she called his office and asked to have lunch. He'd thought she wanted a secretarial job, and he was inclined to give her one. But, no, what she proposed was a proposal. During the raid of The Blue Fox, they'd pretended to be a straight couple. Vera had the idea they could both benefit by doing that more often.

She offered to pose as his fiancée for his family and business associates. In return, he went on double dates with Gigi and her husband, Manny Marker. It was a simple ruse that worked well for six months or so. Then, Patrick began to be annoyed by Vera's independence. She was quick to state an opinion and slow to consider its impact. His family didn't really like her and neither did his co-workers.

And the time he spent with the Markers was increasingly unbearable. In the spring of forty-nine, he began making himself less and less available to Vera. He also stopped bringing her around his family. The less he relied on her the less he owed her.

Meanwhile, Vera's relationship with Gigi was deepening. Vera wanted Patrick to help with getting Gigi out of the marriage. But he wasn't a divorce lawyer. And divorce was not as easy as it was in 1973 when Patrick was writing these. In the late summer of 1949, Manny Marker was putting pressure on Patrick to get Vera in-line and keep her away from Gigi.

And that's where it ended. P13 was one of the tapes that had broken. I could only assume that things continued to get worse. At some point, Patrick cut Vera out of his life. She didn't give up; she continued trying to rescue Gigi. And then Manny Marker killed her.

EPILOGUE

September 30, 1949

The sun was setting in a swirl of Easter pastels. The waves beat against the sand like a pulse. They walked along the water's edge, fingers inches apart, making Patrick want to reach out and take his lover's hand. He knew better.

There was no one to be seen, but that didn't matter. There could be someone unseen in one of the cottages crowding the shore, many of which were still under construction. It couldn't be risked. It could never be risked.

They were quiet. They'd barely said a thing since they left the house Ivan had designed for eighteen-year-old movie star Jane Van Houten, who'd been a second-rate Shirley Temple and was now an aspiring sexpot. Her gratitude—he'd sent the bill to Monumental—resulted in the loan of the house several times a year.

"You're feeling bad, aren't you?"

"I'm fine," Patrick replied, though it sounded the opposite.

"You did what you had to do."

And for a moment, Patrick was back on the phone, a bag of ice pressed against his face, telling Vera it was over. "We can't continue like this. It's too dangerous."

"Patrick, it's perfect. Your family believes you're in love with me. So does your boss."

"And your girlfriend's husband beat me up. Vera, you have to stop seeing her. I don't know what he'll do next."

"I love her. I have to get her away from him."

"He won't let her go."

"Can't we talk about all this at the beach? We'll have time to make a plan."

"Vera, you and Gigi aren't coming to the beach. It's over."

And then he hung up on her. The phone rang immediately, and he didn't pick up. Since then, he'd felt like a coward, a cad. A Hollywood hero would find a way to save the girl, even a girl who loved another girl. But there was nothing to be done. Manny Marker knew too much. It wasn't just his fists that could hurt him. He could be disbarred. He could end up penniless and alone.

As though he'd followed each and every thought, Ivan said, "She'll be fine. She's a smart girl."

And then he reached out and took Patrick's hand.

"Ivan, don't."

They stopped walking and faced each other. Ivan placed a hand briefly on Patrick's heart and then on his own. "Nothing matters but this. The space between us. It's all there is. All there ever will be."

IN THE BOYSTOWN MYSTERIES SERIES

Boystown: Three Nick Nowak Mysteries

Boystown 2: Three More Nick Nowak Mysteries

Boystown 3: Two Nick Nowak Novellas

Boystown 4: A Time for Secrets

Boystown 5: Murder Book

Boystown 6: From the Ashes

Boystown 7: Bloodlines

Boystown 8: The Lies That Bind

Boystown 9: Lucky Days

Boystown 10: Gifts Given

Boystown 11: Heart's Desire

Boystown 12: Broken Cord

Boystown 13: Fade Out

The Boystown Prequels

IN THE PINX VIDEO MYSTERIES SERIES

Night Drop

Hidden Treasures

Late Fees

Rewind

Cash Out

Help Wanted

IN THE DOM REILLY SERIES

Year of the Rat

A Mean Season

The Happy Month

OTHER BOOKS

The Perils of Praline

Desert Run

Full Release

The Ghost Slept Over

My Favorite Uncle

Femme

Praline Goes to Washington

Aunt Belle's Time Travel & Collectibles

Masc

Never Rest

Code Name: Liberty

Fathers of the Bride

Sentenced to Christmas

ABOUT THE AUTHOR

Marshall Thornton writes several popular mystery series, most notably the *Boystown Mysteries* and the *Pinx Video Mysteries*. He has won the Lambda Award for Gay Mystery three times. His books *Femme* and *Code Name Liberty* were Lambda finalists for Best Gay Romance. Other books include *My Favorite Uncle*, *The Ghost Slept Over* and *Fathers of the Bride*. He holds an MFA in Screenwriting from UCLA.